# Let's Try Love

## Anthology

Jessie Chick
KL Fast
ChaShiree M.
M.K. Moore
Paula Phillips
K.R. Reese
Alice La Roux
Fey Simmons
Judy Swinson
C.L. Williams
Terri A. Wilson

Let's Try Love

Copyright © 2019

All rights reserved. No part of this book may be reproduced or transmitted in any form or by any means without written permission of the author.

*Since this anthology and all of the proceeds are for Rhylon I wanted to dedicate it to his momma for all the hours she puts in for his care. I have never met someone as strong as her and she is an amazing mom who does wonders for Rhylon. She sacrifices so much just to make sure her little fighter has everything he needs. She's a mom I definitely look up to.*

# Who is Our Anthology for?

## About Rhylon
*(a message from his momma)*

I was induced at 33 weeks 5 days. He was born at 33 weeks and 6 days. I ran out of amniotic fluids, due to Rhylon's posterior urethral valves (causing his partial bladder blockage). He spent 56 days in the NICU.

He had his peritoneal dialysis catheter put in at 5 days old. Started dialysis at 14 days old. He was born diagnosed with end stand renal disease. It's been 2 long years of dialysis, and hospital stays, surgeries, therapies, daily meds, daily shots. Rhylon's father isn't around so it's only been me and Rhylon for 2 years now. He didn't even make it to the delivery of his first and only child. We're hoping he'll be ready for the transplant workup, in about a year. He has to be 35 pounds and is currently 24 pounds. I would love it if everyone could go give his journey page a like!

https://www.facebook.com/RhylonKades-Nicu-journey-and-beyo.../

# One Click

## by Jessie Chick

When Piper's best friend signed her up on a dating site she never thought she'd find love. Now that's she's met the love of her life she's helping others find love through her dating site Let's Try Love.

# One Click by Jessie Chick

So, you found yourself on Let's Try Love. Well I'm glad you're here and that you decided to find love the untraditional way. I founded this site after I met the love of my life through a different online dating site. If you're skeptical about finding love online, then let me tell you my story.

*Four Years Ago*

*You have four new matches.*

I have what? Oh, I am going to kill Kayla! I opened the next three emails and they were all the same. It was a complete joke last night when I said I would try online dating after the last failed date I went on, but it was the wine talking. I did not want to meet a man online. Who knows if I was really talking to the guy in the picture? Traditional dating was my way of dating and I was fine with it. I needed to call my best friend. Luckily, it was lunch time.

"Hey!"

# Let's Try Love

"Please tell me you did not sign me up on this stupid site and that someone stole my email?"

"Nope, you're welcome, and I'll email you your login. Just give it a try, Piper; you may just find the love of your life."

"Kayla! That conversation we had over wine was just a joke! I did not intend for you to take it seriously. I'm not ready to give dating another shot yet."

"Piper, come on it has been two years since that jackass broke your heart. Don't you think it's time to get back out there?"

"I like traditional dating. Who knows if I'm meeting the guy who I've been talking to online? What if I get catfished?"

"Girl, you watch way too much TV. You are not going to get catfished, just go on one date. What would it hurt?"

"If you'll leave me alone, I'll go on one date. Just one and then I want you to take my profile down."

"Mmhmm, I got to go. I'll call you later."

I knew she didn't need to get off the phone, she was just ignoring me. God she was frustrating, but she was my best friend.

I logged back onto the site and read all the messages that have came in since I picked up my lunch. Some of these messages were hilarious and some of them were creepy.

*"Hey boo, wanna make babies?"*

*"Hey gorgeous, you must be from Heaven. You're an angel."*

*"Let me tie you up and tell you who's boss. I know you'll like that baby."*

They just kept getting weirder. I did answer a couple that weren't completely creepy, but I didn't have hope. Why were there all kinds of creeps on dating sites? I mean, I could deal without the creepy men. That's why I liked traditional dating. You could see who you were talking to and hear them. Online dating just seemed weird and I was ready to quit even without meeting someone. Then two messages popped up.

**New match: Hey, my name's Talon and I don't usually do this, but I saw your profile and you are pretty. I also read that you liked concerts in the park. Maybe we could go to the one this weekend?**

I decided to give Talon a chance, but I wasn't just going to jump into a date with him.

**Piper: Hi Talon, thank you for the compliment. You're pretty good looking yourself. I would like to get to know you first before just jumping into a date. Is that ok?**

I closed my browser down and got back to work. These books weren't going to edit themselves. I waited until I was home and had a few glasses of white wine before I opened the site back up.

*****

I was having a good twenty-minute conversation with Talon when there was a knock on my door. I knew who it was before I even answered the door. I answered the door to my lovely bestie and more white wine.

"So, how's it going?"

"It's going. I met one guy and he seems pretty sweet, but I haven't decided yet."

"Oooh, what's his name?"

"His name is Talon and he looks like a sports guys, but with an artistic side. He wants to take me to a concert in the park this weekend."

"That should be fun! You're going right?"

"I don't know. I don't really know him that well. What if he's not the real him that I'm talking to? What if I get stood up?"

"You won't know unless you try."

Let's Try Love

Just then I got a ping for a new message. This one was from a new guy and his message was interesting.

**New match: Hello, my name is Adam and I noticed that you are really into books. I would love to take you out to a bookstore some time and get to know you over some coffee.**

Kayla was reading over my shoulder and was already shaking her head yes.

"Choose him! I like him, he's right up your alley."

"Yeah and I like bookstores and coffee. Maybe I should give them both a try."

"Both?"

"Yeah you said to take chances so why not give them both a shot."

"You go girl! Get it."

As she read over my shoulder, I agreed to the concert with Talon; and then I agreed to a bookstore coffee date with Adam the next weekend. To be honest, I was looking more forward to the date with Adam than the date with Talon. Concerts in the park were more Kayla's thing than mine, but I guess she needed to fill in my hobbies, so she used some of hers. Adam also looked like more of my type. He was fit, but not overly buff. He had thick, dark hair and wore sleek black glasses that really framed his face. I wasn't too bad looking myself. I was fit, and my hair was a little longer than shoulder length. I also wore glasses, which suited me; I hated contacts. I imagined us fitting well together. I didn't picture myself with Talon. The more I talked to him the more into sports he got.

*Three Days Later*

## Let's Try Love

I was just finishing my hair when there was a knock at my apartment door. I took one last look in the mirror at the outfit Kayla picked out before I answered the door. I was wearing dark skinny jeans, short black boots, and a loose red blouse. My phone dinged as I was opening the door and it was a text from Talon, who I expected to be at the door, but it was Kayla. I let her in as I read the text from Talon.

**Talon: Sorry doll, I'm not going to be able to make it. There's this huge game on tonight and my buddies want to go to the bar to watch it. Catch ya next time.**

Seeing the look on my face, Kayla asks, "What's wrong?"

"I just got stood up, that's what's wrong. I need a drink."

I poured us both a vodka and cranberry and checked my profile to see if I had any new messages from Adam. We have really connected over the past week and I found myself looking forward to hearing him from every day. I also decided that I would finally give him my number. I wanted to let him know that I trusted him enough to share that information with him.

Just like I hoped, there was a message from Adam.

**Adam: I have been staring at the same contract for a client for the last 20 minutes, save me!**

I laughed as I typed.

**Piper: Text me, and I'll see if I can save you. 976-553-9256.**

I waited for his response, but didn't receive anything for about ten minutes. Then my phone chimed with an incoming text.

**Adam: So were exchanging numbers now?**

**Piper: I thought it would be easier than having to log onto the site every day. Plus, I only talk to you on there, so I figured why not give you my number.**

**Adam: Well I'm honored. So how is your night going?**

Let's Try Love

**Piper: It's going. I'm having drinks at home with a friend.**

Adam and I texted as Kayla and I drank and talked about how cute he was. He was seriously good looking and he had a good job. He was a contractor that owned his own company that built and designed most of the houses in Golden Brook, Mississippi. The more I talked about him and thought about him, the more I liked him. After being stood up tonight though, I was nervous about our date next weekend. What if he stood me up too?

*One Week Later – The Date*

This time Kayla was waiting with me before Adam showed up. I was a nervous mess and didn't want to be alone if I was stood up again. I zipped up my shoes and did one last look in the mirror before the knock on my door. Of course, I didn't make it out of my room quick enough to answer the door.

"Hot damn, Piper, you didn't tell me he was this hot!"

I'm going to kill her. "Kayla!"

"What? He's cute!"

"Thank you, I think." Adam said laughing.

"No, thank you, for gracing us with your presence," Kayla said.

"Hey Kayla."

"Yes?" She answered still staring at Adam.

"Leave."

She gave me her "how rude" look and thankfully left. *God, I loved her.* With her gone, I got a good look at Adam and she was right. He was gorgeous. He was wearing dark jeans, a red shirt, and black converse type shoes, and those glasses. I don't know what it was about the glasses, but dang he made them look sexy.

"You look beautiful," Adam said.

"Thanks, just something I threw together."

I was wearing my favorite skinny jeans, a loose top, and my favorite short boots, and, of course my glasses.

"Shall we?"

"Yep."

I locked the door and Adam opened the passenger door of his Nissan GTR. I was already impressed. As he drove, we talked about anything and everything. I found out he is an architect and owned his own company, he has two adopted dogs, and he reads every chance he gets. I told him about the little boutique I worked at and that you can always find me with a book on me.

Then we got to the reasons we were on Date for Two. *I know it's a ridiculous name for a site.* I gave him my spiel on how I didn't really sign up for the site.

"Well after all my failed traditional dates, Kayla thought I needed to try something untraditional. I told her I'd give it a shot and here I am."

"At least your best friend set you up. I was set up by my mom and sister."

"You're kidding?"

"Nope, I'm serious. They ambushed me with it at dinner one night. It was mortifying until I saw your profile and then I thought, 'maybe this won't be so bad.'"

I smiled at him as we pulled up in front of the bookstore ice cream shop. It was my favorite place to be when it came to books and ice cream. We ordered our ice cream and picked a table in the corner near the window. Talking to Adam was easy. He knew how to keep a conversation going and there was never a dull moment.

"So, what made you love books?" I asked.

## Let's Try Love

"It was because of my dad. He always had a book in his hand. He never read the newspaper, or watched much TV, but he was always reading. He introduced me to *Fahrenheit 451* when I was 15 and I was done for. I've been reading ever since. What about you?"

"It all started with The Little Engine That Could. My mom read it to me every night and it got me hooked on books. I've read anything and everything I could get my hands on. It also brought on my dream to be a famous writer. In fact, hang on just a second."

Adam gave me a 'where are you going?' look when I got up from the table and went to the local author section of the bookstore. I pulled down my book *Small Town Love* and brought it to the table. I set it in front of Adam and smiled as he read the back and then started reading the first chapter.

"I'm assuming you like it?"

"Shhhh, I'm reading."

I laughed and let him continue through the chapter. Men usually don't like romance, but here I was on a date with a gorgeous man that is reading a romance.

"Piper, this is amazing."

"Thank you."

"Please tell me you're working on another book."

"I am actually, but you'll have to wait for it to come out."

We continued with our date and, before we left the bookstore, Adam purchased my book and made me sign it. Our next stop was the little diner on the corner for coffee. This date was going perfect and I never wanted it to end. So, when we pulled up in front of my house after coffee, I wasn't ready to get out of the car.

"I had a great time tonight and I'd love to see you again."

"I'd love that too."

Adam leaned over a placed his hand on my cheek and kissed me. *I swear the world stopped with that kiss.* We sat forehead to forehead until my phone chimed. I groaned and checked the notification. It was Kayla. I could kill her. Then Adam laughed.

"What's so funny?"

"Your friend is waiting for you."

I looked over my shoulder and, lo and behold, she was standing there waving me out of the car. I felt like a teenager whose dad was flashing the porch light. Adam kissed me lightly and then got out to let me out of the car.

"I'll call you." Adam said.

I walked to my doorstep and smacked Kayla on the arm.

"You ruined a perfect moment."

"So, you don't give it all to him on the first date."

"No shit."

She laughed, and we walked into my kitchen. I uncorked a bottle of wine and gave Kayla every detail of my date. I gushed like a teenage girl and told her it was the best date I had ever been on.

"I told you so."

"Told me what?"

"I told you dating online would work. It was your first date from the site and it was the best one you've been on."

My phone chimed with an incoming text.

**Adam: I had an amazing time tonight. Thank you for changing my thoughts on dating.**

**Piper: Me too! And thank you for being the best date I've ever had.**

**Adam: Well I'll just have to top it with the next date.**

**Piper: Now that sounds fun. Can't wait to hear what it is.**

# Let's Try Love

**Adam: When I figure it out, I will let you know, but it will be soon.**

**Piper: Can't wait!**

I couldn't help but smile for the rest of the night. Maybe online dating was the way I needed to go from the beginning.

*One month later*

Dating Adam was like dating your perfect man. He called me every night, and we talked for hours. Our dates were always fun, even if they were just laid-back dinner dates and a movie at my place or his. I even let him see a sneak peek into my next book I was writing, and he couldn't wait to read the full thing.

I still checked the site periodically, but no one piqued my interests like Adam did. So, I decided to delete my account. That was until I saw Adam out with another woman. I was enjoying ice cream at the bookstore and working on my book when they walked in. I kept my head down so he wouldn't see, but I was hurt. I thought we were only seeing each other, not going on dates with others. I finished my ice cream, put my laptop away, and got up to walk out the door. Unfortunately, he saw me and his eyes went wide. He wasn't expecting to get caught. I left the store and it took all my strength not to cry until I was in my car.

"Piper! Wait!"

I didn't want to, but at the sound of my name I stopped and waited for him to catch up.

"It's not what you think."

"Oh, so you're not at the same spot you brought me to with another girl?"

"Well it is, but it's not a date. She's a client. I'm building her and her husband's house. See," he said pointing to the girl, and now man she was hugging on the sidewalk. "I would never do that to you. I was actually going to tell you that I left the site."

"You did?"

"Yes, I know it's only been a month, but I only want to date you."

"I was about to delete my profile and then I saw you walk in with her, and I just didn't know what to think."

"Everything ok, Adam?"

"Yes, everything's fine. I'll be with you in just a second."

He wiped my tears and I told him to get to his meeting and call me or just come over afterwards. He kissed me gently and told me he would see me later. I got to my car and felt like a complete idiot. I should have known he wouldn't do that. I got home and immediately got on the site and deleted my profile. Adam was it for me.

*Two years later*

These past two years of dating Adam have been the best years of my life, but now we were moving in together and I was excited. It meant I got to come home to the love of my life every night and I was totally ok with that.

I unlocked the door to our house and noticed there were no lights on. Not even the lamp I usually leave on in the foyer. I dropped my keys in the little bowl and flipped the lamp on. That's when I noticed the flower petals on the floor. I followed them to the living room and flipped the light switch on. All our friends and family jumped out and yelled "SURPRISE!" with Adam at the center of everyone on his knee. I was speechless. I walked to the center of the room and stood in front of him.

## Let's Try Love

"Piper, from day one on Date for Two I knew you were it for me, and I hadn't even met you yet. I was so happy you said yes to a date, and when I met you, I was done for. So, will you do me the honor of being my last date forever? Will you marry me?"

I stood in the center of the room speechless until Kayla said, "Well answer him already!"

"Yes! Yes, I'll marry you!"

He slipped a beautiful rose gold ring with a single diamond in the center on my finger and then picked me up and kissed.

"By the way, happy birthday baby."

I kissed him several times and then asked if I could go change before continuing my party. He set me down and sent me upstairs. There was a light pink dress, a necklace laid out on the bed for me, and some nude colored heels. I changed, fixed my hair and made my way back downstairs. I was handed champagne before all the ladies started to grab my hand to look at my gorgeous ring. I couldn't be happier. I looked across the room at Adam who was talking to my mom and I just smiled. Who knew that I would fall in love with a man because of a dating site?

A couple days after the party we both got an email saying that Date for Two is shutting down. There wasn't enough traffic to the site and they couldn't keep it going. So, I don't know what it was, either my love of a good love story or because I found love online, I decided to start my own dating site. Adam was completely on board and even helped me with the planning.

*Three months Later*

Before Let's Try Love made its debut, I had to get married. Kayla was helping with my hair and Adam's sister was helping me with my makeup. Once all of that was done, my mom helped me get in my dress.

"Don't do it, Momma. Don't you start crying. I'll mess up my makeup."

"I can't help it. My baby is getting married."

I hugged her tight and told her I love her so much and then my dad walked in. His tears just started to fall, and I almost lost it.

"You are breathtaking. Adam is one lucky man."

"Thank you, Daddy."

"Are you ready?"

"More than I'll ever be."

I walked down the aisle with my dad and watched as Adam covered his face to hide his tears. That was just the reaction I was hoping for when I saw my soon to be husband at the end of the aisle. My parents gave me away and Adam and I exchanged our vows. Everyone laughed as Adam didn't wait for the preacher to say the usual, 'I now pronounce you husband and wife, you may kiss the bride.' As soon as he was able, Adam kissed me.

"Well since someone is in a hurry," the preacher laughed. "I now pronounce you husband and wife. You can kiss the bride again."

So, he did.

*Now*

So, see, you can find love online. That's everything Let's Try Love is about. We want you to feel comfortable meeting the love of your life through a computer or an app. Let's Try Love is all about getting to know one another and falling in love just like Adam and I did. It's been two years since Let's Try Love was started and I can't wait to hear about when you find love through our site.

## About the Author

Jessie Chick is a small-town southern author who lives in a big city. She loves telling love stories especially with a country background. You can always find her chilling with her dogs, curled up on the couch writing all the words. She also loves putting the chick in chick-lit.

## Where You Can Find Her

www.facebook.com/authorjessiechick

www.facebook.com/groups/jessiesnerdypeeps/

https://twitter.com/Jessiechick2

www.instagram.com/jessiechickauthor/

## Anthologies She's a Part of

The Plus Sign featuring *Unexpected*
Our Secret Nook features *His Promised*
Casseroles features *Foot Pop Thanksgiving*
My True Love Gave to Me features *Santa's Paradise*

## Books She's Written

Deadly Love (Love in Detroit Book #1)

# Needing Forever

## by KL Fast

Shaye Chanler is ready for love.

Clayton Dickerson is looking for the one.

Let's Try Love is the perfect app to get these two together.

This is a safe and sexy short story...

# Needing Forever by KL Fast

# One

*Shaye Chanler*

We have been busier than normal today and I am almost out of flowers. I own Shaye's Daisies, the only flower shop in our little town right outside of Charlottesville, North Carolina. Ten minutes before closing, an older man, whom I know well, walks into the store with a smile on his face. I can't even be mad at him. Everybody knows everybody around here.

"Welcome to Shaye's, Mr. Hartford. How can I help you today?" I ask him.

"Well, it's a special day for my Lilly and I. It's our fiftieth anniversary and I want to surprise her with her favorite flowers. Do you have any pink daisies?" My heart melts.

"You're in luck! I just got a shipment of them today. How many would you like?"

## Let's Try Love

"Fifty of them please," he says grinning. "One for every year that she has been in my life."

"She is a lucky lady," I tell him while getting his order ready.

"No, my dear girl. I am the lucky one, she is my world. Lord knows I have no idea how that woman has put up with me for all these years." I laugh and hand him his flowers.

"Alright, here you go. That will be ninety-six dollars, including tax."

"Small price to pay to see her smile," he says, handing me his credit card. I run it and give him his receipt.

"Aren't you sweet. Have a nice evening," I say. I am so friggin' glad tomorrow is Friday. I'm not open weekends, because nothing is in Plain Springs, North Carolina is open on the weekends. Weekends are spent in Charlottesville, which is only twenty minutes away.

"You too, dear. Tell your grandparents I said hello," he says before leaving.

"Of course," I respond then I lock the door behind him and flip the sign to closed. I have had enough of today.

I want someone to love me like that. I need someone who wants to promise me forever. After the Chinese I ordered gets here, I make my way upstairs to my apartment. I plug my phone in and grab one of my favorite beers.

I take a sip of my drink and look at the website I found while searching for dating sites. Let's Try Love is the third site on the Google page. After reading reviews on their page for an hour, I finish three more beers while reading all of them. Now I have a buzz going and my inhibitions are gone.

"I don't want to see your nasty ass cock. I need forever, not a cock fest." I snicker and hit enter. I have been trying to find "the one" but

## Let's Try Love

instead I have been getting dick pics left and right with guys asking if I liked what I saw. *No, you no tiny-dicked motherfucker, I did not.*

What I don't understand is how some of the guys that send them are proud of their tiny weenies. I put my computer away, pick up my beer bottles and go grab another beer then make my way into my living room and put in the next disk of NCIS: LA in my Blu-ray player. Fuck me, Marty Deeks is sex on a stick.

I grab my phone off the charger and plop down on the couch. I quickly set my alarm so I'm not late to work in the morning then download the Let's Try Love app.

"Okay let's see if I can find Mr. Forever," I say to Snooky, my pit boxer mix. He sighs and puts his head on my lap. "Yeah, I hope we find him too." Four beers in and I am three sheets to the wind. My alarm goes off right, next to my damn ear and I scream, falling off the couch. I land on my side and groan. "Fuck me, that hurt like a bitch."

What the fuck happened last night? I sit up and the room spins. *Don't hurl, don't hurl.* I tell myself over and over as I stand up. Snooky is sprawled out on my bed, snoring. Once in the bathroom, I do my business, then get in the shower trying to wash away my hangover.

After a few minutes, I get out to get ready for the day. Then I take Snooky out for what I hope will be a quick walk, but of course, he takes his sweet ass time. He pays no mind to the thousands of tiny knives stabbing into my temple. I push my sunglasses further up my nose.

I really should pace myself. I am not much of a drinker and I have no idea why I drank so much last night but I am so regretting that right now.

"Snooky hurry up, mommy has to go to work." He stops barking and wags his tail. He loves coming into the shop with me. He might

## Let's Try Love

weigh seventy pounds but he is the biggest softy you could ever meet. He loves people and all of the attention they give him.

We make our way back to the shop where I grab him some water then I go in search of my phone. I hear it ping letting me know I have a message. Good thing it pinged, otherwise I would have never looked under the couch for it. I grab some coffee and unlock my phone. The page opens up to an open message tab.

**Promisingalways32: This might sound crazy but I think its fate that you signed up tonight."**

**Needingforever22: really, how so?**

**Promisingalways32: I was about to deactivate my account when I came across yours.**

**Needingforever22: and my profile made you change your mind?**

**Promisingalways32: oh yes believe it or not women do the same thing.**

**Needingforever22: Same thing?**

**Promisingalways32: Send unwanted nip pics.**

**Needingforever22: Ha, it doesn't surprise me women are just as pervy as men.**

**Promisingalways32: lol, would you like to go on a date with me tomorrow?**

**Needingforever22: Sure just know I like to eat steak and potatoes so no nasty vegan crap.**

**Promisingalways32: Haha, Steak and potatoes it is... pick you up around 7?**

**Needingforever22: Okay.**

"What the fuck, I told him where I live like some kind of dumbass he could be some kind of crazy person." I glare at Snooky like he actually had something to do with this. "Why didn't you stop me?" He

## Let's Try Love

huffs and walks into the kitchen. I exit out of the messenger box and go onto his profile page. Sweet baby Jesus! He is gorgeous.

Fuck, I guess it's a good I'm tired of playing it safe.

I grab my coffee cup and make my way downstairs Snooky following behind me. "If you think he is a creep you can bite is balls off okay?" I tell him. He barks once and wags his tail.

Time to get to work. Seven will be here before I know it.

## Two

*Clayton Dickerson*

"Hey, boss, where'd you go?" I look up to see Stan, my assistant, looking at me weirdly.

"Nowhere. I have been here all day," I respond, returning his weird look. God, if he wasn't my brother in law, I would have told him to go fuck himself. Other than being nosy, he's the best damn assistant I've ever had.

"Your body might be here but you sure aren't. I have been calling your name for the last five minutes," he says impatiently. I shake my head to clear it.

"Sorry, I just have an important, um, meeting tonight and it needs to go perfect." I hedge. I'm not exactly lying. I am meeting someone.

"You have a meeting? I didn't see it on the calendar. Did I miss it?" he asks concerned, while frantically looking through his iPad.

"No, you're fine. It is a personal meeting." He visibly relaxes

"Okay, if there is anything you need just let me know," he says walking out of my office. The damn goddess from last night has had me up all night. I knew the moment I laid eyes on her picture that she was going to be mine. I haven't been with a woman in longer then I can remember.

I was too busy trying to get my law practice up and running. By the time I was done doing that, I was suddenly thirty-two and looking for *the one*. That is extremely hard to find when women know how much you are worth, so I tried something new. A dating site, Let's Try Love. It was so out of the realm of normal for me, but I figured that it couldn't hurt to try. It was a little unconventional but I am desperate. I am tired of being alone and tired of not having someone I can call my own.

I have the house, the car, and the job. Now it's time for me to get the girl. I've been on the app for over a month only getting crazy ass women trying to sell me sex tapes of themselves.

I had given up on finding anyone on this site when her profile came up. I knew it was fate and had to take a chance. I rub my temples, accepting the fact that I will not be getting any work done today. I take off my tie and unbutton my first two buttons of my crisp white shirt. I lost the jacket as soon as I came in from the courthouse hours ago.

Beautiful Shaye is everything I've ever wanted in a woman. I give up working, since it's five-thirty, grabbing my jacket, I head out into the common area.

"Are you sick?" Stan asks, looking up from his laptop.

"What?"

"You never leave before eight. Are you sure you're okay, man?"

"Yes. The meeting, remember?"

"Oh, right. I'll head out now too if that's okay?" he asks. "I want to take Clint out to dinner tonight." Did I mention that Stan is married to my twin brother, Clint? Their son, Rudy, is only two months old. They had him via surrogate. They aren't sure which one of them is the actual father but man he is so cute. If I am honest, that's what got me thinking so much about having a family.

"Of course. Give my love to him and Rudy. See you guys at Mama's on Sunday." It's Nascar season and if the Dickerson's love anything as a whole, it's freaking Nascar.

"Will do." I walk outside. I haven't seen the early evening sun in weeks, but it's nice out. Getting into my Mercedes G Wagon, I pull out and head home. I am meeting her at O'Flannigans in

## Let's Try Love

Charlottesville. The restaurant is casual and nearby but I want to shower and change before meeting her. My house is on the outskirts of town, about fifteen minutes from my office.

At home, I shower quickly and get dressed. I feed the cat, Bob. Bob, the girl cat, Dickerson is her full name. She's actually my sister, Talia's cat. Talia might be insane but she is brilliant. Talia is studying abroad in Portugal this semester. Since my parents have two Bull Mastiffs, I volunteered to cat sit. Heading back out, I opt to take my BMW. It'll get me there faster.

I make it to the restaurant in record time. I'm a little early, but I am surprised to see her sitting at a high top table in the bar area. She is drinking a margarita. She looks amazing in a purple dress and sky-high heels. She is looking at something on her phone. I growl inwardly. She better not be making another fucking date on Let's Try Love. I don't know what I'd do.

"Shaye?" I ask startling her. She looks at up at me, and my heart does a little flip. Man, I sound like a pussy right now, but it's true. Her eyes are so blue they look violet.

"Yes," she says standing. She hugs me in greeting and I take the opportunity to smell her hair. She smells like summer: coconuts and fresh air. "It's so nice to meet you, Clayton, or do you prefer Clay?"

"Clay is fine," I say sitting down. She sits as well. She clenches her thighs together, squirming in her chair before crossing her ridiculously long legs under the glass top table. My cock swells at the mere thought of them wrapped around my waist. "You look beautiful."

"Thank you," she says biting her plump bottom lip and blushing. She picks up her menu and looks it over. I do the same.

"So, what looks good to you?" I ask. The only thing I want to eat is her. Damn, she is beautiful.

"Um, I'm not actually hungry… for food," she says quietly, setting her menu back down. This time, I do growl. Out loud. She jumps but doesn't take her gaze off of my face.

"Me either, doll. What should we do about it?"

"Take me home?" she asks.

"Let's go," I say, signaling for the check.

Besides, I can always feed her later.

# Three

*Shaye*

I have never been so bold in my life but I want him the minute I locked eyes on his honey brown ones. I was hooked. He grabs my hand and we walk out of the bar.

"We'll come to get your car tomorrow I can't stand that thought of being away from you," he says, pushing me up against the side of his car. His hard cock throbs against my lower stomach and I moan. He growls and kisses me. I wrap my arms around his shoulders and kiss him back. He tastes like sin and I can't get enough of him. Someone honks at us, "get a room," they shout out of the passing car. He pulls away from our kiss. I can feel the blush running across my cheeks and I can't help but laugh.

"Oh my God." He chuckles and opens the car door for me.

"Come on, doll, let's get you home," he says helping me into his car.

"Okay, hurry though. I feel like I am going to combust," I say breathlessly. My thighs clench together causing him to groan. After shutting the door, he gets in on the other side. He throws the car into drive and pulls out of the parking lot.

"Pull your dress up and spread your thighs, baby. I can smell that sweet pussy cream from here and I need a taste." I whimper and do as he asks he lets go of the steering wheel and runs his hand up the inside of my thigh. When he finds that I am not wearing any panties, he sucks in a sharp breath.

"Fucking hell, you are so wet for me. You want my cock in this tight little love hole, don't you baby?" he growls, slowly thrusting one of his thick fingers into my pussy. I moan and my hands wrap around his wrist

"Oh God! Yes, I want it," I mewl. He pulls his finger out then rubs it over my clit before thrusting it back in my hips buck up and I moan.

"That's right, sweet girl. Let me hear how much you love it. Your little virgin pussy is going to feel so good wrapped around my aching cock." My mouth pops open.

"Ah, how did you know I was a virgin?" I ask breathlessly. He curls his finger up and hits my g-spot.

"Because your greedy pussy is just begging to have my cock destroy it for another man," he growls I moan loudly and my eyes close as he brings me to an orgasm I sit there panting as he takes his finger out of me. I open my eyes and watch as he brings his finger to his lips and licks my pussy cream off of it.

Fucking hell, that should not be hot but holy fuck was it ever. I reach of and run my hand up his thigh and over his bulge his hands tighten on the wheel.

"Fuck," he curses. I lean closer to him and kiss his neck.

"You planning on being the only cock I ever have? Because that's the only way you're getting this pussy." I whisper into his ear before biting his ear as I cup his bulge squeezing it. He pulls into an open driveway and throws the car in park. Before I know it I am unbuckled and thrown over his shoulder my dress rides up over my hips and my naked ass is right by his face. He turns his head and bites me. I moan and spread my thighs a little. "Oh." My back suddenly hits a cold fridge door and I whimper. When did we get inside his house?

"Can't make it to the bedroom, need you right now," he says in a gravelly voice. He wraps his arm around my waist and holds me up as he quickly undoes his belt and pants then shoves them down his thighs just far enough. My wet pussy clenches with anticipation. My legs wrap around his waist. My stiletto's dig into his ass and he doesn't seem to mind.

"Fuck me, Clay." His hands tighten on my hips.

"I'm fucking keeping you forever, Shaye. You are always going to be mine." He growls, thrusting into me to the hilt, his heavy balls resting against my ass. My nails dig into his back and I scream out. He starts kissing my neck.

"Shh, it's okay baby," he says his hands going to my ass. I nod my head, breathing heavily. He pulls out a fraction of an inch then thrusts back in. I moan at the feeling of being stretched open. "Your sweet pussy feels so good around my cock, just like I knew it would."

I moan as he pulls out almost all the way then slams back in. I cry out in pleasure. He groans.

'I'm not going to last long doll. All I can think about is feeling your womb with my babies. Fuck you're going to look so fucking sexy round with my child." My pussy clenches and I whimper.

"Please, I want it harder. Fuck me, Clay. Fuck your babies into me," I demand, biting down on his neck. He growls and starts pounding into me over and over. All I can do is hang on as he fucks me onto his cock. "Oh God, oh God, just like that please, please," I beg mindlessly.

"Fuck your sweet pussy is starting to clamp down on my dick. You're already trying to milk my cum, aren't you? You're a greedy girl."

"Fuck yes. Give it to me," I scream as an orgasm comes crashing through my body. My head falls back and my hands latch onto his shoulders for dear life. He roars my name and I feel his cock get impossibly bigger as he comes. Rope after rope of his cum fills my womb. I shudder and another orgasm hits me. His head drops to my chest. Running my hands through his hair, I whimper when I feel his cock start to get hard again. "How are you hard again?" He chuckles and looks up at me.

"I have a feeling my cock is never going to go down again." I giggle and kiss him. When he pulls back he looks at me with a serious look on his face, I begin to worry.

"I'm never letting you go." My eyes fill with tears.

"Good thing, cause I wasn't ever planning on leaving."

He walks us to his room where he makes love to me three more times before I collapse on his chest, about to pass out. He runs his hands up my bare back and sighs in contentment.

"I'm going to love you forever, Shaye."

"I hope so because I'm going to love you always," I say kissing his chest.

# Four

*Clay*

Last night was the best night of my life, hands down. Shaye is everything I've ever wanted and then some. We drift off but suddenly she sits straight up.

"Shit. I forgot about Snooky," she says frantically.

"You can watch the Jersey Shore here, baby."

"Oh, God. I do love that show, that's where I got the name, but I am talking about my dog. I've never left him alone overnight before. I am being the worst fur-mommy right now."

"It's alright. We'll go get him. I'm sure Bob will be okay with it."

"Bob?"

"My sister's cat. She's around here somewhere," I say getting out bed.

"Bob is a girl?"

"Says the girl who named her dog after a fist-pumper in a short dress," I say laughing.

"Hey, it was the best telenovela from two thousand nine to two thousand twelve. Just try to deny it."

"Alright, you win," I say putting my hands up in surrender. I move to my dresser and pull on a pair of basketball shorts and a t-shirt.

"Where's my dress?" she asks getting out of bed, crawling around on the floor. Her naked ass wiggles in the air and I groan.

"You best get up, or we'll never leave this room. Let's get Snooky and then come back to bed."

"You say that like it's a bed thing."

"A bed thing?" I question, holding in my laughter.

"Freudian slip," she says shrugging.

"Right. Let's go."

She tells me her address, and I plug it into the GPS. She only lives five minutes from me. I pull into her driveway. She pops the passenger door open.

"I'll be right back," she says.

"Pack a bag. You don't live here anymore." I know that I am being high-handed but, fuck I am already obsessed with her.

"Excuse me? This is where I work."

"I see that Shaye's Daisies."

"So, I live upstairs," she says.

"No, you live with me now," I say.

"Oh. Is this your way of asking me to move in with you after one night?" she asks, looking confused. When I don't say anything, she continues. "I'm not saying no, I just want to clarify."

"Hell yes. I realize how fucking crazy this is, but I don't care."

She leans over and kisses me.

"I'll be right back."

"I'll come up with you," I say getting out the car. I follow up the stairs to her apartment. I can hear her dog scratching at the door.

"He sounds big," I say.

"He is, but he's a big teddy bear,' she says pushing the door open.

Snooky is a gorgeous dog. While she packs a bag for herself, I make myself useful getting the dog's things ready. Twenty minutes later, we are back home. Bob and Snooky get along great. I take my girl back to bed, where I love her for the rest of the night.

****

# Let's Try Love

Three weeks later, Shaye is completely moved into my house and it's like she's always been there. While I was at work today, I went to a local jewelry store on my lunch break and bought her an engagement ring. When five o'clock rolls around, I am out of the office like it's on fire. When I get home, she is already there and something smells amazing.

"I'm home, Shaye," I call out.

"In the kitchen," she shouts back. Walking into the kitchen, I see that it's a disaster area.

"What happened in here?" I ask.

"I'm making dinner. I am not very good at the cleaning up part."

"I see that," I say. It looks like every single pot and pan that I own is in the sink as well as the six sitting on each burner on the stovetop. "I'll clean up," I say taking my jacket off and rolling my sleeves up. "What are we having?"

"Parmesan crusted salmon, loaded mashed potatoes, asparagus, and salad," she says.

"Sounds like a feast," I say as I fill the sink with hot, soapy water.

"It should be. I got the recipe from my mom. I've never actually made the fish before, but the potatoes are my specialty."

"I am sure it will be amazing," I say getting to work tackling the dishes.

"This is kind of domestic," she muses.

"It is, isn't it? What's the occasion?" I ask.

"I was tired of going out," she responds. I am too if I'm honest. Each night that we've been together we've either gone out, brought takeout home or eaten at one of our parents houses.

## Let's Try Love

"Also, I have some big news. I'm pretty nervous about it actually. We haven't talked about it much, but I'm bursting to tell you," she says excitedly. I finish up the dishes and turn to her. The look on her face portrays her excitement.

"Tell me."

"I'm pregnant."

"Can you tell that soon?" I blurt out. That's not exactly what I wanted to say. Her face falls and I feel like a giant bag of dicks. "That's not what I meant baby. I'm sorry. I am so fucking happy," I say.

"Are you sure? We didn't exactly talk about it, except in like a sexy way," she says blushing. I chuckle.

"I am positive. You've made me the happiest man in the world. I love you." She looks up at me.

"I love you, too." I was going to do something special for a proposal, but this is better. The perfect moment.

"I love you," I say again. She smiles and kisses me softly. "Be my wife?" I ask pulling the ring box from my pocket.

"No shit?" she says before slapping her hand over mouth. I laugh again.

"No shit. Marry me."

"Yes. Of course. Fucking yes," she says jumping up into my arms. I support her by gripping her ass. I kiss her face.

Thank God, she said yes, because I don't know what I would have done.

"When did you do this?" she asks looking down at the diamond her finger after I've set her back down on her feet.

"At lunch today, though I have been thinking about it since the day we met."

"It's perfect. You have good taste, Mr. Dickerson."

## Let's Try Love

"So do you, Mrs. Dickerson."

"Mrs. Dickerson? God, I *love* the sound of that."

So do I.

I never thought that a dating app would find me the love of my life, but I'll be forever grateful that it did.

# Epilogue

*Shaye*
*Ten Years Later*

I sit on the back porch breastfeeding Grace, our sixth child, watching Clayton and our other five children play on the playground. They have already had dinner and since it was still light out, I decided they should come out and waste some of the energy before bed.

Clay had specially built for them. It's in the shape of a boat with swings on one side and the inside is basically a tree house. They spend most of the summer trying to camp out here. We can barely get them in the house. I am not going to complain though after all that, the house tends to stay cleaner when they are outside. Unless I am cooking then the kitchen is a complete wreck. Luckily, Clay just kisses my cheek and cleans up after me as I go.

My life is better than I could have ever imagined. How can your dreams turn out even better than you thought they would be? Grace sighs and I know she is done. I put my boob back in my shirt then put her on my shoulder, lightly patting her back.

"How are my girls doing?" I look up to see Clay walking towards us.

"Hey baby. We are good. How was work?" I ask as he leans down and kisses me.

"It was good. I actually have some big news that I want to talk to you about"

"You are going to retire aren't you?" I have known that he hates being away from us and he is ready to be retired. I have just been waiting for him to decide what he want to do. His eyebrows shoot up.

"How the hell do you always know what I want to talk about?"

"Because I am your other half, my love. Not to mention I have super mommy powers that make me know everything," I say laughing. He grabs Grace from me then sits down next to me I turn to the side and drape my legs over his.

"You truly are amazing, baby. I don't know how you do it all. You run this house, take care of our kids, and still run the shop. You amaze me more and more every day." I blush. He's so right for me. He always knows just what to say.

"I love you, husband."

"And I love you, wife. How about you go take a bath and I can take care of the kids." I grin.

"Hell yeah. You know I love our new bathtub," I say getting up. He got us a huge tub that could easily fit four people. It even has jets! He redid our master bathroom for Mother's Day last year and it's now one of my favorite places in the house. I lean over and kiss him soundly.

I make my way to the bathroom and get the tub going. While it is filling up, I toss a bath bomb in it. Then I turn on four of my fake candles, the ones that use the batteries. I fucking love them. I don't have to worry about tipping one over in the bathtub and burning the shit out of myself.

Once the bath is full, I turn off the light and get in. Sighing in content, I soaking up the hot water. I must have fallen asleep because the next thing I know I am in Clay's arms and he is taking me to bed.

"You are one tired mama, love." I snuggle into his chest.

"Where are the kids?" I mumble he kisses the top of my head.

"They are all asleep since you had already fed them dinner, I just gave them all a fast shower and now they are all piled up on the living room floor, in the fort that they built. And Grace is in her crib."

## Let's Try Love

I wrap my arms around his shoulders and kiss him.

"You are the best daddy ever."

"Thank you baby. I am still trying to figure out how they conned me into letting them all sleep in the living room," he says perplexed.

"They are turds and know if they give you their best puppy dog eyes that you can't say no to them." He chuckles and puts me on the bed.

"I can't even argue with that they all have me wrapped around their fingers," he says going to the closet and getting me a pair of underwear and bringing me one of his shirts. I put both of them on while laughing. I get under the covers.

"Hurry up and come snuggle me." I tell him as he starts taking off his clothes.

"Okay, I will be right back." He goes into the bathroom and takes a fast shower, himself. When he is dressed, he climbs into bed behind me. Then pulls me close. His hard cock digging into my ass.

"Always so hard for me.' I tease pushing my ass against him he groans and his hand goes to my hip, squeezing it.

"He is always ready for your sweet pussy baby."

"Fuck me until I pass out," I demand, pushing his sweats down. He drapes my leg over his hip and yanks my panties to the side. He slams into me from behind,

"Fuck, your pussy feels so good wrapped around my cock."

He pounds into me over and over until I come screaming his name. He isn't far behind me. He kisses my shoulder and pulls out of me. We both groan at the loss. He rights my panties, and caresses my ass.

"Thank you. But I don't think I've passed out," I say laughing before giving him a quick kiss.

"I fucking love you Shaye. So much. You are my always." He laughs with me before wrapping his arm around my waist. I snuggle closer to him.

"I love you too, Clay. You are my forever."

We are forever and always.

I fall asleep in his arms with a smile on my face knowing that there is no way I could have ever asked for a better life.

# Acknowledgements

Thank you to my husband, Seth. You have always been my # 1 fan. Thank you for supporting my dreams.

MK Moore, my partner in crime. Thank you for pushing me out of my comfort zone. Thank you for dealing with my crazy ass when I am on a deadline. Thank you for being a kick-ass best friend. I love your face .6 times…

And to my readers. Thank you for sticking with me this far!

-KL

# More by KL Fast

**Kissing Junction, TX series written with MK Moore**
*-Candy Corn Kisses*
*-Thankful Kisses*
*-Candy Cane Kisses*
*-Champagne Kisses*
*-Chocolate Kisses*
*-Midnight Kisses*
*-Shamrock Kisses*
*-Summer Kisses*
*-Cowboy Kisses*

**Clearwater Curves Serial written with Elisa Leigh, C.M. Steele, & MK Moore**
*-Delicious Curves (Book # 4)*

**Hauntingly Romantic Serial written with Elisa Leigh, C.M. Steele, & MK Moore**
*-Hunting Luna (Book # 1)*

**Seven Brides of Christmas Serial written with MK Moore, Elisa Leigh, Sylvia Kane, Shelby Reeves, Elizabeth Princeton, & Vanna King**
*-A Groom By Christmas (Book # 1) written with MK Moore*
*-Winter's Christmas Bride (Book # 5)*

## About the Author

KL is a twenty-five-year-old doing what she loves. She's making her dreams come true one book at a time. She is the wife of a chef and the mother of an amazing son. She is a full-time author who does a little housework on the side. She can be found perusing social media when she should be writing. If you like Hot AF Alphas and Sassy Heroines with seamy yumminess and sweet Happily Ever After's than her books are right up your alley.

FACEBOOK: www.facebook.com/KLFast2020/
BOOKBUB: https://www.bookbub.com/profile/kl-fast
INSTAGRAM: KLFAST2020
Email: klfast2020@gmail.com

# More Than Enough

## by ChaShiree M.

*AraLynn*

I don't expect to find love. Especially on a dating site. But I long for companionship. Someone to laugh with, talk to and maybe, just maybe, they won't be too disgusted to touch me. But miracles like that don't happen.

Right? Well apparently, they do on 'Let's Try Love'. Or that's what it feels like every time I am with him.

I found him there.

Fell in love day by day.

But I can't help wondering……Do people really find true love in dating sites?

*Mike*

I decided love wasn't for me. Ladies want glamour, material things and stuff I will never be able to afford.

My mom had other plans.

After finding my Goddess on Let's Try Love, I decided to through caution to the wind and go after what I wanted.

Her. Everyday. For the rest of our lives.

I just hope she believes me. Because no matter what she says.

She is MINE!!!

# More Than Enough by ChaShiree M.

## One

*AraLynn*

My fingers brace over the keyboard, heart pounding, mind racing, and nerves dwindling with each second, I don't type. It is my current state of being in the moment. I had heard about the 'Let's Try Love' dating site from a lady at work, who supposedly has a cousin that met her now husband on said site. You know how these things go. It's always a friend of a friend of someone else. Although skeptical, I have nothing to lose at this point. Let's be honest; anything is better than the weirdos my best friend Crystal keeps trying to hook me up. Can't be that bad you say. OK!!

The first guy was sweet when we communicated over the phone. We ended up talking for about a week, about any and everything. For some reason, I ignored the fact that he kept asking about my weight and the kind of sweets I liked. I assumed he was trying to make certain I wasn't one of those girls he would take to dinner and order a salad minus the dressing and the meat. When we did finally go out, he took me to a place called Le Chocolat. I was slightly confused because I was pretty sure they only served dessert. But hey, what did I know?

When we got to the restaurant, and after receiving the menu, my original assessments confirmed. I decided to go along with it since I was there already. After we ordered, things took a swift turn when he tried to feed me fondue dipped pound cake. I politely told him no thank you, but he insisted again. In my mind, I am thinking, 'Ok AraLynn, he is trying to be sweet. Let him be sweet' so I ate the cake from his hand.

It was weird enough as it was, but when he moaned and began to shake as the cakes devoured in my mouth, I began to freak out on the inside. I quickly glance around to see if anyone was watching us. I mean in a way I wanted witnesses. There needed to be people who could say I was there in case he takes me out back, chops me up, and eats me. At the same time, I didn't want people seeing how low I had stooped in the dating pool.

As I turned around to face him, I was running through excuses in my head on ways to get out of here as fast as possible. Instead, I am met with a slice of pie in my face.

*"You said you like chocolate. See the frosting. Lick it. I want nothing more than to see you lick it for me. Oh god. Your little tongue is peeking out and licking the frosting with your chubby cheeks all rosy because you love it. Oh yes."*

Oh no!!! Standing immediately, I pushed my chair back so fast I almost gave myself whiplash. There was no way I was saying

## Let's Try Love

anything to him. I grabbed my purse and hightailed it out of there like my thong was on fire. I had almost made it to the door when I am stopped by a moan. It not a single moan mind you, but a chorus of moans. I paused to find the source. What I saw was.... I don't know how to describe it. All around me there were plus size women with men feeding them food. Not only were the men feeding them, but the women and the men were also getting off on it.

I had no idea what alternate universe I was in, but I wanted out.

When I finally made it home, I called Crystal and gave her a piece of my mind. I don't judge people and feel everyone is entitled to their kinks. But seriously, I have been reduced to Fideism?!

That wasn't the last time she tried to hook me up.

The final straw was when she introduced me to a man named Hector. We texted and talked over the phone, and everything was normal. He **seemed** rather 'boring' if you will, which was a relief. One night he detailed how our first date would be, and his request had the wheels turning.

*"Just don't wear open-toed shoes or flats with rounded or pointed toes."* WTF. Deciding to reserve my concern for a second, I simply asked him why. His response....... *"Well, I have plenty of time to see your feet later. Right? Just not on the first date."* And with that statement, I'm done. The date never happened, and Crystal was banned from playing matchmaker for me ever again. I did tell her I thought it's a reflection of her, that every guy she tried to match me with has had some weird fetish or another.

She didn't find that funny.

It is now a year later since all that craziness, and I am ready to find...someone. I would love to get married, have babies, and live a HEA. But in this day and age of videos, exercise fanatics, and girls that don't eat, no one is going to want a size 16 wife. One with a soft, pudgy stomach, nonetheless. So, I will settle for a companion. Someone I can go to the movies with, maybe snuggle during a movie marathon at home, and talk to on the phone. Hopefully to even feel a bit... feminine. Having sex would be awesome, but I'm not holding my breath.

Taking a deep breath, I start filling out the profile. It's not as bad as I expected. The questions are fairly innocuous, and I don't feel as if I am purging my soul. Actually, I enjoyed myself a bit. The easiest part was answering the questions about any potential matches. I am not shallow, so that part was easy. My picks were an average looking man because I didn't dare pick an athlete or anyone like that. Talk about a suicide mission. I don't care about income or education. The thing I want the most is for him to be a nice person with a good sense of humor and like to go out and seen with **me**. The rest of the questions were the same.

Then it came to the picture part. I don't have many pictures to share because I don't take them. Everyone knows the cameras adds 10 lbs. and I needed that like I needed a hole in the head. Lucky for me, Crystal and my mom don't take no for an answer, so I at least have a couple. After flipping through the ones, I have I pick the one that makes me look less like a cow and upload it.

Phew. Well, no turning back now.

Now, I wait.

# Two

*Mike*

"MOM!" Where is that meddling woman and pain in the ass? As I am walking through the house, my stomach begins to grumble. I smell meatloaf. No one makes meatloaf like my mama.

"In here Mike." She says trying to use her sweet voice on me. I call bullshit. That woman is as charming as a snake. I have seen her outwit plenty of women in my shop who are trying to 'make eyes' at me as she calls it. She spits nasty, just as sweet as a caramel cake.

She thinks she is slick because when I walk into the kitchen, sitting on the counter is a caramel cake. My favorite, see... slick. She only makes caramel cake when she knows she is in the dog house and wants to sweeten me up. Not this time. She has gone too far.

"There's my boy. Come over here and kiss your dear old mom." It doesn't matter how mad I might be, and I am not ever going not to kiss my mama. The woman birthed and raised me as a single mom after my dad died when I was 10. She worked day and night to make sure we got to keep our house and didn't go without what was needed. For that alone, I will always show her how much I love her, even when I want to strangle her.

I lean over to kiss her before backing up against the counter. Crossing my ankles and folding my arms across my chest, I give her my best 'I'm peeved' look.

"What's got your drawers twisted boy?" She asks as she is feigning innocence.

## Let's Try Love

"Mama, why do I have a profile on a dating site?" She stops stirring the beans for a split second but quickly recovers It was long enough for me to see that she is a little nervous.

"Now see here my boy, you know I am an old and ailing woman. I don't know anything about intranets, wide webs, and such. How am I to know?" Ailing my ass. She is healthier than a damn OX. Ailing. She must think I'm 'special'.

"Mama! What did I tell you? I told you that I wasn't interested in seeing anyone. Who the hell needs the headache from a whining woman, who complains about all the crap she wants that I can't give her?"

"If I knew what you were talking about and I don't, but if I did, I would say I have heard great things about this 'Let's Try Love' site."

"Ah ha. Gotcha!! I didn't say what it is called. Now listen here; you take the damn thing down."

"Oh, are they cursing their mamas nowadays? You listen here young man because you are not too old for me to put you over my knee."

"Mama!!! My leg wouldn't even fit on your thigh at this point. Now are you going to take it down or what?"

"Not!" Damn it. She's, so exasperating.

"And why not?"

"Because I think you are a plum fool. There are plenty of women who don't care about things such as money. I think you're scared of getting hurt. Well, I'm sorry, but that's life son. I am not getting younger, and I want grandkids before I'm too senile to know who they are."

Her and those damn grandkids. She sure is laying it on thick, isn't she?

"Now. I suggest you go and sit in front of the computer and look at the matches that popped up today. I flagged a couple I thought looked promising. Now go on. Dinner will be ready soon."

Did she dismiss me? Damn woman. Never mind that I have told her over and over I am not interested in dating some shallow and too done up woman that won't eat anything but salad while talking about shit I don't care for.

Then why do I find myself going to the damn app on the computer and looking at the pictures my mama flagged. Scrolling through still has me annoyed, and I wouldn't have known about it if it wasn't for my buddy Rod. He's one of my employees at the shop. His baby sister is on the site and came across my photo, then mentioned it to Rod. I was livid of course, but it didn't take a genius to figure out who did it. Although….

"Now, you are right about one thing. When I saw you three days ago, you didn't even know what a 'www' was. How, pray tell, did you manage to do all of this? Who helped you?"

"Say what now? How do you know I didn't just turn into a genius all of a sudden?" Now she fancies herself a comedian? It is all too much.

"Mama," I demand. And when she looks at me a bit sheepishly, I have my answer.

"Has Anzel been sniffing around here again?" Anzel is her next-door neighbor. He is a widower, and he and my mama have struck up a friendship in their old age. I figure that they fancy one another and actually it doesn't bother me any.

"I will have you know that it was Heather who came over to help an old woman learn her way around the new stuff. She is such a sweet child and is always checking up on her grandpa. Grandkids are wonderful. Not that I would know." She mutters that last part.

Ignoring her meddling ass, I sit back down and continue scrolling through the list. So far, they all look par for the course. Like they are angry or starving. No thank you. I am about to turn it off when the pop-up window comes up with a new match.

"AraLynn." Well shit. It has to be a mistake. Someone is playing a joke. Right? I mean, it has to be. There is no way that this angel is single and in need of a dating site. The picture before me is of a woman. I mean, a real woman with curves and all. If I put a plate of pancakes, bacon, and eggs in front of her, she would not feign calorie watching to get out of eating.

Holy shit. My not so little cock is in my pants thumping and panting away, while I am looking at this curvy Goddess. No woman that I can recall has ever made little Mike stand at attention as quick and hard as she has. I can imagine grabbing ahold of her sexy big hips as her ass is on my face. Then my cock slams in and out of her juicy pussy.

What the hell. I cannot have a hard-on at my mama's house. Before I can second guess myself, I like her picture and press a button that signifies an interest.

As I sit in the chair staring at her picture, and all I want to do is take my cock out of my pants and stroke it while picturing her taking her clothes off. I can feel it weeping in my boxers and demanding I go and take its state of distress out on her little pussy.

Shit. Now I wait.

# Three

*AraLynn*

"Ara, are you listening to me?" I can barely hear the screech coming from Crystal at being ignored. The truth is I have not heard anything she's said in the last five minutes. I started out listening, I swear I did, but then my phone chimed from an email that was from the dating site. I clicked it open to an image of holy hotness.

The picture of the man staring at me is one who is more than swoon-worthy. I am talking Liam Hemsworth hot. Considering it is popular opinion that Chris is the hotter Hemsworth, I disagree. Liam has a brooding darker look and bedroom eyes that makes him by far the hotter brother. Let's also not forget to mention that his body's built for sin. Sure, Chris's built like Thor-ish, I get it, but I don't need all those bulging muscles. I need simple and healthy not conceited. Liam is healthy and seems less than full of himself.

There is something about the man in the picture, that tells me he would be kind at least. Clicking the link for details, I am shocked to see that he has pressed the button to initiate contact.

Holy hell!! Not sure what to do, I start to read his ice breaker question.

**'If you could do anything in the world for fun, what would it be?'**

Huh. I have never been asked that before, but to me, it is the easiest question in the world.

**'Take a cooking class.'** I answer. It's true. I consider myself to be a pretty decent cook and make a mean homemade Mac and Cheese with a white sauce. But I would love to take a class to learn how to make a fancy dish. And what would be more fun than taking a couple's class?

I know it sounds unconventional and unromantic, but again I am a simple person. In my life, I have never expected a lot of things out of it. There are no illusions as to what men see when they look at me. Half the time, the ones that hit on me are more interested in my boobs. Which does make sense, considering they make it in a room before I do? They stand at an enormous DDD with a 40 circumference. I can't expect anything else, can I?

Oh well. I know he won't respond because no guy wants to take a cooking class, but at least I was true to myself. Getting ready to stand and stretch my legs, my phone buzzes. I hadn't logged out of the app yet, so it shows the message.

"Holy crap!!! He responded." I didn't realize I shouted until Crystal is in my face.

"Who responded to what?" I try to move because I am not ready to share the information. But I am too late.

"You signed up for a dating site? Ara. I am proud of you. You are putting yourself out there. Good for you. Now, show me the hunk who answered your profile." Her enthusiasm makes me want to cry. It is why I keep her around. She has never made me feel as if I am not anything but a size ten like her. She has always been a very supportive friend in my life even when we were little kids.

I flip the phone around to show her the picture and start cringing in anticipation of her response. Crystal is a bit discerning when it comes to men. She has certain expectations and a type I know he won't fit.

"Ara, he is handsome. You two would be hot together." My mouth literally, drops open. Who is she and what has she done with my bestie?

"What?" She sees my face and hunches her shoulders.

"I just…. I mean…nothing. Never mind. So, you think I should answer him back?"

"Hell yea!!! Why wouldn't you?"

"Well look at him and look at me. A man like him cannot want me for anything other than the obvious. Right?"

"Ara. How many times have I told you this? You are beautiful. Curvy is the new in. And there is nothing about you that needs to change other than your confidence. Now, if you don't answer that message, I will do it for you."

Now, I really do start crying. She hugs me and tells me how much she loves me. Then she tells me how she prays every night that I find a man worthy of my heart. When I finally stop sniffling, I open the message and gasp.

**Sounds like a fun night and a great way to get to know such a beauty as yourself. I know the perfect place. If you would be so inclined for tomorrow night? Say seven? I can either come and pick you up or if you prefer since this will be our first meeting, I can send you the address, and you can meet me.**

I am not sure how to respond. Not about the date, because I am saying yes to that. But about the picking up part.

"Tell him you will meet him. He may be cute, but we don't know if he is a serial killer. So…"

"Good point."

**I will meet you if you would give me the address.**

I wait a couple of minutes, and sure enough, he responds. It is as if he is sitting by his phone waiting for me to respond as well.

**Le Contrare. Do you know it? It's on State and Randolph.**

Holy moly!!!! He can get us into Le Contrare!! There isn't a person in the whole of Illinois who doesn't know about that restaurant. It is the poshest restaurant in Chicago and almost impossible to get into. The chef himself makes the popularity of the restaurant more. Chef Alex Gallos. He won a season of Iron Chef America and then went on to the win it in Canada as well. He has worked under the likes of Wolfgang Puck.

**Of course, I know about it!!! You can get us into there??!!! Wow!!!! I am excited. Sorry for all the exclamation points. Just really excited. Ok, see you then at seven.**

"Crystal, I think I am in over my head." This is typical of me. I get excited about something and then immediately talk myself out of it with self-doubt.

"Why do you say that?"

"He can get us into Le Contrare, and I'm not fancy enough for a place like that. I knew he was too gorgeous to be ordinary and I think I need to cancel the date. It's not like we have already met, right? No harm no foul."

"You listen to me woman. You need to get your ass in that room and find a dress. Something cute and flirty, but not slutty. You are starting to get on my last nerve about this. What about you is ordinary? You finished college as Cum Laude and got accepted into the most prestigious nursing school in the country, but you turned it down to take care of your ailing mom. You are the most beloved teacher at the preschool where you work and volunteer at the shelter every third Sunday. No one is a more caring person. Now cut the shit and stand up straight."

Well huh. I want to say something smart to her, but she would probably pop me or something, knowing her. I love her though. She never fails to talk me off the ledge.

Now if only I could take her with me on my date.

# Four

*Mike*

Shit. I am extremely nervous. It has been a better part of two years since I have been on a date. It's not that I didn't have the opportunity but seeing the drama around me of the men in my shop and their women has turned me off. So, then what the hell am I doing?

With that thought, my cock decides to sit up and answer the question. Apparently, because a woman has caught my attention in more ways than one, he wants his piece. Screw my nonplussed ass, he says — disrespectful ass.

I've been sitting in the kitchen of the restaurant for the last hour trying to calm my nerves and to make sure the date goes off without a hitch. In the deep core of my body, I need to impress her.

"Calm down Mike. Shit. I hadn't seen you this worked up, since senior year when you were going to ask out Mary Noro to prom." My cousin Alex says, chuckling at me.

"Shut up. Make yourself useful and tell me what you are going to have us cooking tonight."

"Ah, dear cousin. I am going to teach you two how to make Tuscan Chicken with Fettuccine noodles."

"Sounds like a pansy-ass dish to me," I say and grin as I walk away. I like giving him shit. The truth is, my cousin is and always will be my best friend. Our fathers were brothers, and therefore we grew up more like brothers than cousins. I am incredibly proud of all he has accomplished, and I am his biggest supporter and investor though it's as a silent partnership.

"Whatever. Mama's boy. Does she know you are here for a date tonight?"

"NO! And you keep your big ass mouth closed. Don't go spouting off to Auntie either, because you know her, and mama is like Thelma and Louise."

"Don't I know it." He mutters.

I look at my watch and realize she should be pulling up at any moment and walk out of the kitchen towards the entrance. Before I can make it to the front of the restaurant, she is coming through the door. Holy Shit!!!

She walks in looking the sexy Goddess she is, and I swear my heart is beating in chants. *Get her. Claim her. Own her. Mine. Mine.* ***MINE.***

Needing to stop and take a breath before I decide to charge over, throw her over my shoulder, and take her out of this place where all the men are staring at her tits and ass in the obscene dress she is wearing. I turn my back before she sees me to take a few deep breaths — Son of a bitch. My dick is so hard he could pound cement how the fuck is I supposed to hide my fucking erection.

"Mike?" I hear it whispered behind me. Shit. It looks like I have no time to figure it out. I turn slowly, while willing my cock to act like he has some manners. The fucker has a mind of his own.

"Yes. AraLynn? So glad you could make it." I say like a schmuck. I hold my hand out to shake hers. But when she tentatively puts hers in mine, I am hit with a jolt of lightning that flows up through my arm and straight to my heart. This is the moment my life has changed. I won't even mention the delinquent in my pants.

I know she feels it too when she gasps ever so softly and bites her bottom lip. So much for telling the greedy fucker in my pants to behave. Every instinct in my body wants to suck the offending lip

# Let's Try Love

from between her teeth into my mouth and see what she tastes like. Looking at her, I can picture any number of decadent sweet things. All of which I would devour. Especially her pussy.

Get a grip, Mike. Now is not the time to think about the honey in her pants. Clearing my throat, I lean in and kiss her cheek, which immediately turns a beautiful rosy color. My fucking mistake is in inhaling her scent. Cinnamon and Roses. Fuck. It is completely fucked. There is no way I will be able to leave without tasting some part of her body. It's fucking potent.

With my hand at the small of her back, I usher her to the back of the restaurant reserved for special classes and functions.

"How did you get us a class here and at such short notice?" She asks.

"I know someone who works here, and he didn't mind doing me a solid."

"Must be some friend. Is he a waiter here? Is he working right now?"

Jealousy, like I have never felt before, is raining down on me. The possessiveness that only she seems to wake wants to corner her in a closet and tell her whoever it is doesn't matter. The only man who will matter from this moment forward in her life will be me. I almost do it, but her next words stop me.

"I would like to thank him before we leave." So, fucking sweet.

Before I can answer, we are in the room.

"Welcome. I am……"

"Chef Alex. Oh my gosh. I am a huge fan and watched you win both your titles. Holy moly. It is a pleasure to meet you." She says far too enthusiastically for my liking. My hand is on her back, and I can feel it wrapping around her waist and pulling her slightly back, to my front. My cousin, the ass, smirks at me. He knows me better than anyone.

"Mike, you should have seen him on Iron Chef America. His focus was super sharp. He blew the other three competitors out of the water. What brought you to Chicago to open a business? I am sure you had offers from everywhere." Although I am feeling a bit jealous, her enthusiasm is infectious, and I find myself thoroughly impressed with her detail.

"Well, a little known fact is that I was born and raised here, and my family still lives here. Isn't that right cousin?" Cheeky bastard.

She turns to me with her mouth open.

"Chef Alex is your cousin? Wow."

"Yea. My first cousin. He and I are more like brothers though. Sorry I didn't tell you. Just...you know. Private and all."

"No. I totally get it. I do understand." She says with a blush. When she looks down, and her eyes close, I can see her lashes on her cherub cheeks looking like succulent lolita. Her eyelashes are even sexy. Long and full. They remind me of Marilyn Monroe. I lift her chin with my finger, because in here in this room I can get a look at her up close. As soon as her eyes meet mine, I suck in a breath. I am stunned by the most beautiful jewels looking back at me. I am lost.

Staring back at me is the bluest eyes I have ever seen. No. Blue is too tame. More like a cerulean. They are big, round, and very expressive. Hers are truly the window to her soul. Through them, I can tell she is gentle and unsure. About what I don't know, but I intend to find out and eradicate it.

"You ready to get the cooking baby," I ask rubbing her bottom lip with my thumb. When her tongue very innocently comes out and licks it, while nodding her head, I growl not giving a fuck if we have an audience. I lean into her ear and make sure my day-old stubble runs across her neck. She shivers at the touch and proximity, letting me know I am not alone in the rapidly growing intensity.

"Mmmm…. baby. You might want to be a little more discerning about when you use that tongue goddess. A man like me is only held tight for so long before he unleashes it. And it won't matter where we are. Now, let's go cook before I say to hell with this and take you in the changing room." She moans at my words, and I notice her legs are rubbing together. Fuck. If just my words have her rubbing herself together, she is going to be one hot little sex kitten once I get her under me.

"All right kids. Let's begin. I thought we could make Tuscan Chicken tonight. Something easy enough for you to replicate later as a stay in night. Sound good?"

I nod. She uses words.

"Sounds great Chef Alex."

"None of this Chef Alex. Just Alex. Besides, by the look of things you are going to be family soon."

I roll my eyes at the shit starter, but I cannot deny that my head, heart, and cock all agree. When I look over at her, once again she is blushing, and I have to remember to count in my head. Her innocence is going to be the thing that gets her fucked hard and often.

Fuck. This is going to be torture.

## Five

*AraLynn*

"While the chicken is cooking, go ahead and sauté the mushrooms. Right about now would be the time to drop the pasta in the boiling water. Salt the water to taste."

I have been dreaming of taking couples cooking class for a long time, and with someone who wanted to be there. Now that I am, and from a nationally known chef no less, and with a man as hot and attentive as Mike, all I can think about is how good he smells.

When he was whispering in my ear earlier, my body went on high alert. The minute I smelled him, I wanted to rub myself on him like a wanton hussy and beg for his touch. His finger rubbing on my lip was so freaking hot that I felt stuck to the spot I was in. But, his smell. He smelled of fresh soap, and …... something like oil. I have no idea what it is, but it smelled manly, and I wanted it all over me.

Don't get me started on his words. They were dirty and hit their target. My pussy. As soon as he opened his mouth and told me to watch where I put my tongue, I knew I was a goner. My pussy began dripping and twitching at the same time. I tried to rub my legs together to squelch the throbbing, but damn it didn't work. Now here I am with this gorgeous man, and it feels like it's a dream.

"You were telling me you grew up with a single mom." See attentive. He does listen to me.

"Yea. I never knew my dad. Whenever I would ask my mom about him, she would say, 'We were not what he needed'. I could see how sad it made her, so I stopped asking."

## Let's Try Love

"Wow, babe. I'm sorry you never knew your dad, but I am glad to know you had a good childhood." He is sweet. Since we have been here, he has been such a gentleman. He gets me glasses of water, so I don't dehydrate in front of the hot stove. Ludicrous, but sweet. At one point, the chicken was browning and jumped out the pan, stinging me a bit. He made such a fit that Alex stopped the lesson to get the first aid kit. Mike then cleaned my arm and put ointment on it. If that wasn't sweet enough, he insisted on being the one to finish the chicken so it wouldn't pop on me again.

'You've been asking about me all night, mister. Tell me about you. What do you do for work?" He tenses almost immediately, and I want to take back the question. I'm not sure why he reacted to it, but I want to go back before the question. I am about to say never mind when he takes a deep breath and answers.

"I own a car repair shop over on Lake St."

"That's awesome."

"Yea."

Ok. I don't know what to say now, so I choose to say nothing. I am confused. I don't know what happened. We were having a great time, and then one question changes it all. I feel the tears forming, and I refuse to cry in Alex Gallos's kitchen over Tuscan Chicken.

"I'm going to go to the lady's room." I can hear the shakiness in my voice. As I am about to turn the handle, he hands grab my shoulders. I don't have to look to know it's him. I can smell him and crap he smells good.

He turns me towards him and pulls me into his arms. Being wrapped tight in his arms, I can almost believe he cares. It feels good to be held, but somehow, I know it's more about the person holding me.

## Let's Try Love

"I'm a sorry baby. I didn't mean to be short. It's not you. You are perfect."

Snorting before I can stop myself, I look up, and all thought leaves my head. This man just called me perfect. As flawed as that statement is, I can see by the sincerity in his eyes that he believes it.

"I'm not perfect Mike."

"Oh, Angel. You have no idea, do you? How beautiful and absolutely sexy you are? My dick has been achingly hard since I saw your picture. You cannot image, how much I want to kiss and suck your bottom lip into my mouth over and over until it swells."

"So, what's stopping you?" Who the hell is this woman? I am shocked at what came out of my mouth and drop my head to hide the mortification. His hands in my hair bring my head back and not a second too soon because his mouth is inches from mine.

"Good question baby. Absolutely nothing."

His mouth crashes onto mine, and I swear I hear Zayn Malik and Taylor Swift singing about living forever in my head. This is the kiss to end all kisses. His mouth is soft, seeking, and comforting. It's sweet. But forget sweet.

Opening my mouth was apparently all the invitation he needed. The kiss becomes forceful and almost sinful. His tongue snakes its way in my mouth consuming all I have, like a missile looking to destroy. He finds it when my tongue decides to join the party, and we do a dance. My arms go around his neck to give me the leverage to go up on my toes. Not sure what I am trying to accomplish, but I need to be closer to him. His hands are everywhere — my head, my back, and finally my ass.

Moaning is the current acoustic, and I hear it everywhere. Then again, it is coming from both of us. His hands squeeze me harder while pulling me into his zipper. Holy hell!! If the bulging behind that

## Let's Try Love

zipper is any indication of what he is hiding, I should be afraid. But somehow, I know he won't hurt me. It definitely, turns me on, and I rub myself against it over and over, while trying to get some friction for the part of me that is aching. His arms lift me off my feet, and I'm wrapped around him.

I have no idea how long we are standing in the hallway kissing and sucking each other's face off; but when he pulls his mouth from mine, I find myself chasing it trying to bring it back. He puts his forehead against mine. We both are breathing as if we just ran a marathon.

"Shit! AraLynn. I'm sorry. I didn't mean to lose control. You deserve better than getting mauled in the hallway of a restaurant."

"Mike, I was a more than a willing participant. Stop it. Ok. I liked it. No. I loved it."

His face is unreadable, but then he leans in and kisses me chastely on the lips. He wraps his arms around me and holds me tight as if he knows something I don't.

"Come on baby. Let's finish this class. I don't' know about you, but I am starving."

"Me too. Lead the way."

If only I knew what was holding him back. I keep asking myself of all the heartbreaks I have endured, why does this one after only one date seem like it could hurt the most?

Dinner was delicious. We had a lot of fun talking and laughing. He is a really funny guy, and I learned he loves his mama, who raised him alone after his father died. She was the one who signed him up on Let's Try Love. He hasn't dated in the past two years, which shocked the hell out of me, and he loves horror movies. I love this because so do I. Crystal hates them and would never go with me. So maybe, I finally have someone to go with.

# Let's Try Love

The walk to my car is somber. Neither of us wants the date to be over.

"You have plans tomorrow AraLynn?" OMG!!

"No. I was going to make spaghetti and watch the Criminal Minds marathon."

"No shit. You like that show?"

"I love that show. It's interesting watching them solve cases and find the perps. Not to mention sometimes the villains themselves are a trip. And, the eye candy doesn't hurt. Ya know." I tease. His nostrils flare, and he pins me against the car.

"You don't need no fucking eye candy. If you have a sweet tooth then, I got the magic stick right here. I don't want you dreaming about anybody but me. Got it?" Oh my god. Why is his possessiveness so hot? I am so turned on he could open my car door, demand I strip, and fuck me with the door open, and I wouldn't care. Something about this man does it for me, and it's only the first date.

What is wrong with me?

"Answer me, baby."

"Yes. Yes, Mike. I got it."

"Good. Now, how about I get off work early tomorrow, say five and come by your place? Is that ok?"

"Yes."

"Ok. Get in the car and go straight home. It's late. Text me when you make it home and your address for tomorrow. Be careful baby."

With a kiss on my lips and nose, he opens and closes my door for me. I see him standing there until I turn the corner. His care for my safety is an aphrodisiac by itself.

Lost in thought, I almost miss my turn. When I check my rearview mirror, I notice a red convertible following me. I am sure it's nothing,

## Let's Try Love

but I swear I have seen that same car parked across from my job and it was at the restaurant this evening.

Shaking my head, I laugh at myself. Why would someone be following me? Silly Ara. Snorting again, my mind ventures back to Mike and then it hits me. Shit!! He is coming to my house tomorrow. Oh no!! What am I going to wear?

# Six

*Mike*

For once in my life, I am anxious for work to be over. As soon as the clock hits three, I am out the door. My men are even shocked.

"You are leaving, boss?" Carl asks with incredulity.

"Yes, I am. I'll be back tomorrow. You know how to find me if you need me." I didn't even make it to the door good before my assistant Carol came barreling out.

"You wait for one second Mister. I have been your assistant since the day you opened the doors. Never once have I seen you call it a night before everyone else. Hell, most nights I can't get you to piss without you snarling at me to 'stop nagging you.' So, what gives? And don't tell me any bullshit. I can smell bullshit better than a cowboy."

Damn. She is a nosy ass woman. Her, mama, and my aunt are freaking cackling hens together. If not for that, I would have put her out a long time ago, and I tell her that every time.

"If you must know miss, who can't mind her own business, I have a date. And if you don't quit harassing me, I am going to be late, and then you really are fired." I must confess as I am watching her mouth pop open and close over and over as if she is at a loss for words was enjoyable about damn time.

"Well I'll be….as I live and breathe. Go on then a boy. Get outta here. I don't want you blaming me for you screwing this up." I should fire her ass. Damn, what a thorn in my side. She is lucky. I love her like a second Aunt.

# Let's Try Love

I make it home in record time and barely get out of the shower when my phone rings.

"Hey, mama."

"Don't you hey mama me, Brutus. How come I had to hear about your date from Carol? You couldn't tell your mama. The shame of it all." Oh, now she wants to play the wounded mama. That's OK because I have something for her meddling ass.

"I don't know, mama. Maybe I didn't tell you about the date for the same reason you didn't tell me I was registered on the damn dating sight in the first place."

"That was for your own good."

"Not telling you is for my own good too." Take that.

"E tu Brute." Here we go with the damn Shakespeare. She always spouts that old ass shit when she wants to cry foul — fool woman.

"Mama, I love you. But I have to get ready. If you want grandkids sometime soon, you better let me get to my woman."

"Well shit. Carol was right. You like this girl. Alright, get going then. I do want to meet her Mike."

"I know if it goes that far."

"Don't start that bullocks. You know you deserve this. I love you."

"Love you too, pain in my ass."

Dressed an hour t early, I start pacing my living room. I start trying to talk myself out of going out. Somewhere between getting dressed, drinking a beer, and pacing, I begin to question my decision. Looking at my modest house, I am not sure what I have to offer her. AraLynn is... everything. She is beautiful, sexy, funny, and by all accounts smart as hell. A woman like her deserves a man who can give her the world. I consider myself a lucky son of a bitch to have a chance.

## Let's Try Love

The thought of her walking around my home with her stomach protruding and hard, tits were swollen and leaking as her body prepares to give birth, and her face aglow with happiness and contentment. Deep down inside my soul, I need to be the man on the inside for her. The thought of another man coming along and giving her everything and then some fills my veins with rage. I will kill the dead fucker who thinks of touching my woman.

Well shit. I guess my decision is made and I need to start as I mean to continue. Determined and no longer trepidatious, I say fuck it. I grab my car keys and hop in the car. I wasted what.... about a good hour pacing. It's cool. I will have to sit outside her house until it's time.

The closer I get, the surer I am that I am on my way towards my future. I will make it my life's mission to make her the happiest woman alive. When I park in front of her house, I see her car outside. I have been to the town of Berwyn before but never paid any attention to the houses. Her home is red brick, and the outside is quite quaint. It's not big by any means, but it's... charming and suits her. I can't wait to go inside and see how much of the inside is also her.

Continuing to peruse the neighborhood, I notice a red convertible sitting next to her driveway. I wouldn't think anything of it since the houses are built very close together. He could be a visitor to one of the other houses, but he was staring directly at her door.

My hackles rise, and my blood pumps with the need to protect my woman. He must have heard my car door close because he speeds off before I can confront him. Now, I am not waiting to go inside. The overwhelming need to know she is ok has overridden anything else. I hit the buzzer and wait as my muscles tense and fill with adrenaline.

I hear the locks click, and though I am happy she is home and seems fine, I am pissed she didn't ask who was at the door.

## Let's Try Love

"Hey. Come in." Fuck, she looks good. She has on a tan short skirt with a red shirt hanging off her shoulder. For as simple as the outfit is, she looks amazing.

The words are stuck in my throat, hindered by the dryness, and begging for something wet. And I know just where to get it.

"Mike what are you......" I cut off her question with my mouth. To my surprise, she is with me every step of the way. Our tongues are teasing one another, testing each other's taste, and rhythm. My hands move from her back, down to her waist as I walk her backward to something solid. She wraps her arms around my neck while moaning into my mouth with every swipe of my tongue against hers.

Finally, we reach a wall, and I pull my mouth from hers, though I don't want to.

"Tell me to stop baby. You say the word and I will. Fuck. I don't want to, but I will do it for you. I will wait as long as you need me to. But know this, if you don't stop me now I can't guarantee I won't fuck you up against this wall. Tell me what you want."

"You. I want you. Mike."

"Done."

I take her mouth again, but with her words, something inside of me has been unleashed. Kissing her exposed shoulder, my finger slides under it and across her soft stomach, which turns me on like a motherfucker. There is something about knowing there is no artifice to her, that keeps me hard as granite. She sucks her stomach in as if trying to hide it from me. It pisses me off.

"Don't hide from me, baby. There is not a part of you; I won't love and worship. You understand?"

She nods her head with a face red and heads down. Oh, hell no. She will not feel anything other than fucking sexy as hell. I step back, intending on changing the way she sees herself, starting now. I can see the hurt flash across her face as she assumes, I changed my mind.

"Look at me AraLynn." She slowly lifts her head, unsure and so vulnerable.

"Take your shirt off. Slowly." Her eyes ask me questions, but I simply look at her and wait. Finally, after a few seconds, she grabs the hem of her shirt and slowly raises her arms taking the shirt with it. As it goes over her head, I get a second to look at her and holy fuck. Her tits are a thing of wet dreams. Through her lace bra, I can see her nipples are hard and pointed, begging for my mouth. It takes will power I didn't know I had, to not fall to my knees and worship those fucking globes. But, I will soon.

Once her arms have lowered, I can see the struggle inside of her not to cover herself.

"Good girl. Now take off your skirt."

Taking a deep breath, she drops her skirt and shivers. It is a fucking turn on. I know she is shivering because he is scared of what I think, but hell if it doesn't make me hard as fuck knowing I will be the one to bring her into her sexiness.

"Oh, baby. Look at you. You have no idea, do you? No idea, how hard I am working to hold myself back right now. Look at all of you from your mesmerizing face to your mouth-watering tits. Even your stomach makes my dick weep. Every, womanly full inch of you is what I have been jacking off too since yesterday. So, don't ever hang your head or hide from me. Your body belongs to me now, baby and I won't have you disrespecting my possession. Understand?"

My words must have reached their target because her chest is rising and falling in quick succession as a red flush spread over her.

I walk back to her and use my tongue to demonstrate my meaning. Starting with her lips, I graze my tongue across them. When she opens, shaking with desire, I lick the inside of her mouth, while making sure to suck her tongue out and into mine. After a few minutes of this, my tongue moves on to her ear. I am nibbling on it.

"You have no idea what you've unleashed in me baby," I whisper in her ear. Continuing my exploration, I lick down her neck taking a second to bite her in a few different spots, making sure to leave her nice and red.

"Mike." She says. Her voice is husky and needy. There are no other parts of our bodies that are touching, which makes this more erotic than if I was fucking her on the floor with her legs touching her ears. That's coming soon.

Finally, I make it down to her boobs, and I am ravenous. Grabbing the straps, I rip them from her body — Son of a bitch. Her nipples are even more perfect than I thought. Pink as an eraser, and hard pebbled from my teasing. But it's her round fat areolas that have me rubbing my hands down my face. Mouth, watering to suck her whole tit in my mouth and eat it for lunch. What the fuck.

"Fuck baby. You are fucking perfection. And all mine." I descend on her tits like a rabid fucking dog. I'm no longer in control. Being eye to eye with her fat ass boobs did me in. I suck each nipple into my mouth and instantly hit with the taste of sugar cubes. I knew she would be sweet.

My hands finally find their way to her body, and without abandoning her sweet lusciousness, I rip her panties off. I need nothing of her to be hiding from me. The mewling coming from her mouth has me opening my zipper and pulling out my panting cock. I can smell her pussy as it sends out bat signals and shit.

"Oh god, Mike. Yes." I leave one nipple and go to the other one, giving it the same treatment. When her hands pull on my head, I push further into her; it makes me feel complete.

My hand slides up her juicy thigh where I encounter her sticky sweetness. The evidence she's as turned on as I is amazing. Now I need to taste her desire. Reluctantly and with much protest from my baby, I pull her nipple from my mouth with a pop.

She looks down at me under hooded lids, flushed, and overcome looking like a pinup girl.

"Open your legs baby. I'm going to lick all your cream from your thighs, and then I am going to lick your greedy pussy. Now spread your fucking legs."

She spreads them fast and with a sigh. I waste not a second. Starting at the inside of her knee, I lick up one thigh and bask in the sweet cream she has provided me. When I have licked that one clean, I bite her thigh making sure to mark her. Then I go and do the same to the other.

"Mike. Please."

# Seven

*AraLynn*

This man is going to be the death of me, but what a way to go. Never has a man made me feel as sexy and wild as him, even though it's true I have yet to have sex. I have always gotten as far as making out, and maybe a few pieces of clothing is being removed, but when they see what is underneath……fat, cellulite, and love handles……they usually find some excuse and bail. Hence the reason I wasn't looking for this part of the companionship, but the closeness to someone. This though…. this is out of the realm of what I thought I would ever experience.

His bites are driving me crazy. I have never felt such fire in my veins before and having him on the floor, worshipping me like some plus-sized queen has my blood firing on all cylinders. Rushing to the surface and aiding in my willingness to give it all to him.

"Open wider baby. I need to fit my shoulders here." I widen my stance praying he continues. If he quits now, I might die or kill him.

"Ah. There she is. So, fucking pretty baby. Glistening as it looks like she is covered in sparkles. Her personal pussy glitter. Mmmmm."

"MIKE!!" The first lick is like a match. My body jerks forward as if to fall. His hand shoots out and pushes my torso back onto the wall, while the other is holding onto my ass. His mouth has yet to move from the place where he is feasting on me. Holy moly!!!

"Sweet fucking pussy. Tastes like my mama's pancakes. You are going to be my favorite breakfast baby."

Mercy. His mouth is just as filthy with words as it is covered in my juices right now. My body moves of its volition, demanding the friction it needs to finish. I should feel embarrassed about using his face as my totem, but fuck if I can muster the emotion to give a hell.

"That's it, baby. Take what you need from my mouth. Use it as your personal fuck toy. Cum baby give me your cream. Cause as soon as you finish; I'm taking you upstairs and making you my personal push cushion."

"Yes, Mike. Yes. I want that. Oh god." I don't know what I'm saying, but I would say anything to hold on to this feeling. His tongue is fucking in and out of my pussy like I imagine his dick will do. And that is only where I can feel it at the surface. I know I am about to experience something unprecedented. He can feel it too because he sucks my clit into his mouth adding teeth to the action and the bomb goes off.

"AHHHHHHHH…...yessssssss………." I am lit. There is no other way to say it. My brain is seizing as the sensations overtake every nuance of my being. I have no control over my body right now, and in truth, I would give over complete control to him if this is the outcome. When my body has had enough, I feel myself falling when I am swept into his arms as if I weigh nothing.

We make it to the bedroom, and he lays me down on the bed as if I am as precious porcelain. Long forgotten is the insecurities of my body. If I wanted to, I couldn't lift my arms right now.

"Oh, baby. That downstairs was for you. So, you never doubt what I feel for you. This…is for me. Grab your knees baby and pull them back to your ears. I need to be in you now. Eating your fat juicy pussy has made me ravenous to feel your cunt wrapped around my cock."

With no hesitation, I grab my knees. Watching as he strips off all his clothes, my mouth waters more with each article that drops to the floor. To say he is ripped is an understatement. His chest is manly. I am covered in hair, not too thick but enough to run my finger through when I am laying on top of him in post-coital bliss.

His hands unzip his pants, but his eyes never leave my pussy. In fact, he has been licking his lips the whole time, breathing hard, and visibly shaking as he tries to hold himself back. That is the last thing I want. I want him as out of control for me as I am for him.

Deciding to push him, I take my finger and slide it over my pussy, up and down collecting my juices as I go.

"Fuck," he says almost to himself. Feeling bolder, I bring it to my mouth intent on tasting myself when he practically jumps on top of me.

"NO! It's my pussy. My sweet sticky cream. Give me your fingers." Holding them out for him, he shoves my fingers in his mouth and I could cum right now.

"Mmmm baby. I was trying...but you fucked up. I'm sorry."

Before I could figure out the apology, he impales himself inside of me breaking through my hymen in one shove. The pain is piercing, but nothing compares to the feeling of having all of him inside of me.

"Oh, God!!!" I cry.

"Shhhhh.... I'm sorry baby. I didn't know. Why didn't you tell me? Son of a bitch Aralynn. You feel, so good. I don't know if I can hold on the baby. Your tight little pussy is sucking the life from my cock right now. Fuck. Never felt anything so good."

I test out the feeling by squeezing my walls and am jolted by the zing of pleasure that shoots through me.

"What the fuck. Don't do that. I'm barely holding on."

"It's ok Mike. You can move. I feel so full. I need you to move."

He doesn't wait. He is moving in and out, over and over, while his mouth seeks mine. There is not a part of my body right now not touching his. It feels incredible. So lost in the moment, I meet his thrusts wanting this to be as good for him as it is for me.

"Look at your greedy girl. I just broke through your barrier and already your demanding everything from me. Fucking hungry pussy. Shit. I can't hold on baby. Your snatch is too hot and wet. My cock is on overdrive. I promise to make it up to you."

He leans back and batters into me as his life depends on it. My nails find traction in his skin and the hiss that leaves his mouth, followed by the speed with which he fucks me is...EVERYTHING. I can feel an orgasm just on edge and suddenly he pushes me over. His finger finds my already swollen clit and pinches it, then…. blackness.

I am not sure how long I am out, but when I wake, he is kissing my face and telling me to look at him. I open my eyes, and the look of concern on his face is beautiful.

"There she is. You scared the hell out of me Ara. I feel fucked up because I couldn't stop myself from cumming before checking on you." I giggle at his confession.

"That's so hot Mike," he smiles at me tentatively and then rolls me on top of him. This...this is what I have been missing — the intimacy of having someone to snuggle with.

"You sure you're ok?"

"I'm fine. In fact, I'm more than fine. I wasn't sure you were going to show up."

"And why the hell not?"

"I don't know. When we were together last night at the restaurant and talked on the phone earlier today, you seemed to be holding back. Like you were unsure of something."

I know now is probably not the best time for this, but if this is going to go any further, I need to know that I am what he wants. It says something that I just gave him my virginity after knowing him less than 48hrs, but something about him makes me feel safe and gives me hope. I have never believed in love at first sight, but I feel something very close it, and I don't want to run from it.

"Ah. Damn baby. I didn't realize I was transparent. It has nothing to do with you. You are perfect. Perfect for me in every way. From your beautiful smile to your luscious body, to the way you look at me down to your untouched pussy that I just violated. You are perfect. I just wasn't sure if I was right for you."

"Why would you say that?" Finding it ludicrous that someone like him would think such a thing.

"I own my repair shop. True. And I make a decent living. But nowadays, women want luxury and decadence, and that will never be within my purview. You are a fucking queen, and you don't even know it. You deserve all of that, and I won't be able to give it to you. That was fucking with me for a while."

As he is telling me this, his finger is rubbing back and forth across my lips. I feel the desire rising to the surface, not that it is far away when he is around. But this needs to be addressed.

"Mike. I could care less about things. I want someone who will love me, curves and all. Make love to me daily. Make me smile around the clock and will be faithful to me. I want children and a house filled with love, honesty, and trust. That is all. Can you give me that?"

His eyes stare into mine, searching for something I don't know. But when he sees what he needs, he leans over and takes my mouth in a kiss only to be described as erotically beautiful. He doesn't just kiss me. He claims me with that kiss. His mouth takes mine on a sensual journey. He nibbles my lips making sure to suck them into his mouth over and over. His tongue mates with mine, showing me how to be claimed. His hands hold my head, not giving me room to think. Who knows how long this goes on? When he pulls back, he looks me in my eyes, and my heart thumps out my chest. In his eyes, is something akin to love and god do I want it.

"Yes, baby. I want that man to be me more than you know. I want to share all of that with you and more. From the moment I saw your picture, having you in my future was the prominent vision."

A heart so full, I tell him the truth. "Then what you have is more than enough for me. Especially considering you did just fuck me until I passed out and preceded to cum inside me with no condom on. I can feel it leaking out." I say giggling. I am so happy right now; anything would make me giddy. And being honest, nothing would make me happier than to have babies with this man.

"Leaking out is it. Hmm...let's see if I can do something about that."

# Eight

*Mike*

Two weeks. Fourteen days. That is how long AraLynn and I have been together. It is also, how long I knew I was in love with her and wanted to be with her for the rest of my life. We have spent every night together since the first night. We both agreed to leave our mothers out of it for the first few weeks. We wanted to give ourselves a chance to get acquainted and build a level of trust before the crazy lady's in our lives wreck their special brand of havoc. Finally, last night I introduced AraLynn to my mom. It turned out exactly as I expected.

We pulled up to the house, and of course, the old reprobate was sitting outside like the one woman's neighborhood watch. She is equipped with binoculars and all. Crazy ass. As we were walking up to the porch, she started squinting her eyes and immediately my hackles rose. See, she has never needed glasses a day in her life so that damn twitch was a put on.

"Mom. I would like for you to meet my Aralynn." AraLynn who had been holding onto me so tight, loosened her grip enough to hold out her hand.

"It's so nice to meet you, ma'am. Mike talks about you all the time."

"Don't believe nothing that boy says. Oh yes, son. She will do just fine. Nice, childbearing hips. It seems this one likes to eat. Well done indeed. Come on in here pretty girl and talk to me, while I get the roast done for this spoiled ass boy of mine. I will give you the recipe before you leave tonight."

## Let's Try Love

"MOM!!" This is why I waited. I knew she would pull some shit like that.

"Don't mom me. My dryer is not working. Make yourself useful."

An an hour later, the dryer was fixed, and those two were as thick as thieves. Ara had been nervous all day. I told her mom would love her. As a matter of fact, before we left mama's house and Ara went to the bathroom, mom gave me the engagement ring that dad gave her and her blessing.

"That's a good one. That is one sweet girl. She is going to make you a great wife and mom. I'm happy for you son." Well shit.

Now we are on our way to her mother's house. From what she says, her mom is a lot like mine but a bit more reserved. Whatever. The end game stays the same. As soon as I can get her to fall in love with me, I am trying her to me in every way possible. I have been working on one of those ways every night. For all the praying I have been doing, she is more than likely carrying my child now. Shit. It is not the time to be thinking about that. Every time I do, no matter where I am, I want to take her to the floor and fuck her through it.

"You ok babe?" she asks me. She is obviously sensing my tension. Thank god she can't figure out why.

"I'm fine baby. Why do you ask?" Maybe because she saw your cock jump asshole. Keep your hands on the steering wheel.

"You got quiet is all."

"Sorry baby. I'm fine. Just a bit anxious." It's true. But I am also apprehensive about this damn red car that keeps showing up everywhere we are. It is beginning to get more unnerving and pissing me off.

There is no time to dwell on it since we are pulling up to the house. I help her out the car, and we walk up to the door. We don't get to ring or knock before her mom is answering the door.

## Let's Try Love

"Hey, mom."

"My baby girl. Come on in." We step over the threshold, and instantly my stomach smells German chocolate cake. Her mom just became my new favorite person.

"Mom, I would like for you to meet Mike. Mike, my mom." I extend my hand to her hoping this initial contact goes smoothly.

"It's a pleasure to meet you, Ms. Jansen. AraLynn has told me so much about you."

"All good things, I hope. It's nice to meet you as well. But please. Someone who can put a smile like this on my baby girls faces daily, can call me Olivia or mom." I exhale a breath I didn't know I was holding. Thank fuck.

The rest of the evening goes off without a hitch. I find myself looking out the window every once in a while but see nothing. I want to believe it has all been a part of my imagination, but I know it's not. Someone is following my woman, and I am going to get to the bottom of it.

We make it back to my place pretty late, and she decides to stay the night. Not that I was going to let her leave anyway. The truth is, I want to say fuck it and ask her to move in with me, but I know she will think it is too soon. Not having her permanently at my place or me at hers is driving me crazy. In such a short period of time, she has burrowed herself inside of me, and I need her to be my wife like I need air. I am so caught up in my thought process; I miss the question.

"Mike, did you hear me?" Shit!

"I'm sorry baby. My eyes were otherwise occupied." I said licking my lips. Though I was thinking about something else, it is not far-fetched that I was eye fucking her as she undresses. This is the routine. My eyes see, my hands seek, and my cock catches.

"Well handsome, I was saying mom wants us to come over for dinner next Friday night. She is inviting Crystal and wants you to invite your mom. What do you think?"

"Sounds good to me baby. Now, how about we stop talking about your mama and you bring that pussy over here so I can see if it tastes like the cake we had tonight."

She saunters her sexy ass towards me, forgoing the t-shirt she was going to put on. Knowing exactly what I want, she lies on the bed with legs spread and waiting. The need I have to be face down inside her pussy is more than desperate. Down on my knees, I lick her from asshole to clit.

"Shit. Mike." She hisses. Over and over again I satisfy my need to have her in my mouth. Her hand finds its way to my hair, and she smushes my face further into her pussy, taking what she wants from me.

"That's right, baby. Take what you need. I'm going to turn you into my cum slut one way or another. No other man will ever own this pussy. Will they?"

She gyrates on my face up and down in a desperate dance, while racing towards her finish. I pull slightly back, denying her until she gives me what I want.

"Mike, please. I am almost there."

"Then tell me, baby. Tell me what I want to hear. Who owns this pussy?" Licking her harder and harder being careful to avoid the spot she needs me most, but also making sure to get what I want. When I slide my tongue inside and mimicking what my cock is about to do in very short order, I can feel her walls squeezing and trying to latch on.

"Please. Please. Please…. Yes. Yes. Yes."

# Let's Try Love

"I know you need it baby, but I do too. Tell me. Who is the only man that will ever own this pussy? Tell me, and I give you what you need."

"You Mike. YOU!!!" Finally!

"Good girl." Sucking her clit into my mouth, I insert two fingers as I sweep across her g-spot and watch as her body goes into a hundred different shocks as she continues to face fuck me. Her cream gushes out of her and drenching my face. No facial has ever felt or tasted better. I lick her through her termers. As she is coming down, I start kissing and rubbing my face over each inch of her body. I am making sure to rub her juices into her skin, so I can smell it all night while she is wrapped in my arms. When I make it to her lips and stare into her eyes, I am struck with one thought…... Tell her before you lose her. Taking my time to try to convey it without using words, I kiss her with my whole heart. Licking her lips and inside her mouth, I pull back and look into her eyes while holding her head.

"I love you," I say as I slam my cock into her balls deep. Fuck. Fuck. Fuck. She still shouldn't be this damn tight. I pull all the way out and rut back in over and over. Half-crazed.

"Oh yes. Mike. You always fill me so much. So good. Don't stop."

"Never baby. Never gonna stop. You're mine." I should be gentle. I just told her I loved her but having it out in the open somehow makes me feel even more out of control. I beat her pussy harder and harder. Grinding into her clit at the same time.

"Yes. Yours. I love you so much, Mike. I'm cummming."

"Cum baby. I'm with you. I'm with you. Ahhhhhhhhhhhh."

We cling to each other in the afterglow of our declaration, and my one final thought is…… maybe we made our baby while saying I love you.

# Nine

*AraLynn*

Since saying I love you, things have been full steam ahead. He finally got me to agree to move in with him. He was so sweet about it. We went out to dinner and a movie. When we got back to his place, there was a big note on the door that said 'Would you move in with me? Circle yes or no'. It was old school, cute, and made me cry. I once told him one night when we were lying in bed, how awful school was for me. Holding nothing back, I told him how much time I spent alone because the kids ignored me and none of the boys liked me. I even told him how I used to get sad because I never got one of those notes asking me to be their girlfriend with a yes or no. So, coming back to his place and seeing that was a beautiful surprise.

He would have had me move in the same day if I would agree to it, but I am the holdout. It's not that I am having doubts about my decision. That's not it at all. I love him. Mike is the sweetest, hottest, and sexiest man I have ever met. He is intuitive, thoughtful, and he really listens to me. The best part of all is how the man loves me. He loves me with every fiber of his being, listens to me, and treats me like his queen. I would be a fool to walk away from him. No, my hesitation in not moving yet is because I want to wait for our moms to meet first.

I know I sound weird and old fashioned, but my mom is all I have had my whole life. As happy as I am, I want to honor all she has been in my life by giving her the respect of not doing something like this without her having met his mom.

## Let's Try Love

I am headed to my mom's house as we speak to help her prepare for dinner. I wish Mike could come with me but seeing as how we are going on vacation starting Monday; he wanted to get some things done in the shop. So, he is meeting me in a couple of hours.

"Hey, mama. How's your day been?"

"If it isn't my baby girl. I am just fine. Got the Lasagna in the oven and the salad is in the fridge. I am making the green bean casserole as we speak."

"What can I do to help?" The fondest memories of my childhood are of helping my mom in the kitchen. Something about cooking and being around all the smells makes me feel happy.

"Can you start the 7-UP cake?"

"Absolutely." Moving about the kitchen, mom and I get into a grove as we finish up.

*Ding Dong*

"What time is it Ara?"

"Four. Maybe Mike got off early." Allowing the excitement to take me, I don't bother looking before I open the door. Probably should have.

"You get off early......... oh, you're not Mike. I'm sorry. How can I help you?"

"Dios Mio. You look just like my mother."

"I'm sorry. Do I know you?" I would remember meeting a man like him. He is handsome. Movie star handsome. He stands at about 5'12" 185 lbs. Though he is not huge, he carries his slight build well. You can tell he has money because of the cut of his pants, though they are not business-like in nature. His hair is impeccable, and he smells nice. But, the thing about him that I can't quite put my finger on is why he looks familiar. His eyes remind me of my own, though that can't be right.

## Let's Try Love

"No hija. You don't, but you shall. Is your mother here?"

"Oh. You're a friend of my mom. That makes sense. She hasn't mentioned you before, but come in."

"I imagine she didn't. Wait. Let me look at you. Que Bonita. So pretty." I don't know why I am blushing, other than having men compliment me so openly and without ogling me is foreign, before Mike.

"If you'll follow me." I walk him to the kitchen, still confused about what is going on.

"Who was at the door AraLynn?" I am about to answer when this...man...does it for me.

"It is me, sunflower."

I have never seen my mom react so intensely. Her body suspends as if frozen and she is holding her breath with her back turned to us. I feel as if I made a mistake letting him in. But then she turns and says his name with so much pain and love, that it takes me back.

"AraMando. What…. how….you found me?"

"Finally, mi amor. I have only been looking for you for 21 years. It seems you took something that belongs to me with you when you left." I am about to ask him what he is talking about when his next question suspends all the time.

"How did you think it was ok to give birth to my child and never tell me. I never pegged you for being selfish sunflower. But this, this is something else altogether."

Child? I am her only child. He must be mistaken. My mother has never given birth to another child. Surely, I would know. Which means it would have to be me and…….

"Oh, God." I turn to my mom willing her to tell me this is not true. I need her to tell me my father knew about me and just didn't want us. She needs to tell me she didn't leave him without telling him about my existence. But as soon as I look into her eyes, they fill with guilt and tears. It seems I now know what he is saying is the truth.

"Mom. How could you?" I barely get out. I am too shocked and filled with...betrayal to yell.

"I did it to protect you. Your father's parents hated me. I wasn't of their culture and from the wrong side of a wrong Podunk town. They called me trash numerous times. I endured it because I loved him. I loved you Mando." She says now talking to him.

"You have a funny way of showing it. I leave for work one morning to come home to you gone. No letter, message, or anything. You change your last name making it virtually impossible for me to find you. If that is how you show love, then my daughter must have suffered greatly."

"You-self, righteous son of a bitch. You threw me away by sending your mother to pay me off. How could you? Is that what you really thought of me? I wanted your money?"

"What?!? I did no such thing. I loved you, Olivia. You were the sun in my otherwise dreary world. I would never dishonor you like that. I had no idea my mother did such a thing to you. Why didn't you come to me? You had to have known how much I loved you. Why would you believe such a thing and tear both our hearts out?"

"I thought...she said...oh god...what did I do?" She falls to the floor her heart wracked with pain. Realizing the life, she had always wanted was there the whole time.

"You're my dad?"

"Yes. Hija. I am your father and glad to have found you. May I hug you?" I can't talk from crying, but I nod.

He walks over and embraces me as if I am the most precious thing he owns. It makes me weep more. What I wouldn't have given for a father when I was growing up, that could have shown me what protection feels like. Maybe my self-esteem wouldn't have been so hard to come by if I had a dad in my life to tell me I was beautiful. After kissing my forehead which makes me more emotional, he releases me to pull my mother off the floor out of her weepy state.

"Mi amor. We have lost a lot of time, and there is much we need to discuss. But know this. There has been no one since you. You had taken over my mind from the moment I first met you when we were but young adults ourselves, and you haven't left it for a moment. Don't pull away from me."

As he talks to her, he is holding her in his arms, and I have to admit my mom has never looked more serene. She still looks wrecked. No doubt she will be coming to terms with her decision back then for a while, as will I. But she looks, almost.... happy. Like she is now complete.

*Ding Dong*

Shoot. Mike, his mom, and Crystal are on their way. This is going to be more interesting than we planned.

"Sorry. We are having a dinner party of sorts. My boyfriend and his mom are here. My best friend will be joining us."

"Bueno. My brother is also on his way here. He was coming to be of an.... emotional support. May we join you?"

"Uh... sure." Why not. The more the merrier. Oh boy.

# Ten

*AraLynn*

Pulling up to Olivia's, I am immediately on alert. I see the red convertible sitting outside her house, but there is no one in it. Anxious to get inside, I open my mom's car door and practically sprint to the door as I pull her the whole way.

"Calm your britches boy. She's not going anywhere in the time it takes us to make it to the door." I ring the bell. My palms are twitching and sweaty, as I hope nothing has happened.

"Hey, Mike." She answers the door, voice barely audible. Her face is covered in tracks from tears. I am ready to rip someone's head off for making my woman cry; I cannot help but admire how beautiful she looks, even when she is crying.

"Baby what happened? Why are you crying?"

"Come in. It's a long story. I'm just glad you're here."

"Where else would I be."

Walking inside, everything seems in order until I turn to my left and see two men I have never seen before, standing in the doorway to the kitchen.

"Hija is this your Mike?" What the fuck did he just call her? And who the hell is he?

"Who the fuck are you?" AraLynn gasps beside me. I can feel her squeezing my arm as if to hush me but fuck that shit. There are two men in her mother's kitchen, dressed like they are walking the runway or some shit. It's obvious they have money. Men like them think they can buy their way into everything. My woman is not for sale.

## Let's Try Love

"Mike, please. This is my...my father. AraMando Cortero and his brother. My uncle, Hector."

"Father? I thought…..."

"I did too. He has been looking for my mom since she walked away from him. He didn't know she was pregnant with me."

"The red convertible…..."

"My apologies. That was me. My brother has spent the last 20 years of his life in limbo without the love of his life. When the PI we hired said he had found her and a young woman, I came down myself to see first. It couldn't be denied. She looks just like my mother." The one named Hector says.

"Wow." I am stunned and feel like I walked onto a soap opera.

"I am sorry to have crashed your dinner. But I couldn't wait another moment to meet my beautiful daughter. And to hold my sunflower again. We can go if you like?" I am about to insist he stay because I know how important this is for AraLynn when the doorbell rings.

"This is a fucking one stop shop right now," I mutter.

Ara walks back into the room with Crystal, and suddenly the air feels electrified. I don't know where the feeling is coming from at first, and neither does anyone else. But when I look towards Hector, his gaze is permanently fixed on Crystal. She too has not blinked from his stare.

"Carajos!" Hector expels. He saunters his way over to her, slowly stalking his prey. Sensing danger or a least unsure of what is happening, she begins backing up into the wall.

Crystal hits the wall with nowhere to go, and he stands in front of her, almost touching and invading her space. I am about to intervene on her behalf. But the boom of his words stops me.

"Hola Mi Tesoro. Hoy es el primer día del resto de muestra vida."

## Let's Try Love

"Ummm...I don't speak Spanish." She whispers.

"My apologies my treasure. I said today is the first day of the rest of our lives."

"What? I don't know you." I need to put an end to this before we end up on the wrong end of a porno.

"Well, it's nice to meet you, gentlemen. I for one am interested in hearing the story and eating. Ms. Olivia, this is my mother, Judy."

"Oh my. Where are my manners. I am so sorry what you must be thinking of us, walking into this mess. Please come in. It's a pleasure to meet you. Your son is amazing."

With that settled, poor Crystal still looks like a deer in headlights as she walks into the dining room. She sits as far away from Hector as she can. That doesn't deter him. He simply lifts her out of the chair and plops her right on his lap, as she belongs there. Well shit. This is going to be fun to watch.

By the end of the evening, everyone's laughing and talking. Bonds are being formed and plans made. Well exceptt Hector and Crystal. I can see this being a chase for a while to come.

"You ready to go, baby?"

"Yea Mike. Let's go home." Hearing her say home sounds too damn good.

# Eleven

*AraLynn*

This, sucks. I have been bent over the toilet for the last hour. It has been like this every day this week. I heard on the news that the flu is going around. Mike has been wonderful, though I have been telling him to stay away from me because I don't want him to get sick like me.

"Baby. I don't think this is the flu. The flu comes and goes. Maybe it's something else."

"Like what Mike? You think maybe food poisoning?"

"No. I'm thinking maybe something that will last for the next nine months." He says as his face looks like the cat that got the cream.

OH MY GOSH! How did I not figure this out?

"Here., I bought this on my way home from work. Go take it." I love this man. Most men would be apprehensive or anxious at best, learning if they are going to be a dad. Not my man. He is preening like a peacock, and we don't even have confirmation yet.

After taking the test and washing my hands, I walk out of the bathroom to wait the three minutes with him. There I find him on his knees. My hand immediately goes to my mouth as I try to hold in tears. It doesn't work.

"Mike?"

"You changed everything I thought I knew about myself AraLynn and made me want to try harder, to make this life worthy of you and the family I want to have with you. Every day, you let me know the life we live is enough for you. But it isn't for me. AraLynn, I love you

## Let's Try Love

more than I could ever put into words. Will you do me the honor of becoming my wife?"

OH MY!!! I have been dreaming of this day since I was a little girl and my wedding of course. To be faced with it in this way, with this man, is well…. everything!!!

"We don't know if I'm pregnant yet?" I don't know why I won't just say yes. I think the last little part of me needs to know it's not because there might be a baby.

"I don't care. I was planning to do it tomorrow while we were out to dinner. But I think now is just as grand. So, will you?"

"YES!!! I love you so much, Mike. Any life I live with you will be more than enough because you love me with your whole heart. That is all I have ever wanted."

Looking down at the ring as he slides it on my finger, I am momentarily at a loss for words. Down on my knees, I wrap my arms around his neck and kiss him. I want this kiss to convey everything that is inside my heart, but it won't come out of my mouth. Our tongues do a slow dance, sucking, and mating in motion. This moment is not about sex. It's about a confirmation of everything we feel for one another.

"Come on baby. Let's go see the results." Together we walk into the bathroom, and our lives change yet again.

"I'm going to be a mommy!" I say throwing myself into his arms.

"And I'm going to be a daddy!!" He says with as much enthusiasm.

There we stand. Wrapped in each other's embrace, knowing that as long as we have each other, we have everything we need.

## THE END

# Other Books by ChaShiree M.

**Birds of Paradise Series**
*The Life She Left Behind*: https://www.amazon.com/dp/1979517657
*The Life She Wished For #2*:
https://www.amazon.com/dp/1987411889

**Part of the ScentSations Empire Series**
*Cinnamon*: https://www.amazon.com/dp/B07J4V5KHN

**Part of Cupid's Aim Series**
*Love's Lost Embrace*:
US: https://www.amazon.com/dp/B07ND7KKMD
UK: https://www.amazon.co.uk/dp/B07ND7KKMD
AU: https://www.amazon.com.au/dp/B07ND7KKMD
CA: https://www.amazon.ca/dp/B07ND7KKMD
IN: https://www.amazon.in/dp/B07ND7KKMD

**Works written with MK Moore**
*Moosehead Minnesota Series*
*Marry Grinchmas*: https://www.amazon.com/dp/B078KM7BC5
*Sterling and Kennedy*: https://www.amazon.com/dp/1977027164
*A Rose for Max*: https://www.amazon.com/dp/B07B5PNYZH
*The Time Between Us*: https://www.amazon.com/dp/1718873093

**Queen of Hearts Ink Series**
*Inked Heart*: https://www.amazon.com/dp/1717383165
*Inked by Him*: https://www.amazon.com/dp/B07DV5L1Q6
*Inked By Her*: https://www.amazon.com/dp/B07FTD3R1W

Let's Try Love

*Ink My Soul*: https://www.amazon.com/dp/B07GFD7LTM

**The Jorgensen's**
*LOKI*: https://www.amazon.com/dp/B07PBNRJQY

**Other Works by ChaShiree M.**
***Charity Anthology (Suicide Prevention)***
*Letting Hope Enter*: https://www.amazon.com/dp/B07G7GG1RV

## About the Author

ChaShiree M. lives in Chicago Il. With her family.

She believes she has just begun to find her voice in writing and this makes her very excited.

She loves to read in her spare time and when she isn't doing either of those, she is traveling to different book events with her friends.

She is caring, loyal and sarcastic as hell.

And she loves to meet new people.

You can reach, follow and talk to her with the following links:
FB Page: https://www.facebook.com/ChasShiree/?ref=bookmarks
FB Readers Group:
https://www.facebook.com/groups/ChasShireeslifers/?ref=bookmarks
Bookbub: https://www.bookbub.com/profile/chashiree-m
    Amazon: amazon.com/author/chashireem
    Goodreads: https://www.goodreads.com/ChaShiree

# One Night...

## by M.K. Moore

Tymber McKay doesn't want to be alone anymore.
Hayden Weston wants it all.
Let's Try Love was the perfect app for these two.
Swiping right has never been so easy.
This short story is safe, sexy, and insta-everything.

# One Night... by M.K. Moore

## One

*Tymber McKay*

I never thought I would be doing this, but I've got to face facts, I am at my wit's end. Let's Try Love is the hottest new app and I'm in the process of signing up for it. I heard about it at the coffee shop this morning. The ladies in front of me in line were touting its accolades and I just knew I had to try it out. I am only twenty-one years old, and I have my whole life ahead of me, but I can't be alone anymore. I just can't.

After drinking an entire bottle of wine, I'm lying on my couch, in my sweet *Harry Potter* pajamas, filling out the extremely personal and quite long questionnaire. I have never been on a date, but I've got my reasons for doing this. The biggest and most glaring reason is my brothers and sisters. Have you guessed that I'm the youngest and the black sheep of my family? I have six older siblings and they are all leading perfect lives, with perfect spouses, and their perfect children. I hate how bitter I am about this.

All of my brothers and sisters are married and they either have kids or are expecting them. I am *so* beyond tired of my sisters and their pitying looks over family dinners. Sometimes, I feel like I am stuck in a Jane Austen novel. Once a week at least, all I hear is about my lack of a husband. It's not like I don't want one. It's not like I don't want to be a mother more than anything, but without prospects it's hard.

I make it a priority to as honest as possible when answering the questions. I take a tasteful selfie and post it. I don't hate it, but I don't love it either. I look like shit. My exhaustion is evident, but I am an insomniac. What you see is what you get. These questions are pretty thorough. My interests? Shit, I have so many, I just list my top five: Cooking, baking, knitting, reading, and football. Recently, I graduated from the University of Tennessee with a degree in Medieval French and a minor in British Literature. Why? Because I am obsessed with both. I know there is no practical implementation of either unless I want to be a professor, which I definitely don't. I speak four languages, besides English and sarcasm: French, Vietnamese, Spanish, and Mandarin. I feel like an accomplished lady from *Pride and Prejudice*. Caroline Bingley comes to mind. Accomplished but not exactly marriage material. I could probably go out and meet someone, but that's not really my style.

I finally finish filling out the questions and hit submit. Of course, nothing happens. It's a bit underwhelming actually. I don't know what I expected to happen, but when nothing does, I toss my phone aside and do what I do when I'm stressed. I clean my entire apartment

## Let's Try Love

from top to bottom. My family takes up an entire floor of The Sorensen Heights Tower. The thirty-eighth floor to be exact. Mine, 3810, is the last apartment on the right. My sister Rachel, her husband Brad, and their three kids are my immediate neighbors.

At three-thirty, I hear my favorite niece, Brianna crying. A few minutes later, there is a soft knock at my door. Answering it, I see that it's my brother-in-law.

"Hey, Brad," I say softly. I knew it would be him. He looks exhausted, but he still manages to offer me a smile. Brad is actually my best friend. We don't hang out much anymore, as it should be, but he'll always be my best friend. We met in high school. I was a sophomore and he was a senior, the same as Rachel. They started dating when I introduced them a few days later. I've never had those kinds of feelings for him, but I am glad he loves my sister so much.

"Rachel has an early day. Can you work your magic here?" he asks handing me the still crying Bri and her bottle. I am kind of a baby whisperer. They all bring me their babies when they are inconsolable.

"Of course," I say, putting her on my hip, she sniffles and settles into my shoulder. "You wanna come back in the morning? I got her tonight." Most nights, I have a kid here and fuck if that doesn't make me long for my own. I even have my own stockpile of clothes and diapers here.

"You are a life-saver, Tymber. You are going to make some guy very happy one day," he says with a smirk on his face.

"Gee, thanks jerkface. Go back to bed," I say laughing and shutting the door in his face.

"Hi, Bri-baby. You ready to go to bed?" She is eighteen months old and just starting to form sentences.

"No, no, no," she says burrowing deeper into my neck.

## Let's Try Love

"Alright, how about some cartoons and this bottle."

"No, no, no," she says again. That's pretty much all she says.

"Alrighty." I say, putting her down on my bed. She takes her bottle.

"Ba." Her cute little baby voice gets me right in the feels.

"That's right Bri-baby. Some soothing milk for my favorite girl," I say turning the tv on. I put a Disney movie on, but she's already out. Her little snores are adorable. I watch the movie I cued up for her, even though I've seen it a million times. God, I need to get a life.

Just as I am about to drift off my phone dings. Looking at it, I see that I have a match on Let's Try Love. I read over the profile and instantly I know who it is.

*Holy shit.* It's the Tennessee Goliaths quarterback, Hayden Weston. I'd know that man anywhere. He's the sexiest man I've ever seen. Despite being a super fan of the team, I've never met him. How the hell will I be able to keep my cool? As I swipe right, this feels like the biggest thing I've ever done.

Is this real life?

# Two

*Hayden Weston*

Staring at the bottom of another empty bottle of Jack, I do something I never thought I would. The Let's Try Love dating app was recommended to me by a teammate and now I find myself filling out the lengthy questionnaire. I am tired of meeting women who want to date me based on what I can give them.

As the quarterback for the Tennessee Goliaths, I have met my fair share of crazy fans. I have never been nor will I ever be interested in women like that. I think the last date I went on was my sophomore year in college and it ended in disaster. At twenty-eight, I am ready to start a family. I am tired of being alone and as arrogant as it sounds, it's hard to meet someone genuine when you are famous.

As soon as I finish the questions, I submit it. Within seconds I have a match. Looking over her profile, I am entranced by her beauty. Her green eyes call to me even in the picture. I swipe right, but I can't stop staring at the picture. She messages me almost immediately.

**TeneseeLuv Hi. I've never done this before.**
**SavageQB Me either.**
**TennesseeLuv So what should we do?**
**SavageQB How about drinks tonight?**
**TennesseeLuv Where should I meet you?**

There are several places I could suggest, but most of the bars in Nashville are tourist traps owned by musicians and sports players, so I suggest a dive bar out in Henderson.

**SavageQB Do you know Tandem in Henderson?**
**TennesseeLuv Yes. Perfect; 8?**

**SavageQB See you then.**

As a football player, I get hit on wherever I go, but I am not interested in easy pussy. I want what my parents and my grandparents have. I want to find the one woman who is meant for me and love her until I draw my last breath. Groupies who fuck their way through entire teams is not what I am looking for at all.

I am not saying I saved myself for marriage, but I want my wife to know that there was never anyone before her and there won't be anyone after her. Is it so terrible to want that? I get shit for it from my teammates, but some of them are on their third wives, so forgive me for not taking anything they say to heart.

Somehow, we manage to chat on and off throughout the day. We talk about everything. I am surprised by how much we have in common. I am intrigued when she doesn't say much about the fact that I play football. I feel like I've known her forever and I've not yet met her. She is the most interesting woman.

Before I know it, it's time to meet her for a drink. I have never been this excited about something before, including our super bowl trip last year. We didn't win, but I feel like this going to be even bigger than that.

After a quick shower, I grab my keys and head out. I decide to take my 2019 Bentley Bentayga. The SUV gets excellent gas mileage. It was extravagant purchase. I've been playing professional football for seven years and other than paying off my parent's mortgage, on their house in Chattanooga, I haven't bought much. Just necessities. I felt like I deserved this car. I have two other, less expensive cars, but this one is my favorite. It takes me about twenty minutes to get to the bar, looking around for her, I see her sitting at the bar. Her tight black dress and knee-high boots make me want to fuck her right here. My cock is hard and I haven't even spoken to her yet.

## Let's Try Love

"Tymber?" I ask, sitting down on the worn barstool next to her. Her gaze roams over me. She is even more beautiful in person. Her wavy brown hair is down around her shoulders. I want to reach out and touch one of the curls to see if it's as soft as it looks, but I don't. I don't want to scare her. The powerful thoughts running through me right now would do just that.

"Hayden?" she asks, nodding.

"Yes. Nice to meet you," I say extending my hand. When she puts her tiny hand in mine, I feel the heat between us. We stare at each other as it sizzles. I am drawn to her on a level I didn't know that I had. I want to take her home and chain her to my bed. I never want to let her go. At least not until she admits that she's mine.

"You too," she finally says.

"What can I get you?" The bartender asks interrupting us. He sets coasters down in front of us.

"I'll have a bottle of Bud Light, please," she says. I don't like the way his eyes roam over her like I am not even sitting here. I clench my fists at my side.

"I'll have the same," I say gruffly causing his eyes to snap to mine.

"Can I see your id's?" We both hand ours over. "Coming right up," he says sliding them back over to us.

"So, what do you do?" I ask.

"Did we not talk about that earlier? I don't actually have a job right now. I just graduated from college in January. I haven't found anything that suits me yet."

"That's understandable. There's still plenty of time to decide."

"Yeah, tell that to my mom," she says laughing.

# Let's Try Love

"I'd be glad to," I say. I boldly reach out and put my hand over hers. She doesn't move away from me and I suddenly feel about a thousand feet tall.

"I promised myself I wouldn't get all fan-girly, but what's it like playing football? What I mean is, how much pressure do you feel walking out there every Sunday?" I frown for a second. No one has ever asked me that before. I typically get the glory type questions.

"It's a lot of pressure, but the best kind of pressure. I thrive on it," I answer honestly.

"It shows. I've seen every home game you've played. I have season tickets. I can see it each and every time you take the field." When I don't say anything, she makes a sound in the back of her throat. "I'm not a crazed fan or anything, I just notice things."

"I didn't think you were." I chuckle and her responding giggle goes all through me.

"Good. I imagine those types are kind of scary." The bartender sets our drinks down and walks away to help another customer. We both gulp down some of the beer.

"They can be. I don't get that vibe from you at all," I say after setting the bottle on the coaster.

"Oh good. I recognized you right away, but I tried to play it cool. I was afraid I came off as insane."

"Not at all."

As we continue to talk, my initial assessment of her continues to be true. She is amazing and just what I've been looking for.

I finally know what my dad has been talking about all this time.

I am falling for this girl and I can't stop it. Not that I want to.

We finish our beers, yet we linger continuing to talk. Eventually, she puts her hand on my thigh.

"Do you want to get out of here?" she asks.

## Let's Try Love

Has there ever been a better set of eight words strung together?
No, there hasn't been.
Even though she doesn't know it yet, she is mine.
Forever.

# Three

*Tymber*

I don't know what made me act so rashly, but it feels right. His cock is hard under my hand and I am playing it cool on the outside. On the inside, I am dying. I did that to him. He's even hotter in person and I don't ever want this one night to end. He needs a haircut. His brown hair falls into his eyes, and I want to push it away. How dare those errant locks cover those intense blue eyes?

"That sounds good," he says. Suddenly, I get this vision of him doing this sort of thing all the time. Picking women up in bars and taking them home. I am irrationally jealous.

What should it matter what he did before he met me? I know it shouldn't but it does. I don't want to be one of many. I want to be special.

"Um, do you do this a lot?" I ask hesitantly.

"Do what?"

"Take a lot of women home?"

"No. Never."

"Never?"

"Can I tell you a secret?"

"Yes. of course."

"Don't go selling this to the tabloids, now," he says leaning closer to me. His lips brush my ear and I almost melt into a giant puddle right then and there.

"I won't," I promise.

"I've never been with a woman before," he whispers in my ear and I gasp. Surely, that can't be true.

## Let's Try Love

"Ever?"

"Never. You are going to be my first and last, Tymber. Are you ready for that?"

"How is that possible?" I ask incredulously.

"I was waiting for the one."

"And I'm the one?"

"Yes," he says without hesitation. Should I believe him? I decide to. Guys don't say shit like that right? I turn my head and my lips find his ears.

"I've never been with a man before," I say.

"Jesus. I am going to destroy you," he responds.

"Promise?"

"Absolutely. Let's get out of here. Do you want to follow me to my place?"

"I took an Uber." Is it weird that I am not nervous in the slightest?

"Even better," he says taking his wallet out and dropping a twenty on the bar. I grab my purse just as he grabs my hand again. I hop down from the barstool. He all but drags me out of the bar. He opens the passenger door of an extremely fancy SUV. Before I get in, I screw up the courage and kiss him. I moan into his mouth as our tongues touch. Oh. My. God. I could combust right here. I have no idea how long we kiss for, but eventually, he pulls away from me and walks around the car in order to climb into the driver's seat. I buckle up before he starts the car. When he does so, I am greeted with Blake Shelton's "God Gave Me You" and I know we are soulmates. Before I know it, we pull up to a fancy apartment building downtown.

"You live here?"

"Yes. For about six years now."

"Awesome," I say.

## Let's Try Love

He pulls his car down into an underground parking garage and we take the elevator up to the penthouse. He kisses me the entire time. The doors open into his living room. I kick my boots off, the entire time we are kissing like it's suddenly illegal.

"Are you sure you want to do this," he asks.

"Fuck yes." I don't need rose petals and Kenny G, but losing it to a man I love isn't too much to ask, is it? I always thought I was waiting for marriage, but that is just unrealistic in this day and age. No man is going to get married without testing out the merchandise first. I wouldn't want to be saddled with a man I have no chemistry with for the next fifty plus years, but I do want my first time to be something that I remember for the rest of my life. The spark between us is enough to set the world on fire.

"Tymber," he says, his voice is full of lust.

"Hayden." I don't know why I do it, but I pull my dress over my head to show him just how much I want this. How much I want him. I wait with baited breath while he looks over my body. He sucks in a breath. My boobs are perky, almost too perky. I never wear a bra unless I have to, and since this was a long sleeve dress, I didn't need to. I pull my black panties off and stand naked before him. His eyes widen.

"Holy shit. You are gorgeous."

"Thank you," I say unbuttoning his white dress shirt and tossing it to the ground. He pulls off his undershirt and kicks his shoes off along with his socks. I fumble with his belt, but I finally get it open, letting his pants fall to the ground. He's not wearing any boxers or anything, so his hard cock stands straight up and my mouth waters. I lick my lips while I stare at him. Holy fuck. He's huge. I've never seen anything like it, even in porn.

He's gotta be at least ten inches, maybe more. It's thick and there's precum beading at the tip. I tentatively reach out and touch him. He shudders under my hand. I wrap my fist around him and pump it a few times before dropping to my knees in front of him.

"You don't have to do this, love," he says. I look up at him and smile.

"But I want to. I need to," I say before pulling him into my mouth. I've never done this before, but his groan tells me that I'm doing something right. His precum hits my taste buds and it's amazing. I can't get enough of him. I call upon every blow job scene in my favorite books. I want this to be good for him. I want him to want more from me. I suck him into the back of my throat before backing off. Over and over I do this. His hands grip my hair, hard. He's pulling me in the way he wants. Like a puppeteer, I do what he wants.

"I'm gonna come, love." His warning is cute, but I want to taste it. I want it on my tongue, then I want it to be a part of me.

Who am I right now?

# Four

*Hayden*

Seriously, her mouth is amazing. She is sucking my cock like her life depends on it. Her little hand gently squeezes my balls while she takes me down her throat. She doesn't have a gag reflex. With my hands tangled in her hair, I direct her, though she knows just what she's doing. I can't think about that shit though. I am jealous of anyone who came before me, though I'm certain that she's a virgin too, a lot of women don't think blow jobs matter.

Her big green eyes stare up at me while she does this. I feel my orgasm building up from my fucking toes. I've never felt anything like this before. Finally, I can't take it anymore and I tell her that I'm going to come, but she sucks me harder, so I have no choice but to come down her throat. The feeling of her swallowing my load while still sucking is a euphoria I never knew existed. I pull out of her mouth, but she is still holding my hips, so I don't get far from her. She licks her swollen, red lips, before gently licking my cock clean.

"Thank you," she says rising from her knees. Is this girl for real? Did she really just thank me for letting her suck my cock? Shouldn't I be thanking her? How'd I get so lucky? I was half in love with her just chatting with her. Now that I've met her, I am so far gone that while I know it's insane I don't give a fuck.

"You're mine, Tymber."

"I'm yours," she agrees readily.

Kissing her, I lift her into my arms and carry her to my bed. I lay her in the center of it. Spreading her thick thighs, I lick her from clit to ass. Her taste hits my tongue and I know that I'll never get enough of it. I am in awe of the fact that she got wet while sucking me off. She moans, gripping the sheets. I hold her down by gripping her hips while I eat her pretty pussy. I lick her clit until her pussy juice drips down my face, down her ass, and on to my sheets.

"Fuck, you taste amazing," I say.

"Let me taste," she says pulling me up to her and kissing me. Filthily, she all but licks inside my mouth, moaning at the taste of herself. God, I need to marry this girl and soon. She is perfect for me.

"Are you ready for me to fuck you," I ask.

"Yes, stop teasing me, Hayden."

I line my hard cock up with her tiny pussy hole, and slide into her slowly. Motherfucker, she is tight. Her wet heat is going to unman me before I pop her sweet cherry.

"Holy hell. I feel like I am having a heart attack. This feels amazing," she says.

"You feel amazing, love." I clench my teeth to keep from coming. I realize I am not wearing a condom, not that I have any in the first place, but with her I never want anything between us.

I lean down and kiss her before slamming through her virginity. I pause. Not only to allow her some time to adjust, but to also keep from coming like a one-pump chump. She cries out, but when I look down at her she's smiling and doesn't appear to be in pain. She wraps her legs around my waist, using her heels to dig into my ass, letting me know to move. I do. I pull all the way out of her and slam back into her. Over and over.

"Oh, God," she chants again and again.

"I am going to fuck my kid into you, Tymber. Tell me to pull out if you don't want that."

"Don't you fucking dare pull out me. Give me your babies. Breed me."

## Let's Try Love

"Holy shit, little girl. I am going to do just that," I say. Who the fuck is this girl?

Breeding sounds so fucking primal. Animals and cavemen did that shit, but fuck if I don't feel both animalistic and like a caveman as I fuck in and out of her. I take her hands in mine and pull them above her head. I kiss her neck. Moving down her chest, I pull her tight pink nipple into my mouth, biting it a bit. She arches her back and moans- long and loud.

"I am going to come, Hayden. Please don't stop. I love you, I love you," she screams. I feel her juices on my cock.

"That's it. Keep coming on my cock. Give me those sweet juices." I feel my orgasm rising and I fill her cunt with my seed. I pull out of her, moving to the other side of the bed, pulling her with me.

We are both breathing heavily. Her head his on my chest. My hand caresses her back and her damp hair. "I love you too, Tymber." It's crazy fast but you know what it doesn't matter. We have the rest of our lives to figure shit out.

"I can't believe I said that," she says laughing.

"Did you not mean it?"

"No, I definitely meant it."

"Then don't worry about it. I feel the same way. Despite the insane timing or lack thereof, it is what it is. I always knew it would like this for me."

"I didn't," she says. "I thought it would never happen. I imagined my life snuggling nieces and nephews, never knowing that kind of joy for myself. You want to know the real reason I don't have a job?"

"Yes," I say. I am curious.

"I want to be a mother. I want that to be my job. Deep down, I've always known that. That's why I picked two obscure ass things to study in college. I am practically unemployable on purpose."

"There's nothing wrong with that, Tymber. You know your own mind and heart. I think that's amazing. I am also ready to start a family. Get married."

"Well, I hope so. You came so much inside of me, it's leaking out," she says laughing. She runs her fingers through my chest hair.

"I'll get you a ring tomorrow," I say. Her fingers pause.

"I'm sorry. What?"

"You're marrying me, love. No way I'd let you go now."

"We don't have to get married or even engaged to be together. I don't want you to regret anything."

"Love, you have nothing to worry about on that front." I kiss her soundly. Damn, I'll never get tired of that.

She falls asleep in my arms, right where she belongs.

I could get used to this, I think as I cover us up.

# Five

*Tymber*

I don't regret telling him that I loved him last night. Shit, I always thought instalove was something authors made up, but boy was I wrong. I didn't even know I could feel this way about another person and so fucking fast, but here I am. Muscles I didn't know I had are sore as fuck this morning, besides the obvious ones. Even with that, I've never felt better.

"Will you come to dinner with my family tonight?" I ask over coffee in his huge gourmet kitchen. I want him to meet my family more than anything. I know they will love him. We are all Goliaths fans.

"Of course, love. Should I bring anything?"

"No. It will all be taken care of."

"Are you spending the day with me?"

"I need to change, but we can hang out at my apartment," I say. I need a shower as well.

"Sounds good." I am just wearing his flannel shirt. It's like a dress on me, so I gather up my dirty clothes and we head out. In the garage, we take a different car than last night. This one is a two door sports car with a name I can't pronounce. I give him directions to my building. Green Hills is pretty much a traffic jam at this time of day, so it takes us a while to get there. We make a quick stop at a jewelry store on the way.

"Are you coming in with me?"

"No, I want to be surprised by what you come back with," I say.

## Let's Try Love

"Okay, sit tight love. I'll be right back." He kisses me and hops out of the car.

Fifteen minutes later he's back. He holds open the box and I gasp. The ring is fucking huge. It's a platinum princess cut engagement ring. He slides it on my finger.

"Marry me?" he asks.

"Fuck yeah," I say kissing him. We get going again and I marvel at how heavy the ring is.

Once inside the building, we take the elevator up to the thirty-eighth floor. On the way over, I explained that my family has the whole floor, so he isn't surprised when there are about ten kids aged 18 mos to eight playing in the hallway. Most of the apartment doors are open, but I don't see any adults. The kids come up to me one by one for daily Auntie Tymber hugs and I indulge them because I live for them too. When I turn around, just to see if he is overwhelmed, he is carrying Brianna and holding the hand of of my nephew Benji. My ovaries explode.

"Guys, this is Hayden," I say introducing them to him.

"Where have you been," Rachel says laughing from her doorway. "Brianna had a fit when you didn't answer your door."

"I was out. Aww, Bri-baby. Did you need me?" I say holding my hands out to her. She leans over and I lift her up.

"Yes," she says and I gasp. She was on that no kick for a while.

"I'm sorry, baby. I'm here now," I say as she buries her head in my neck.

"She only slept for like two whole hours last night."

"Well, I was super busy, but how about a little nap Bri-baby?" I say, but I can tell she's already sleeping.

"I hate you, you know that. Why doesn't my baby like me?" she whines. I know she's kidding.

"I don't know Rach, maybe she knows I'm the fun one."

"Maybe."

"Rachel this is Hayden. Hayden this is my sister. I am just going to put her down in her bed, be right back."

"Nice to meet you. You look familiar," Rachel says, looking him over. I don't like that. "Did we go to high school together?"

"No. I play for the Tennessee Goliaths."

"You're Hayden Weston?"

"Yes."

"Holy shit, Tym. You bagged a football player?"

"Jesus, Rach. Could you be any less tactful?"

"I could, but I won't."

"Gee, thanks." Hayden laughs so I know he isn't offended. "We'll see you at dinner," I say.

"Okay. See you later," she says going back in her apartment. I follow her and put Brianna down. Then I free Hayden from the kids. I take him to my apartment, where we get back in bed for the rest of the day.

I must drift off because when I open my eyes the sun is setting and there is a banging on my front door. Since I am not dressed, I throw on a robe and answer the door.

"You're late," my mom, Denise, says.

"No, I'm not," I say after glancing at the clock on the stove.

"Fine. Rachel tells me you have a man in here. Is that true?"

"Yes, mama. It's true."

"Well, I want to meet him," she says. I smirk.

"He's indisposed," I say. "You can meet him later."

"What the hell is that?"

"What's what?" I ask, feigning innocence.

"That giant rock on your finger?"

"Oh. I'm getting married," I say. She grabs my hand, examining the ring.

"My last baby is getting married?" She's about as subtle as Mrs. Bennett.

"Yep."

"Oh my God. I thought this day would never come." I roll my eyes. I am twenty-one, not seventy-one. She's so overdramatic.

We eat dinner with my family. Everyone bombarded him with football questions, but eventually, we escape back to my place.

"So what do you think? Are they deal breakers?" I ask getting ready for bed. He's staying so that's something.

"Not at all. I'm an only child so I think this is going to be great," he says.

"You say that now," I say laughing.

"I mean it," he says pulling me in for a kiss. "Loving you is going to be the easiest thing I've ever done."

"I love you too, Hayden. This is so intense," I say.

"It is, but I have a feeling it's going to be worth it, love."

"I think so too," I say agreeing with him.

Being by his side for the rest of my life sounds just about perfect.

Who knew signing up for Let's Try Love would actually work out in my favor?

# Epilogue

*Hayden*

Five years and three kids later, I've gotten everything I ever wanted and a few things I didn't know what I needed. My profile on Let's Try Love was only active for one day, but I don't think I would have found Tymber without it, so I will always be grateful for it. Tymber and I endorse the app whenever it comes up because that's how much we believe in it.

I am still playing ball, but this is my last season. I am moving into broadcasting next season and I couldn't come at a better time. At thirty-four, my body isn't what it used to be. I started playing peewee ball at five and I've given everything to the sport I love. I've broken so many bones over the years, that I can tell when it's about to rain now. I've made enough money over the years on top of what I already had to support our family a hundred times over. Even with all that, it still wasn't an easy decision, but it's time to hang up my cleats.

After we got married, we moved to the Green Hills area. On one side of us, a county music star lives with his wife and kids and on the other, a teammate of mine, Asher Tipton lives alone. I enter the house through the garage after a long day at practice. The scent of something amazing cooking makes my stomach grumble. I was so busy today that I forgot to eat lunch. I'm exhausted, sweaty, starving, and in dire need of a shower.

"Babe, I'm home." I am greeted with shouts from the kids.

"Daddy," our oldest, Zia shouts from in front of cartoons. She is four and our little ringleader.

"Hi guys, where's mommy?"

## Let's Try Love

"She is in the bathroom, again," Zia says. Riley and Rachel sit next to her on the couch, but they aren't as talkative yet. Tymber has been sicker with this pregnancy than with the last three. I lean down over the back of the couch kissing my girls heads. They are so engrossed in the cartoons that they barely notice me.

"You stinky daddy," Zia says without looking away from the tv.

"I know baby. I'll take care of it," I say laughing as I leave the room and head towards the master bathroom. Zia keeps me on my toes. I never know what's going to come out of that mouth. She is the spitting image of her mama. I am going to be in so much trouble in about twelve years, I just know it.

"Babe, are you okay," I ask walking into the room. I see her standing in front of the sink.

"Oh yeah, just perfect," she says before brushing her teeth. "How was practice?" she asks. I hate that I wasn't with her when she feels like this.

"Long, boring and I'm pretty sure I broke my thumb. Do you need to go to the doctor?" I ask. She is paler than usual and I don't like it.

"Nah. I'm fine now. And again, really with the thumb?" she asks kissing me. I love her lips on mine. Good thing I get to kiss her for the rest of my life.

"I can move it, but it's bruised, so we'll see what it looks like in the morning. Oh, did I tell you I love you yet today?" I ask kissing her again. She really is the greatest thing that has ever happened to me.

"About fifty times, but it just so happens that I love you too. Dinner is almost ready," she says going out into the kitchen. I hop into the shower. Once done, I am feeling much more human and less stinky as my baby girl put it.

After dinner, we put the kids to bed. It's a long process, but we get through the baths and the stories in record time tonight. The girls were tired, which bodes well for us. They should all sleep through the night. Tymber didn't want a nanny and we only use babysitters when we have to. Even then, it's usually one of our mothers or her sisters. They have finally started treating Tymber with the respect she deserves. No more pitying looks over pot roast.

I all but drag her to our room. Undressing her slowly, I pull her down to the bed and move over her. I kiss every inch of her body, my hard cock digging into either her or the mattress. She has only gotten more beautiful with each baby she gives me. Her curves are amazing and I can't get enough of them. I trace them with my tongue. Her moans are almost too much for me.

"Hayden, please. I need to come. I've missed you all day," she begs.

"You don't have to beg me, Tymber. I'll always give you whatever you need." I kiss her with everything in me. I love this woman more than life itself. I'd do anything for her.

"Promise?"

"Promise," I reply, kissing down the column of her throat, her chest, her rounded belly. I gently pull her clit into my mouth and slide two fingers into her slowly.

"Oh, God," she moans. I coax her orgasm from her before sliding my cock into her wet cunt.

Rising up on my knees, I slam into her over and over, giving her just what she needs. What we need. I feel her pussy clench around my cock and I come with her, filling her already full womb with my seed. I'll never get tired of this woman.

## Let's Try Love

Everything we've done has been at hyper-speed. We met and fell in love on the same day and then got married barely a week later. Our story is unique and it's our own. I wouldn't change a fucking thing.

After several hours of taking her again and again, she falls asleep in my arms, just where she belongs.

Signing up for Let's Try Love was both the easiest and the best decision I've ever made. Because of her, the next fifty plus years will be better than I ever thought possible.

# Acknowledgements

I want to thank my husband, Daryl. You are so supportive of my dreams and I love you so fucking much for like ever.

Thank you, Mama, for all of your support! I love you.

Karlee, thank you for being a friend. #GoldenGirls reference. But seriously, thank you!!!! Love you .6 times!!!

Elisa, Love you, my #unicorn friend!!!

JENNY!!! You are the best damn alpha reader a girl could have!

To my arc team, no matter how many arcs I send in a short amount of time you guys pull through! Thank you so much for hanging out with me!

To all of the readers, you guys are the ones that make this possible! Thank you for reading me and taking the time to review. You don't know how much seeing your words of encouragement help me when I am struggling!

Love Always,
MK

# Other Books by M.K. Moore

**To Love Series**
*-Brother in Law to Love*
*-Heel to Love*
*-Wife to Love*

**Royally Yours**
*-A Princess for Hans*

**Love In Norlyn**
*-Madame President*

**Regret, South Dakota**
*-My Aubree*
*-Her Forever*

**Owned**
*-Christmas Auction*

**Turn Me On**
*-So Good*

**-Xander's Treat**
*-One Night Wasn't Enough*
*-Thanksgiving Ever After*

Let's Try Love

## Clearwater Curves Serial written with Elisa Leigh, C.M. Steele, & KL Fast
*-Fancy Curves (Book # 2)*

## The Caribbean Rivalry Series written with C.M. Steele
*-Stealing Destiny (Book # 2)*
*-Taking Her For Granted (Book # 4)*

## A Hauntingly Romantic Halloween Novella with Elisa Leigh, C.M. Steele, & KL Fast
*-Hunting Gypsy (Book # 3)*

## Kissing Junction, TX series written with KL Fast
*-Candy Corn Kisses*
*-Thankful Kisses*
*-Candy Cane Kisses*
*-Champagne Kisses*
*-Chocolate Kisses*
*-Midnight Kisses*
*-Shamrock Kisses*
*-Summer Kisses*
*-Cowboy Kisses*

## The Gallucci's written with KL Fast
*-Anthony by KL Fast (Out Now)*
*-Trinna by MK Moore*

## All for Love Series written with Elisa Leigh
*-Daddy Captain*

Let's Try Love

**Moosehead Minnesota Series written with ChaShiree M.**
*-Marry Grinchmas*
*-Sterling and Kennedy*
*-A Rose for Max*
*-The Time Between Us*

**Queen of Hearts Ink Series**
*-Inked Heart*
*-Inked by Him*
*-Inked by Her*
*-Ink Me*
*-Ink My Soul*

**The Jorgensen's written with ChaShiree M.**
*-Loki*
*-Bill*

## About the Author

MK is married to the love of her life. She lives in Tennessee with her husband. She is an avid reader and loves telling steamy stories she deems filthy contemporary. She loves meeting readers, so come hang out with her!

FACEBOOK: https://bit.ly/2PlRV6t
TWITTER: @smutyourmouth
BOOKBUB: https://bit.ly/2QgXZCE
BOOK + MAIN: @mkmoore
INSTAGRAM: mkmoore0320
SNAPCHAT: mkmoore032010
Email: mkmoore032010@gmail.com
For more flirty, filthy fun check out my Facebook group with KL Fast: https://www.facebook.com/groups/KLMKGPR/

# Third Time Lucky

## by Paula Phillips

After finding her best friend Tammy with her fiancé, Skye heads back to her hometown and her friend Aria suggests a night out which leads her to a one-night stand. Months later, Skye's new work colleagues talk her into signing up on Let's Try Love, imagine her surprise when she's matched with her one-night stand Tucker Hollywood.

# Third Time Lucky by Paula Phillips

Life can deal us the worst cards, just when we think that we have our life's plan all sorted out – something goes haywire and blows up the plan to smithereens.

One moment I was happy and had my whole life planned, I was engaged to the most amazing man Luke, and we had a beautiful house and a tiny little dog named Braveheart, and I had an awesome best friend Tammy and living it up in the city.

Then just like that, it was all over when I walked in one day after a tiring day at work and there sitting on the kitchen counter was a plain white envelope with my name written on it in black writing – Skye. I should have known at that moment, that something was up as the house was eerily quiet and something felt off – I just couldn't put my finger on it.

I wandered over to the kitchen counter as my fingers started to tremble and I picked up the letter, inside it read. I'm sorry, I've fallen in love with someone else – Luke. Want to know what the worst thing was, that somebody turned out to be my best friend – Tammy. What a bitch. Here I thought she was helping me plan the wedding of my dreams, when in fact she was fucking my fiancé behind my back. Probably doggy style too as I had always hated that position. What kind of woman wants to be treated like a dog? A bitch.

After my stunned shock, I guess you could say I fell apart and spent the next few weeks in the house Until I realized I would have to move back home with my folks as there was no way I could afford to live in the city on one income. Gosh, I was pathetic – here I was at 30 years old and moving back home to live with my folks. I felt like one of those cliched girls that you read about in the chick lit novels, the ones whose lives completely shatter and they have no idea what to do – so they move back in with mummy and daddy.

First things first, I had to hand in my resignation at Books A Plenty where I had been the assistant manager. I was going to miss the customers as I had an old lady who loved to bake me muffins and cakes. She enjoyed baking but couldn't eat it herself, so I was the lucky recipient and then had to call the real estate agent to help sell the house. Lucky it was just my name on the mortgage as I doubt, I would have been able to do all this so easy if Luke's name was added. Another red flag, I should have picked up as he always liked everything to be in just my name. I could trust him to pay his share happily. Jerk.

The next step was the worst; I was holding my breath as I sat there and opened my contacts on my cellphone and looked for Mum and Dad's number. Maybe it was the gods, but as I sat there trying to get the confidence up to hit dial, my phone started ringing Baby Shark. I was obsessed with the catchy tune, I knew most people hated it with a passion but how can you hate something so upbeat and poppy. It

## Let's Try Love

made me smile though I felt like crap. I took a deep breath and hit answer – "Hi Mum, how're things? Funny story I was about to call you" I managed to get out without breaking down, but then you know how Mum's have this third eye – mother's intuition where they just know something is up. Well, my Mum had it, and the next words out of her mouth were "What's wrong, darling?" I couldn't hold it in any longer as I broke down on the phone. Sobbing hard, I managed to squeak out "Luke's left me, and he's moving in with Tammy, I need to move back home."

*****

*A month later*

As most parents are, my Mum and Dad said of course that I could move back until I find my feet and stay in my old room. I packed up the house as only my things were remaining and here I was now sitting in my car ready to say goodbye to the life I had planned and thought would be my forever and heading back to the Podunk town of Taverners that I had managed to escape or so I thought for good. I was the type of girl at high school, who had always planned to leave town as soon as I graduated as nothing major ever happened in Taverners and I had for a while.

Baby Shark, doo doo doo, Baby Shark. I glanced down at my phone and checked the caller ID – Mum. Should I pick it up or just hit decline? It kept ringing; I reluctantly picked it up. "Hey darling, just wondering where you are?" Mum asked. "I've just finished tying up some loose ends, and about to leave now." I'll be arriving tomorrow and will stop tonight at my friend Aria's Motel – Funky Monkey Lodge. She had inherited it from her parents after they died a few years back and along with her new husband – Max who had been one

## Let's Try Love

of her first customers at the Lodge. They had re-done the rooms and made it a famous holidaying Lodge. It was halfway between the city and Taverners.

Nine hours passed as I drove along the highways and passing through little towns, some kitschy and others blink and misses. When I looked up and saw a big billboard with a giant monkey that resembled a soft toy that I had as a child – Henry holding a suitcase in one hand and a banana in the other, this made me chuckle, I wonder if this was Max's creation as the billboard was advertising the Funky Monkey Lodge. I pulled over to the side of the road and got out my cellphone and dialed Aria's number – "Hey girl, how far away are you? Aria shouted over the phone. I'm about ten minutes away, be there shortly. I can't wait to see you and Max. "Wait a minute, are you talking and driving at the same time" Aria shrieked. Nope, I promise I've pulled over to the side of the road and talking to you. I remembered how Aria gets with cellphones and driving as her parents were killed by a driver talking on their cellphone.

I got off the phone and kept driving until I saw another Giant Monkey, this time I saw double and a statue as they had commissioned by a local artist two Giant monkeys to sit on either side of the lodge's gates. As I pulled up and hopped out of the car, I headed towards the office and in my excitement almost bowled over a guy walking out of the office. Not just any guy either, this guy was hot with a capital H. He had dark hair, piercing blue eyes and what looked like a muscly body under his shirt. My mind started racing with thoughts of what I could do with him; it had been a while since Luke and I had done it. "Skye, you're here" screamed Aria which interrupted my sexual thought train.

I took one more glance over my shoulder, but the guy had vanished, had he been a figment of my imagination. "We are going to

## Let's Try Love

have so much fun" Aria excitedly exclaimed. It looks like my night of relaxing and moping had a pin put in it. All I had wanted to do was sit and wallow and eat lots of ice-cream as wasn't that what the characters in the movies did when their whole lives fell apart. Not in Aria's world, it seemed like her idea of moving on and getting over Luke was to have a night of debauchery.

I settled into my lodge room and pulled out my kindle, if I was going to have a night of debauchery as Aria had put it then I needed to get in the mood and what better book to read than Alexa Riley's latest Closer, her books always got my juices flowing if you know what I mean. They were raunchy, hot quick reads bursting with raw sexual energy. Reading the book had turned me on, and it had been a while since I had been laid. So, I pulled my shorts down and started rubbing myself until I managed to orgasm. I seriously needed to get laid if I had resorted to giving myself orgasmic pleasure.

Knock, knock. I turned and looked at the time; I must have fallen asleep. Just give me a minute; I need to get ready. Aria burst in and looked at me; you're nowhere near ready to go out. This is going to take us longer than a minute. While I was in the shower, Aria took it upon herself to pick out my outfit for the night. I got out and looked at the outfit that she had picked me. I tried it on, "don't you think it's a bit tight," I asked Aria. She looked at me as if to say duh, that's the point.

"Where are we going?" I asked Aria. There's a good bar up the road owned by the Lachlan Brothers; they are good friends with Max. "What took you so long?" Max asked. "Skye, over here fell asleep and we had to get her sexified" Aria responded. Well, ladies, your carriage awaits, don't get into too much trouble. I laughed as with Aria by my side it would be a night of trouble.

## Let's Try Love

We headed to the club, and I met Jack and Michael Lachlan behind the bar. Hey ladies, what will it be tonight? Just as I was about to respond with a pure vodka and red bull, Aria's voice popped up and 'strawberry martinis – stirred not shaken and keep them coming. Over the night, I sat there drinking and chatting away with Aria; she made me feel so much better as I still felt the sting of Luke and Tammy's betrayal- how could they both do this to me. I went to fiddle my ring and looked down; it was missing. I must have left it on the bathroom sink at the lodge. Maybe this was a sign?

While we were drinking, I love Rock n Roll by Janis Joplin played on the jukebox. "Let's dance; it's playing our song," Aria said. This had always been our song as back in high school we did a talent show, and we were inspired by Britney Spears' movie Crossroads and sang a duet of I Love Rock N Roll. We didn't win but it was a lot of fun, and from then on, this became our song. "Are our drinks all good to leave here?" I asked. Aria laughed "of course, they are." I smiled as I realized that the city girl in me was starting to show. I had been away from the small-town life for far too long.

We got up and started dancing; it felt so free to let my hair down and just be able to relax. I had missed all of this as Luke had hated small towns and going out dancing in clubs. He preferred the world of suits and sophisticated bars where they sat and slowly sipped on their drinks making small talk over business stuff. I no longer had to worry about things like that, that was now Tammy's problem. That and the horrible habit he had of never tidying up after himself. I finally had this epiphany that I was free from the restraints of the life I had thought I had wanted for all these years.

As I was busy dancing away, Aria leaned over and whispered in my ear "don't look now, but there is a hot guy at the bar, checking you out." Of course, when someone tells you don't look, the number

## Let's Try Love

one thing you are going to do is look straight away. I peered over her shoulder to see where she had been looking, and I let out a small yelp. "That's the guy; I almost barreled into," I said as I explained to her how when I was walking into their office earlier today, I walked into a guy, that's the guy. He's coming over, what do I do? I asked Aria. She gave me a little shove, which coincidentally landed me in the guy's arms.

Hi, I said straightening myself back up I'm Skye. Hey, I'm Tucker in said in this handsome southern drawl which had my knees feeling a tad weak. I had always been a sucker for the southern accents. I turned my head to Aria as she knew my weaknesses and she had a slight smile on her face as she mouthed "Go for it."

I turned back to Tucker as we walked over to tables where our drinks were, I so needed a top-up of my glass. Tucker had inherited that skill Mel Gibson got in the movie What Women Want as he read my mind and ordered me another of the same. We sat down and started talking and laughing the night away, I hadn't had this much fun in such a long time as whenever we went out it was always with Luke's friends and I have to admit they were still a bit stuffy and bland for my liking.

As the night wore on, Tucker put down his drink and asked me four simple words that would be the start of a domino effect in changing both our lives. Those four words were Your room or mine? It turned out we were both staying at the Funky Monkey Lodge, and our rooms were just down from each other. His being first as he was booked into Room #2 and I was in Room #7. We hopped into a taxi and hightailed it back to the Funky Monkey Lodge and stumbled into his room.

## Let's Try Love

Just like in my fantasy, he opened the lodge door and closed it with my back as he pushed me against the door kissing me like he had been starving for physical connection. He put his hand on my thigh and slowly worked up my dress and got to my panties which he hooked his fingers through and pulled them down. He then stuck them in his pocket and whispered, I'm keeping these for later. He then took his shirt off and his pants and stood there in his black underwear. I felt a tad overdressed but couldn't move as I was entranced by his array of tattoos on his chest and that nipple ring which I was looking forward to swirling my tongue on it later on in the evening.

He then interrupted my thoughts as he huskily said: "we need to get out of this dress." I put my hands up as he pulled the dress over my head and left me standing in my strapless bra. He unhooked the bra and chucked it onto the pile of clothes that had been forming on the floor next to us and pushed me onto the bed. Now he was the one with too many clothes on and a great package I could see growing in his underwear.

He slipped off his underwear and leaned over to the dresser and pulled out a condom, always got to prepare he whispered. It made me wonder if he had been a boy scout in his younger days. As I laid on the bed, he started to travel kisses down my body and stopped at my vagina. I got a bit nervous as Luke had always hated giving me oral. I tried to relax, and when his tongue started swirling around my clit, I felt like I had gone to heaven – boy this guy was a god at giving a girl oral. The gods must have blessed that tongue. I felt like I was going to cum and be staring at the stars in the heavens.

Just as I was about to burst, he stopped and said, I have to save something for later with his cheeky smirk. We switched places as I brought my hand down to his hard cock and put it in my mouth like it was a lollipop that I had been rewarded with. He then slid the condom off as it was apparent we weren't going to do any actual fucking tonight as we were both at our climax and ready to explode as I worked my mouth up and down his hard cock and swirling my tongue around the tip, whilst trying to remember some of the tips that I had read in all of the smutty erotica books that I had sitting on my kindle. I felt him give a little jolt that told me he was about to come too and I felt the wetness pooling in my pussy. One more swirl and aah, I'm about to come he spoke raspily. I opened my mouth wider as I tasted his warm cum on my tongue and running down the back of my throat. As he came, I felt my own about to erupt. Tucker sensed it and gave me another swirl with his gift from the gods – that magical tongue and I came more than I felt I ever had. This was an orgasmic moment to remember.

We then lay back on the bed, and I had a moment of worry pass by that the others in the lodge had heard our wild ride. As I laid there, I had a moment of panic as I had never had a one-night stand before and was unsure of what the correct protocol was. Do I stay or tell him I am leaving or Do I just up and leave? I turned to say to him; I was going when I noticed a little bit of snoring coming from his side. He must have been exhausted as it was now 4 am the following morning. I grabbed my dress and put that on and picked up my bra. He could keep my panties as I had spares and I didn't want to wake him up.

I walked back to my hotel room and set my alarm for 9 am as I needed to get on the road as soon as I could as Mum and Dad were expecting me today. The Haters gonna hate, hate, hate, shake it off by Taylor swift started blaring from my phone. Time to get up, check out and say goodbye to Aria and Max. As I gathered my stuff together and closed the door to Room #7 and wandered down to the office, I briefly stopped to knock on Room #2 but stopped myself. It was just a one-night stand, and it's not like I was ever going to see him again. I reached the office to check out where Aria was working behind the desk. I'm headed off now, I gave her a big hug and thanked her for the night as it was exactly what I had needed.

I hopped into my car and set off to Taverners – my hometown. Part of me was dreading seeing Mum and Dad as they would pull me back into the pity party that my life had been just as I was finally feeling the guts to move on. I turned on my radio and put on 78.7 GRX and listened to Carrie Underwood and Keith Urban's The Fighter.

I was a fighter; I was a warrior; I am healthy and ready to move on with my life. I repeated this over and over to myself as I drove up and saw on the left a billboard welcoming me to Taverners – Population: 5387. Home of the Taverners Brewery, where most of the town work. This meant that I was about 15 minutes away from my childhood home.

I came up to the road and turned right down Holyoake Lane; we were the last house on the left. As I pulled up, I realized it had been at least about five years since I had been home with Mum and Dad coming to see us as Luke didn't like the atmospheres of small towns. I arrived outside the house when the front door opened and out popped Mum and Dad. They must have been sitting at the window waiting for me to enter. Mum wrapped her arms around me squeezing the life out of me as she was giving me her famous sympathy face. "Give the girl some space, Liv" my dad piped out. I turned and smiled at him, he looked and nodded and went to the car to grab my bags. Always a man of few words my dad Patrick is.

*****

*Another month later*

## Let's Try Love

The players gonna play, play, play blared my alarm. Time to get up and head to work, I was in my second week at work. I had managed to get a job at this cute little bookshop which also doubled for the owner's husbands tattoo shop next door. It was called Words and Ink. I loved my job and my co-workers Daphne and Katie and boss Suzy was terrific. I hadn't felt this much at home in my old job, but here I managed to slip right in the mix.

It was the weekend coming up, and I had planned to have another quiet weekend curled up watching Netflix and devouring popcorn as I had the new Titans Season one to binge watch. The girls always laughed and called me an old soul, but the truth was once I settled back home and was away from Aria and Max and that burst of happiness. I started thinking about what Luke and Tammy were doing, and it devoured my every thought. I had to do something as for those first few weeks at home; I was spending day and night in my pajamas and moping around the house.

That's when I saw the job one day in the newspaper, and I had wandered down to Words and Ink to check it out. They had music playing, the best books around and gave off a good vibe. I got the courage up and asked for a job application, and then Daphne told me to wait, that she would get the manager – Suzy. As soon as I met Suzy, I clicked with her straight away, and that buzz that I had with Aria was back. I just knew in my heart that this was the place I was supposed to be and to work at.

Interrupting my daydream, I heard Daphne say "Come out with us tonight," we are heading to the Taverners Inn for Karaoke night. That's what small towns did for fun – quiz nights and karaoke. I tried to talk myself out, but the truth was, I had nothing better to do. I reluctantly agreed and said something along the lines of sounds fun. I just had to stop home and get changed and would meet them at Taverners Inn.

It was odd being back at Taverners Inn as this is where Aria and I used to spend our nights in high school getting drunk and singing along to the jukebox. As I entered the door, I was brought back to my nights here as I looked around and saw that nothing had changed. Even now ten years later the place hadn't changed a bit. The only difference was that it was owned by Billy Davies who had taken over the inn from his parents who last I heard had decided to retire in Cape Daniel as they had owned a summer house at there. Aria and I once visited it when Billy decided to throw a school break party there one summer. Aria used to date Billy's best friend Travis, and I used to date his friend, Devon. Aah, good memories. Gosh, it made me feel old.

Over here, I turned and saw Daphne and Katie waving at me. I walked over to them and hugged them. Just like I had with Suzy, I had automatically clicked with these girls. We wandered over to the bar to order our drinks. Billy looked up, "Skye, hey what you are doing here. Last I heard you were living it up in the big city". I needed to shut this conversation down quickly, so quickly blurted out didn't work out. Can I order a drink? A tad shocked, but getting the idea Billy clicked on – what will it be, on the house? I ordered a Vodka and Red Bull and went to sit down with Daphne and Katie.

As the night wore on we started chatting about everything under the sun from favourite books to author gossip from discovering Sherilynn Kenyon's husband was poisoning her – seriously it was like a storyline from a Lifetime movie to the latest of Dan Molloy aka AJ Finn lying that he had Cancer and then the shock that Anne Perry who had been voted one of UK's best crime writers was, in fact, Juliet Hulme – one of the girls that were convicted in the murder of the

## Let's Try Love

Parker mother in New Zealand, a crime that shocked New Zealand shores so much that Peter Jackson had directed a movie based on it called "Heavenly Creatures".

We then moved onto the topic of relationships which lead to my drunken rant of Luke the ex-fiancé and my ex-best friend Tammy and how they screwed me literally as just months to our wedding I discovered that those two had been having an affair and he left me for her. The positive side of things is thought that I at least found the cheating before the wedding actually had happened and life was looking up for me here at Taverners – well as much as it could. It was an entertaining night out and looking back on it; this was my second girl's night out which would play a part in that domino effect that I was talking about earlier on.

I arrived at work, ready to start the shift and Daphne and Katie were there chatting away. I waved and said Good morning in passing as I went to make my morning cup of Earl Grey. I loved Mondays as that was one of the days, I was in charge. As much as I loved Suzy, it was nice to be the acting boss for the day. Daphne and Katie wandered into the staffroom, and I could tell that something was up.

They both had this weird grin on their faces; I put my hands up as to say nope, I don't want a part of whatever it is that you girls are scheming. "We just want you to be happy," Daphne said, and Katie put her two cents in of 'we were thinking" after your conversation of the bad luck you have had in the love department.

Daphne grabbed my hand and brought me to the office where up on the computer screen Katie had opened up a dating site called Let's Try Love. I stared at the tagline – Swipe + Like = Love. I couldn't do an online dating site, I had heard about people that signed up for these sites. They were desperados and weirdos who couldn't find a date in real life. I had heard of some crazy dating site stories like the one

## Let's Try Love

where the guy had turned out to be a stalker, and she had only one date with him. He started like texting her 100 million times and turning up at her workplace. What if he's a crazed serial killer?

Katie piped up "This site isn't like that at all." My cousin Christina swears by it as she met her husband Corey on this site after a friend told her about it. Here look, they do full background checks, and their terms and conditions are quite explicit and in detail of what to and what not to expect.

As I read more about the site, it turns out it was created by a female named JB who fancied herself a matchmaker and wanted to match people up with their perfect matches. She had a knack for matchmaking. She just knew when two people should get together and used this site as almost like a front for her gift of love matchmaker skills.

With nothing to lose and the stubborn looks on both Daphne and Katie's faces as I knew neither of them was going to give up. If I hadn't created the profile myself, then they would have created one for me and who knows they might have given me cray-cray answers and I could have ended up with a weirdo like an Alaskan bushman or a cursing sailor.

I opened the main sign-up page and started entering the necessary details.

    Name: Skye Lancaster
    Country: Taverners, Pandora
    Phone: 027 789 6572
    Email: skye.lancaster@gmail.com

    Then there were the matching questions:
    Username: BookishSkye

## Let's Try Love

Favorite Animal: Unicorns – though this is debatable as some consider that they aren't real animals. Hello, we have National Unicorn Day every April 9$^{th}$.

Favorite Author: James Patterson, Abbi Glines, Colleen Hoover

Favorite Position: Anything but Doggie style as I am no ones bitch :P

Taking a deep breath, there was no going back as I pushed submit and awaited holding my breath for the matches to roll in.

Opening my eyes and counting to ten, I was surprised at the matches that started piling up. None of the first lots took my interest, and I thought I would be at a complete loss as I kept clicking nope he looks too stalkerish , next one – too fat, ewh – talk about not cleaning out nostril hair ; is he trying to grow his own jungle in his nose , no way what are we ten with his favorite cartoon being PJ Masks and Wait a minute, what the hell what straight man loves cross-dressing ?? It seems like I was destined for only finding weirdos, so much for the girls' adamancy that this site was safe from oddballs.

Scrolling back up on the screen, there in all his perfect glory was none other than my one-night stand Tucker and reading more I learned his last name was Heywood and I laughed as his favorite animal was a Dragon – If he can have a dragon, then I don't see why Unicorn wasn't acceptable. How on earth was it that he was looking for love? He did not lack in the good looks department, and the sex was fantastic not like it was with Luke.

Taking a deep breath, I clicked PM and counted to ten as I gathered up the courage to send him a message. Hey, remember me your one-night stand from a few months back? The chick from the hotel? I backspaced and went for the safe option – Hey FriarTuck,

## Let's Try Love

saw your profile on Let's Try Love, not sure if you remember me but we met a few months ago while we were both staying at the Funky Monkey Lodge. Are you interested in meeting up for a C and C? Cheers, BookishSkye

Looking at the time, I closed the laptop and headed off to do some work as our children's after-school Storytime was about to start and today was my turn to read them the books. Today's reading aloud book was The True Story of the Three Little Pigs, and we were making some cute origami pigs as we were joining in on the celebration of National Pig Appreciation Week. Setting up the table of books with Pigs as characters we had Piglet from Winnie the Pooh, Wilbur from Charlotte's Web, Mercy Watson and Nanny Piggins and of course who could forget Peppa Pig.

The rest of the day whizzed by, and as I arrived home, I heard a ding on my phone telling me I had a new email from FriarTuck. Hey BookishSkye, I remember ☐ Best night ever. Fancy seeing you on here and would love to catch up, how about Friday night at Taverners Inn? FriarTuck.

Friday came, and I was a bundle of nerves and had butterflies fluttering around, I hadn't felt this nervous in such a long time. I arrived, and there he was as hot as ever. We spent all night chatting and catching up as he mentioned he had moved here to work at the local lawyers' firm as he was over the big city life and growing up in a small town, he preferred the homely feel that small towns have. We went back to his place as I had to embarrassedly explain that I was back living at my parents' home and wasn't quite ready for him to meet the parents on the first date, well technically our second date.

Fast forward to a month later, and I was in heaven, I had finally met a guy who loved me for who I was. The sex was utterly phenomenal. I had moved out of my parents home and guess what, readers we are engaged. Tucker surprised me this weekend by taking me to the place we first met which also meant that I got to catch up with Aria and Max and he had reserved Room #7. It was the perfect proposal ever, as he had brought an old book. The old book was sitting on the bed surrounded by rainbow colored rose petals. As I opened the book it had, had the pages hollowed out and when I opened the cover, there on the page in gold pen read Will You Marry Me ? with a purple ring box in the middle of the hollowed pages and as I opened the ring box. Tucker grabbed it and knelt on one knee and said BookishSkye, will you marry me? Of course, I said Yes.

Moral of the Story: Readers, if you feel like you have been burned by love. Don't be afraid to try again and internet dating is not just filled with weirdos. Like a diamond can be found in the rough, amongst the sea of weirdos may be your very own Prince Charming or in my case FriarTuck.

## About the Author

Paula Phillips hails from the small country of New Zealand 🇳🇿. She works by day as a Children's and Teens Librarian and by night she can be found at her version of the Daily Planet - The Phantom Paragrapher Book Blog.

# Who We Are

## by K.R. Reese

Tanner and Alyssa have worked together for a few years. When their best friends convince them to sign-up for Let's Try Love, an online dating site, they didn't expect their anonymous match to be each other. Can they ignore their employer-employee relationship for what's to come?

# Who We Are by K.R. Reese

## Prologue

*Present Day*

"Mrs. Moore, I'm home." Tanner's voice carried through the mostly empty halls to Alyssa's ears. They had only started moving into this home – their first home together – a few days ago; and while some stuff was here, it wasn't put away. Alyssa tried not to think of all the stuff that still sat at both their apartments, either. She wasn't in the mood.

Tanner's arms came around her shoulders, his lips against her ear. "Silence isn't what I expected when I got home. What's wrong?"

"James. Or Brandi. I honestly don't know which one to be mad at right now. I guess I'm disappointed in them both, and worried about James."

Tanner seemed to take his time before responding. There was a time, before they were married, that he was jealous of her best friend. He thought there was more going on than what she was telling him, and it took awhile for them to get over it. Alyssa couldn't be mad at Tanner for it. She was jealous of his best friend, too. But that's what happened when your best friends were the opposite gender and you were starting a relationship.

"What did they do this time?"

She sighed, closing her eyes. "Where do I start? Brandi took off with all the cash James had in the house. They're supposed to get married in *two* days and it looks like she ghosted." She took a deep breath before she continued because it's no secret, she wasn't fond of James' fiancé. "He says she wouldn't do that, that she was excited for the wedding and had gone to pick up more decorations. He wants to file a missing persons report."

Tanner was still silent behind her, contemplating his answer, she guessed. "Well, the police won't let him file a report unless she's been gone for over twenty-four hours. He needs to report the money being gone, though, because that's a good sign that she ditched out. We all know she wasn't there for *him* anyway. It seems he's the only one who hasn't figured that out."

"When can we move the rest of our stuff? We're both taking a vacation this next week. We're paying rent on two different apartments, when we only ever lived in one of those, and we have a house."

Tanner started kissing her neck, distracting her from where her thoughts had been all day. She usually loved when he took her mind off what was bothering her, but she hadn't felt good the past few days, and she wanted to focus on having her belongings.

Pushing away from the chair, the shock on Tanner's face is evident. "Be serious a minute, Tanner. We've been living out of boxes for weeks. We've been going to our apartments when we need something that isn't here. This isn't healthy. We haven't started our life together, even though we're married."

Alyssa felt the burning sensation in her eyes before the tears started to fall. She wasn't an emotional person. These past few weeks had been trying, though, and her emotions were running high.

*At least she hoped that's all it was.*

She needed to talk to Tanner about the possibility of pregnancy before he started pointing out all the ways she was acting differently.

Alyssa could still remember a time when Tanner was just her boss who occasionally flirted with her. She never saw herself here with him now, married, and very possibly expecting their first child.

# One

*Two Years Ago*

Alyssa had been working for StarTech for a little over a year now. James had got her this job, even if he denied it and said she did it all on her own. She knew better. She might've graduated with a Master's in Administration and Communication, but she hadn't worked anywhere relevant for this position. She couldn't be unappreciative, though, because her best friend was always the protector, pulling her out of any and all situations.

*Beep.*

The unexpected notification from her phone sent her heart skittering out of rhythm. James had convinced her to sign up for a dating app where he'd met his fiancé, Brandi. Alyssa wasn't sure that Brandi was truly in the relationship for James, and she never planned on finding out because they couldn't stand each other. She tolerated the other woman because she wasn't going to lose her best friend over niggling thoughts and being uncomfortable. It wasn't her life nor her business.

*Beep. Beep.*

Alyssa wanted to ignore the dating app, *Let's Try Love*, but two beeps meant she had a match and a message request. It had happened a few times over the past few months, but normally they were creeps looking for a quick lay. It wasn't that she was opposed to a hook-up, but it felt wrong without getting to know them some first.

Pulling her phone from her bag, **New Match Found** stared back at her. Clicking into the app, there was a message request from *Tan938*. Alyssa viewed the message without accepting it. If it was another "Let's fuck" message, she'd ignore it and the person on the other end would never know she saw it.

**Tan938: Hi. It seems we're a match. I think? How are you today?**

Alyssa was stunned that it was a normal message compared to what she'd been getting. She didn't want to get her hopes up, though, because she knew it could turn around quickly. Pushing doubt aside, she decided to respond.

**Lys567: Hi. Yes, it seems we're a match. I'm decent today, currently at work waiting for my boss so we can go to meetings all day. Pretty boring. How are you?**

When there wasn't an instant response, Alyssa put her phone on silent and tucked it into her pants pocket. James was getting an earful later, because this had not gone as planned. It had been months, and Alyssa didn't hold much hope that this guy would be any different.

Tanner suddenly appeared in her doorway, causing her to shriek. That beautiful smile of his appeared and Alyssa had to tamp down the feelings it always ignited within herself.

"Well, good morning, beautiful, are you ready to go?"

Alyssa scowled. This was their routine. They flirted. They danced around each other. They never crossed the line, though. James had warned her away from Tanner the moment she was hired. He had given a vague answer of *"she wasn't the girl for someone like Tanner, he didn't want her to get hurt"*, etc. Alyssa had gone with her best friend's word, but sometimes she questioned why. She wouldn't mind a one-nighter with her very handsome, very outgoing boss.

"You know I'm ready. I was waiting for you. Again."

He smiled again, looking toward the windows. "Aren't I supposed to scowl at you for being late? I think this is backward."

Alyssa smacked the client's folders into his chest on her way out the door. "It is backward, sweetheart. I wouldn't have to treat you like a child if you'd act more like the boss you're supposed to be." She stopped outside the elevators, waiting for his footsteps to follow.

Suddenly, he was right behind her, his lips at her ear. "I *am* your boss. Have you ever considered that I like getting you riled up in the morning?"

Alyssa suppressed the groan that almost escaped her lips. Tanner knew the effect he had on women, he couldn't be oblivious to it, but he didn't date. At least not that any of us had seen or heard of. His face was plastered all over every magazine in the city, but he never had a woman on his arm.

"Before you question my authority, Alyssa, you should remember that I know exactly what I'm doing when we argue."

## Two

Tanner was sitting in this meeting with clients that weren't as interesting as the phone burning a hole through his pocket. *Let's Try Love*, the dating app his little sister had signed him up for, had notified him of a new message seconds before he got to Alyssa's office door. It had found a match this morning and he was excited to see how things went.

When Lani had first signed him up, he wasn't happy about it. "This is bullshit, Lani, and you know it. It's not like I can post my picture to the profile, everyone will know exactly who I am."

She rolled her eyes and continued with his phone. "You don't have to post a straight forward picture. You can just post your profile and see what happens. Leaving your appearance as a mystery could be interesting."

"Or it could be creepy as hell and women should run for the hills," he mumbled under his breath.

"Tanner, the app isn't total bullshit. It isn't guaranteed and it isn't for everyone. But that's where I met Anthony and look how that turned out. You're ready to settle down and every woman you meet is after one thing. Once they know who you are, it's game over. You know it, I know it, the fucking entire city knows it. This is an alternative."

Now, here he was sitting in a boardroom trying to pay attention to the client's presentation. Ignoring his better judgment, he pulled his phone out in his binder and opened the message.

**Lys567: Hi. Yes, it seems we're a match. I'm decent today, currently at work waiting for my boss so we can go to meetings all day. Pretty boring. How are you?**

# Let's Try Love

It's interesting that she answered so formal. Was she always like that? What did she look like? Her profile image showed shiny, dark brown hair. He wondered if it was as silky as it looked.

**Tan938: I'm having a pretty boring day, too. I'm in a meeting right now that I'm trying to pay attention to. Your message interrupted my concentration.**

After Tanner hit send, he thought that the message sounded rude.

**Tan938: Don't take that the wrong way, I was happy for the interruption.**

He placed his phone in his lap and focused back on the presentation in front of him. Looking at Alyssa to make sure she was taking notes on what he might've missed, he watched a strange look pass over her face before she started biting her lip.

Alyssa was a beautiful woman. When she had first walked into his office, she was temptation wrapped in a petite package. While he flirted and tormented her, he would never cross the line with an employee. Rumors spread fast and everyone would think she was getting special privileges for screwing the boss. *Too bad his dick didn't have a problem with that scenario.*

Tanner continued to watch Alyssa as she pulled her phone out of her pocket. After a few seconds, she put it away and kept taking notes. His phone vibrated again.

**Lys567: Glad I could be of help in your boring day.**

Something was bothering him, but he couldn't place it. He knew it was something big, something serious. He would have to figure it out later, though, because the presentation was wrapping up.

"Thank you for your time today, my office will be in touch." Tanner shook the other man's hand and they left the building, catching a ride back to their offices. It was silent until they stepped in the elevator.

"You didn't pay any attention to that presentation, even before you started playing with your phone. I'll email my notes and thoughts over to you later."

Tanner wanted to push her buttons. "I wasn't the only one who seemed intent on playing with their phone during that meeting, Alyssa. Did you think I didn't notice?" He watched the blush spread over her face slowly and the shy smile peeking at the corners. "Ooooh, is Alyssa doing something naughty on her phone?"

The glare he received this time was different. She looked him over. Once. Twice. A third time. His mind started wandering to all the places he knew it shouldn't, but he was helpless to stop them. When the elevator dinged, announcing the arrival to their floor, he let her exit first.

"Saved by the bell," he mumbled under his breath.

# Three

*A few months later*

Alyssa had been talking to *Tan938* for the past few months on *Let's Try Love*. She had avoided all attempts at trying to meet because she wasn't ready. James kept badgering her about just going for it, and she knew he was being the logical one in this situation, but she couldn't bring herself to agree to a date. Even if it was just lunch or dinner.

The problem was, Alyssa was pretty sure she knew who *Tan938* was; and if she was correct, nothing could come of the connection they had been sharing. She wanted to set up a 'date' with this mystery man on her terms to see if her assumptions were right. But she needed James as backup, because he was against Alyssa being with Tanner in any sense.

**Lys567: Hiya, stranger. Would you like to meet for lunch today? Maybe around one fifteen at the little diner on 6th street?**

Alyssa tapped her fingers on her desk, waiting for his response. Before her phone beeped, Tanner's head popped out of his office.

"Hey, Alyssa, can you clear my schedule from one to two today, please? I have a business lunch meeting that was unplanned."

She had to clear her throat so her voice wouldn't shake.

"Sure, Tanner, I'll do that now. You'll see the update shortly."

Alyssa went into their shared calendar and cleared the schedule. He only had a few phone calls during that time that she quickly sent emails to reschedule. Her job had become a routine, but she loved it. Before too long, her phone notified her of the message she was expecting.

**Tan938: Lunch sounds amazing. Meet you there?**
**Lys567: Yes! I'll leave now.**

She didn't expect a message in return, and she wasn't leaving the office right away. Alyssa waited for Tanner to exit his office and for the sound of the elevator doors closing. Then she made her way down to her own car to make the ten-minute ride across town.

# Four

It was finally happening. Tanner had been trying for months to get a date with the woman from *Let's Try Love*. Lani had been on his ass about who he was talking to; and every time they talked, he didn't have any new updates. Today would change that. Tanner hoped that the connection they seemed to share through the internet was there when they met for the first time, too.

He was a few minutes early to the café she had suggested, so he grabbed an outside seat since the spring weather had taken over in the past few weeks. Tanner wasn't sure how they were going to know who the other was, but he thought he would recognize her hair or feel some sort of connection when she arrived. He sounded like a sap in his head, but at least he hadn't said any of it aloud. His best friend would have a field day with that news, and he wasn't in the mood for one of Grace's lectures on insta-love.

After a few minutes, a shadow came over the table. When Tanner turned around, he didn't expect to see his secretary standing there.

"Alyssa, what are you doing here?"

She had her head down and she was biting her lip again. That was a tell-tale sign that she was nervous about something.

"Is everything okay?"

Alyssa finally lifted her gaze to meet his.

"We need to talk, but I don't think this is the right place for it."

Tanner thought for a moment. He couldn't leave without meeting the woman he'd been talking to the past few months.

"I'm meeting someone for lunch. That's why I had you clear my schedule. I can meet you at the office later to discuss whatever it is."

Her face turned red again, but Tanner didn't understand her reaction.

"You were meeting me, Tanner."

He stayed silent for a moment, trying to process what she said. There was no way that Alyssa – his secretary – was *Lys567*. Was there?

"Alyssa, I'm a little confused. What are you trying to say?"

A frown pulled her eyebrows together, but she refused to meet his gaze. "I'm Lys567. *Let's Try Love*? I didn't know it was you until a few days ago. But once I figured it out, I knew I had to tell you." She sighed. "Can we please go somewhere to talk about this?"

Tanner nodded, threw money on the table for his water and they left, heading back to the office. Neither of them spoke during the trip in his car. He would send her with someone else to pick up her car later, of course, but right now he hadn't processed everything. *And he was afraid she'd run away before they straightened this out.*

The closer they got to the office, the angrier he became. *Alyssa knew a few days ago* that he was who she'd been talking to. And instead of just telling him, she left him in the dark until it was time to set up a date?

When they stepped inside the elevator, it seemed like the air surrounding them was electrified. Tanner fisted his hands and stepped away from Alyssa. When the elevator doors dinged as they opened, he growled. "My office. Now."

Tanner didn't wait for Alyssa to go first, instead stomping toward the end of the hall. He heard her footsteps close behind. She closed the door behind them, while he just stared at her.

"You. Are. Lys567."

Alyssa straightened, sucked in a breath, and looked away.

## Let's Try Love

He started toward her, expecting her to hesitate. Tanner knew he was intimidating to a lot of people. The fact that she didn't back down didn't sit well with him, but he pushed the thought away. Alyssa wasn't afraid.

In two strides, he was standing in front of her.

"Alyssa," he gulped. "I've wanted to do this since I met you."

## Five

He kissed her – or maybe she kissed him? Alyssa wasn't sure which way was up anymore. His tongue was exploring hers and it felt amazing. When Tanner's fingers tangled in her hair to tilt her head back, her toes curled. His arm wrapped around her waist, holding her steady and she leaned into him.

*Slow down*, a voice told her, and she pushed him away. Alyssa sucked in a breath as he stumbled away from her. He ran both hands through his hair, mumbling under his breath words that she couldn't quite catch. Tanner looked like the world had just flipped on its axis.

Alyssa needed to talk to James. Pronto. She couldn't avoid it any longer, especially if this was going to go any further. The problem was, she didn't now if Tanner wanted it to go any further.

"I don't fraternize with employees. I don't… date." He mumbled, eyeing her cautiously.

She looked him up and down, taking her time.

"Alyssa, I.. I have nothing to offer you. James would kill me if I stepped into this territory with you."

She held up her hand to stop him from continuing. "First, James has no control over what I do with my life. I know he's always been the big brother I never had, he's always been my protector, and I'm sure he warned you away from me ten ways to Sunday. But he doesn't *control* me. I make my own decisions. And right now, my decision is that I want…"

Tanner cut her off with another kiss, dragging her into his lap behind his desk. He stopped and laid his forehead against hers, leaving his eyes closed.

"Say, yes, Alyssa. Tell me we'll just see what happens and I'll make you feel good."

## Six

Tanner reopened his eyes to find her staring at him. A smirk was playing on her lips, but he couldn't decipher what she was thinking.

He let his hands wander. First around her hips, then up and down her thighs. When Alyssa didn't stop his hands from going higher, he pushed her skirt up, revealing black see-through lace panties underneath.

Alyssa grinned. He pulled her down on top of him and she gasped.

Placing his lips against her ear, he whispered, watching goosebumps rise on her skin. "Feel what you do to me, Alyssa," he murmured.

"God, Tanner, yes!"

He rocked her hips against him, watched as her breathing became ragged and frantic. Her breasts were bouncing in front of his face and he wanted more of her.

"Take your shirt off, baby," he said against her collarbone.

His hands snuck underneath her shirt as she fought to get it over her head. His thumb flicked on a nipple through the fabric of her silky bra. A gasp pulled from her lips.

Every time Tanner would make another circle around her nipple, her hips would jerk against him. He followed the path her shirt made as she pulled it off, unbuckling her bra. When her breasts fell free, he sucked a bud into his mouth and applied light pressure. Alyssa threw her head back and moaned. *She was perfect.*

Rather than torturing her more, because he planned on there being plenty of time for that later, he pulled her mouth down to his.

She finally broke their kiss with a moan. "Tanner, I need you," she choked out, reaching for the button on his slacks. "Please."

He stood instead, settling her on the edge of his desk. Alyssa's eyes were wide, unfocused. Tanner pulled her panties down her legs and let them fall to the floor. As he walked to the door, making sure it was locked, he kept an eye on her, too.

"Spread your legs, baby," he mumbled against her lips when he was back in front of her. He splayed one hand across her lower abdomen, holding her in place. His other hand began exploring her folds, circling her clit and going up around her nipples. A constant pattern that had her hips jerking against his hold.

"Tanner," she moaned. "I need to… I need you."

He released his hold and stripped out of his pants and boxers. Leaning toward her again, he whispered against her lips. "I've wanted to do this from the moment your smart mouth stepped into my office that first day, Alyssa." She held her breath. "Talking to you, even when I didn't know it was you, has been wonderful. Amazing, really. God, I didn't think insta-love or whatever it is, even existed. But I love you, Alyssa. I think a part of me always has."

Before she could respond, his lips crashed down on hers and he entered her. The fullness of him made her gasp and she closed her eyes, letting the sensations burn through her. *This* was what she was missing with everyone else. The instant connection, the passion.

Alyssa broke their kiss, but kept her eyes closed. "I love you, too, Tanner."

James was going to kill her, but she'd gladly handle those consequences if it meant she could keep Tanner forever.

# Seven

*Present Day*

Alyssa wasn't feeling well this morning, so she had stayed home. Tanner didn't know what was wrong with her lately, but he intended on finding out. First, he had a meeting with James, and he knew it wasn't going to go well.

When he hired James, it was because of his expertise in the tech world. But he was also Alyssa's best friend who didn't like that she had married him. It was a whirlwind romance, but they had skated around each other for an entire year before *Let's Try Love* brought them together. It was unexpected. Fast. Perfect. Tanner wouldn't change anything.

A knock at the door made him stand. "Come in," he spoke loud enough for whoever it was to hear him. James stepped into his office with a scowl on his face.

"Don't look so disappointed to see me, James."

The other man took the seat across from his desk. "I'm still not happy that you're married to my best friend. But I've learned to live with it and Alyssa strictly told me to stay out of her business." He swiped a hand down his face before making eye contact. "Look, I came here to apologize for the way I've acted since you two announced you were together. I don't know how much Alyssa's told you about our childhood, so I won't get into detail. Just know, I've always been there. I'm the *only* person who has been there. And while there's never been any romantic feelings toward Alyssa, I still care about her."

"James, I'm not…"

He held up his hand to stop Tanner from finishing his sentence.

"Let me finish. Please. I just didn't want to see her hurt. And maybe there was a little bit of jealousy there, too. But know that it came from a good place. She's had it tough, and I pulled her out time and again. Just because your married, doesn't mean I'm going to stop doing that."

Tanner waited to make sure James was finished before he spoke. "I may have married her and we're going to spend the rest of our lives together, but I can't take your place. You're her best friend, and as much as I didn't like that when we first started dating, I'm over it now. I was jealous of you, very much. Alyssa kept telling me that there was nothing between you, but it was hard to believe. You're so comfortable with each other, you know each other's secrets. A part of me wanted to be the one who knew all her secrets, and only me. But I realize that isn't how this works."

James nodded his head before staring out the windows. "My private investigator found Brandi. She's in Atlanta. With some other guy. I guess Alyssa was already right about her, but I was blind in seeing it myself. I don't want to hear *I told you so*, so I haven't told her yet."

A smirk played on Tanner's lips. His wife was very proud of telling someone *I told you so*. She did it often. It annoyed his best friend, Grace, to no end. Speaking of, she should be arriving soon.

"Listen, James, even if Alyssa says I told you so, she doesn't mean it to hurt you. She wants what is best for you, too. She doesn't want to see you get hurt. And I know all about her childhood, as well as bits and pieces of yours. But she only told me what was necessary about yours to fit hers together. I hate to cut this short, but Grace will be here shortly to have lunch. Come over for dinner tonight, we'll talk more then."

"Who the hell is Grace?" Anger exploded into James' features.

Tanner ran his hands through his hair. He forgot that James hadn't met *his* best friend, yet, since she couldn't make it to the wedding.

"She is my best friend. Don't worry, Alyssa wasn't fond of her at first either. But she rubs off on you."

Right on cue, his office door opened, and Grace walked in. "Oh, I'm sorry! I didn't know you were in a meeting. Alyssa wasn't in her office, so I couldn't ask. I'll just wait out here."

James waited until the door closed before turning back to Tanner. "*That* is your best friend?"

Tanner recognized the glint in James' eyes. He had worn that same expression when he first met Alyssa. *Oh, hell no.*

"Don't go getting any ideas, slick. She's off limits to you."

A laugh rumbled through James' and Tanner couldn't hold back his own. "Oh, this should be fun. Alyssa was off limits to you, too, and look how that turned out. I think we should let Grace make up her own mind, don't you?"

James walked backward to the door with a huge grin on his face. "I'll see you for dinner tonight. You should invite your best friend."

Tanner closed his eyes and shook his head. "Asshole," he mumbled under his breath.

"Why am I an asshole and what's this I hear about dinner?" Grace's voice echoed in his office. Tanner had hoped she didn't hear any of that.

"We're going to have dinner tonight with Alyssa's best friend. You should come over, too. Neither of you have seen the new house, yet." Tanner stopped. "Oh, and you aren't the asshole, he is."

Grace was smiling when he finally looked at her. "I already assumed as much, I just wanted to push your buttons. How is Alyssa? It's weird that she isn't here today. And was *that* her best friend?"

Tanner eyed her suspiciously. Grace didn't pay much attention to men. She was career focused and claimed she didn't have time to date. Maybe James was right, maybe she should make her own mind up about him. Who was Tanner to stop it? After all, it could be good for them both. James was stuck in a minefield about Brandi and Grace hadn't dated anyone in years, at least not that he'd known about.

When Grace cleared her throat, Tanner realized he hadn't answered her questions. "Alyssa wasn't feeling well this morning, so I told her to stay home and rest. Yes, that was her best friend, James. He's a pain in my ass and he hated that I married his best friend. But it's settled now and we're on better footing. Anyway, you really should come for dinner tonight, too, it'll be fun."

# Epilogue

*James*

Leaving Tanner's office, he headed straight for their house since Alyssa was home and sick. He didn't know whether she was up for company, but since Tanner had invited him to dinner, he hoped she was.

What was even better was that he wanted Tanner to extend the invitation to Grace. James had never seen a more beautiful woman. While Alyssa had listened and tried *Let's Try Love* by his prompting, he didn't want to try it again after the fail with Brandi. Maybe it was time that he tried traditional dating – dinners, movies, lunch – whatever *that* entailed.

First, though, he had a best friend to check up on and he wanted to know everything she knew about Grace. He couldn't ask Tanner. He had just been warned away from Grace with a growl and furrowed brows. Too bad James was horrible at listening.

## About the Author

K.R. Reese writes contemporary romances with HEAs, and a lot of suspense and thrills. She's the author of the small-town Wilson Creek series and the Rockstar Chaos series, with many more projects in the works. She was born and raised in Ohio, where she still resides with her husband and their children. When she isn't reading or writing, you can find her spending time with her family, doing photo shoots, or listening to music.

## Connect with the Author

Facebook Page: http://www.facebook.com/authorkrreese
Reader's Group: www.facebook.com/groups/reesesroadhouse
Twitter: http://www.twitter.com/authorkrreese
BookBub: http://www.bookbub.com/authors/k-r-reese

# Unexpected Match

## by Alice La Roux

When conventional isn't working, it's time to try something new, and that's exactly what Lila does one night after a disastrous tenth date and too much Pinot. Ava isn't looking for love, she just wants someone to share her bed until the sunrises, not forever. But when the two meet there's an undeniable chemistry. A zing, that brings these women crashing together in a way neither of them expected.

# Unexpected Match by Alice La Roux

## Lila

It's not that I was unlucky in love exactly; just more that nothing ever seemed to stick. It was like going into a department store that everyone loved and raved about, but when you were trying on clothes you realise that everything looks drab and frumpy. It's supposed to be great, supposed to be a fairy-tale but in reality, dating was a drag. There was no magic, no spark—at least not for me, not yet. That's why I'd signed up for online dating. The Let's Try Love site was the one that jumped out, not too lovey-dovey, not too clinically cold and it didn't look like a swinger's site. I wanted to find my 'one' amongst the toads that sat in the pond, glaring at me.

Tonight was the tenth date I'd been on. My roommate, Heather, had helped me pick him. The guy sat across the table from me was okay looking, average height, and average build. He had mousy coloured hair with brown, warm eyes. He was ordinary, but

# Let's Try Love

dull. He chewed with his mouth open and as he talked tiny chunks of chicken flew from his mouth. No. I couldn't date this man. I couldn't even sit through the rest of the meal if he didn't shut his goddam trap.

"Look, Martin..." I say slowly before I take a swig of wine. I need it. I needed an excuse to leave this dreadful meal.

His eyes widen and his mouth finally closes. He swallows and wipes at the corners of his lips with the napkin daintily.

"It's Mark actually..."

"Oh."

I push my salad around with my fork, avoiding his gaze. I'm avoiding the disappointment there because he thought this was going well. He'd told me so twice before our food arrived and again, right before I'd called him by another name.

His face has soured now, but I say nothing.

"Well hey, at least we weren't in bed when you called me by someone else's name," he jokes feebly, trying to warm up the cold atmosphere that's settled over us.

"Look, I'm sorry, but this isn't working for me."

Mark frowns and there's something about the puppy dog expression he's wearing that pangs in my chest. I feel guilty, but I don't want to waste both of our time.

"I thought it was going well, was it something I said?"

I shake my head gently, "No..."

He slams his fork down on the table like a toddler having a tantrum.

"I knew I shouldn't have told you about my ex. It's just, I was with Sheila for so long. She had such a huge impact on my life. But I'm ready to move on, I swear I am!"

"Mark, it's not that. I promise." I lie as I start pulling my jacket on and reach under the table for my purse.

## Let's Try Love

"Then why?" He whines and I swear my skin crawls.

"This is not attractive. It's our first date and you're being overly intense," I say calmly. "That, and you chew like a cow. It's not very nice to sit opposite."

"Wait, you don't like how I chew? That's it?"

I stand, throwing some money down on the table. He's completely missing the point, the chewing is only the tip of the iceberg. I needed to get out of here before he cried. He seemed like a crier.

To my surprise he snorts, "You're one weird chick."

I flash him a small smile before leaving, as if I haven't heard that before. I've heard it all in the two years I'd been trying to date seriously, from 'frigid' to 'emotionless'. I hoped Let's Try Love would've been different, but ten dates in and it wasn't looking that way. I needed to try something a little different, maybe put myself out there a little more. It was time to update my profile.

\*\*\*

A bottle of cheap white wine later, and I start casting my net wider. It's the twenty-first century and my usual dating pool has clearly gone stagnant. Heather plonks herself next to me on the sofa after a long day at the hotel she works in.

"We need more wine," she grins, looking at my empty bottle after clocking what I'm doing. She leans in and places her head on my shoulder so she can get a better view. Nosey bat.

"Women, huh." She raises her brows at me with a secretive smile. "We've all been there…"

"No, we haven't." I frown slightly, was this some rite of passage I'd missed out on? Was kissing girls a 'thing' in school that I'd been oddly oblivious to?

Heather sits up slightly, "Not even in college? A sneaky little grope or a weirdly good snog?"

I snort, "Heather, you've met my super religious parents yeah?"

She nods, she knows exactly what my family are like. I'm the odd one out for wanting to find my own way in life, not dutifully obeying every word from my parent's lips. That makes it sound like we don't have a great relationship, we actually we do. I see my parents twice a month for lunch and my mother calls weekly, but we just work better apart. And I don't tell them every detail of my life.

"True, but isn't that why you dyed your hair pink and got your ears pierced? To rebel?" Heather's turned the TV on now and is flicking through the romance channels. She's a sucker for a happily ever after.

I tilt my head, "This isn't the same thing."

"Then why are you so open to it now?"

I sigh, the wine making me more philosophical than I usually am. "Because all these dates are missing something. That spark, the magic you read about or the lusty, long looks from films."

I'm aware that I'm waving my hand around like it's a magic wand, ready to conjure up some great love. Damn, this wine was going to my head. My other hand grips my laptop tightly. I can't let go. What if Mr or Mrs Right was still just one click away?

"Really?" Heather stands and goes into our tiny kitchenette and grabs a big bag of crisps. "You're using media and fiction to tell you what love is?"

I shrug, only feeling a twinge of embarrassment. "It's not like I've got a whole lot of experience to go on."

She jumps back onto the sofa beside me, "But what do you feel on these dates?" She asks between mouthfuls. "What do you think when you look at the men sat before you?"

I think about it for a second. Every single date has been flat. All ten of them. "Honestly, not a whole lot."

She winks suggestively, "What if one wanted to kiss you?"

I look away, a blush creeping into my cheeks, but not for the reason she thinks. I've already been down that path and it didn't end well.

"That's what happened to Chad…"

"The one you punched and left at the bar?"

"Yeah." I give her a pointed look.

"Oh. Did he press charges after?"

I shake my head. He couldn't, the police had said that I acted in self-defence.

Heather gives a small shrug and shovels more crisps into her gob. "Maybe men really aren't for you…"

I lay back on the sofa and stare at the ceiling for a moment or two. "But what if women aren't either, what if I'm just destined to be alone?" I whisper, mainly to myself.

"Lila, how will you know if you don't at least take a teeny tiny bite of the apple?"

"An Eve reference, really?"

"Just sayin' is all."

We sit in silence for a moment as I flick through the next lot of profiles, my options considerably more now that I'd added women into the mix. I wasn't even sure if I was attracted to women, I mean I noticed them, but I'd never fantasized about them. I'd never actually fantasized about a man either though, that was something I'd always put down to my upbringing.

"What about that one?" Heather says as we stop on the image of a dark haired woman with cool brown eyes and a sharp bob. She looked beautiful in a terrifying kind of way. Everything about her was angles and harsh lines, she screamed driven, successful, take no prisoners. I couldn't tear my eyes away.

# Ava

Sweat coats me and I wish I could say I look glamorous sweating, but I don't. I'm bright red and the salty stuff is literally pouring down my face and into my damn eyes, but I don't care. If I don't run, I go crazy. I need this early morning workout to keep me on track for the rest of the day. Working in the cutthroat world of business means that if you show any weakness, you're dead. I didn't need my emotions to get away from me while trying to climb my way up the corporate ladder. I'm the same when it comes to sex, I know what I like and I like it to be over before my post-workout shower. Relationships are just an added complication I don't have time for right now. There's a promotion in my office for Regional Director and I want it. I deserve it. I haven't worked this hard, for this long, to be passed over. I don't understand why my jerk of a brother has signed me up to Let's Try Love, I don't need a woman right now. Not one who wants to stay over after sex anyway. I need to focus, and stay on track.

    I finish up my workout and head back upstairs to my apartment for a shower. I'm hoping last night's company, Shelly... or was it Shelbie, is long gone. The industry was tough enough without being seen as the hard-ass lesbian, so I keep my private life just that. Fucking private. I use my key card and enter, waiting for a moment or two in the doorway to see if I can hear any noises coming from my room. Nothing. She's gone. I breathe a sigh of relief and jump in the shower, but not before I notice a slip of paper on my pillow with her number on it. Underneath is scrawled 'Sasha'.

    I'm on my way to the office when I get an email to my iPad with the latest candidates from that ridiculous dating site. My brother, Jack, likes to go through my 'matches' with his wife, Nia, and narrow my list down to three each week. Then he emails me, in the hope that I'll message one of them, which I rarely do. I mean I think Sasha may have been from last week's candidate pool, but Courtney, the girl from the night before, was someone I met in the queue of the coffee shop. I know Jack and Nia mean well, and I love them both, but I don't want the white picket fence and the two point four children. I want something that burns, something that hurts so bad, it's good. I want passion, perky tits and an empty bed the next morning—that's not too much to ask for, is it?

That's when I spot Lila in my list. Her soft baby pink hair hangs in loose curls around her face, with big grey eyes that have that deer caught in a headlight look, and I can't help but pause. I'm willing to bet that she's never kissed a woman, let alone given up every inch of her body and her sanity, for one. She has this innocence that's easy to spot from a mile off, and for some reason that makes me want to click on her profile. I want to corrupt her. I want to hear her screaming my name as she clenches her soft thighs around my head. Fuck, I shake myself, it was too early for filthy thoughts. I take a swig of my coffee and pack the tablet away before the taxi pulls up outside my office building. I don't even make it to the elevators when I decide that Lila will be mine. Just for one night. And then she'll never be the same again.

***

I decided not to tell Jack that I sent Lila an invitation for drinks. He'd only get excited, and that would be a waste of his energy and I'd be asked a billion questions the next day. It was only drinks. Except, it was never only drinks with me. This one is different, I can tell just by the messages we've exchanged. She's nervous, unsure of herself and even more wary of me. For some reason that doesn't warn me away, I mean, I should be running for the hills. Inexperience isn't sexy. It's frustrating and a sure way to lead to a disappointing evening, but with Lila I want to take that risk, I want to see just how far I can push her.

When I get home from work I take a shower and wash away the misogyny and bullshit from the day. I hate being the only woman in the office at times. I usually don't like to hang around, a shower is a short functional thing, but with the warm water caressing my skin and my thoughts consumed by a girl with large scared eyes, I'm reluctant to rush. My hands move over my slick skin, anticipation for tonight filling me, curiosity and excitement driving me as I give way to my filthy thoughts. I wondered if I could make her blush with just a look, or how she would react if my hand brushed against her thigh. My mind is filled with hesitant kisses and heated moans as I bring myself to orgasm. We'd already spoken on the phone to arrange a bar and as I come I imagine my name on her lips, a hushed groan that pushes me over the edge.

I arrive at the bar early and to my surprise she's already waiting. Her pink hair is half pinned up and the rest falls around her shoulders in loose, fat curls. She's wearing a tight black dress that stops half way up her thighs, and heels that I want to see biting into my skin as I fuck her. I guess the nerves were getting the better of her as I see Lila down her cocktail and order another. She takes a deep breath and her chest bounces before she slowly exhales. Those were the kind of curves I'd willingly get lost in, she was like a Botticelli painting. She's sipping from her martini glass, trying carefully not to knock off the wedge of lemon resting on the rim as she spots me. She gives me a small smile and a little wave before putting down her drink.

"Hi," she says nervously. "I'm Lila."

I give her an amused smirk. We've spoken on the phone and been texting for days. "I know."

She presses a dainty hand to her lips, "Oh. Yes, silly me…"

"Shall we find a seat?"

She nods, and follows behind as I lead her to a booth in one of the darker corners of the bar. I order a vodka and coke with the waiter who comes over and another fruity concoction for her. After all, a little booze can only help in situations like this.

"I've never been out with a woman before," she says slowly after a few moments. Lila bites down on her lip and that does something to me I can't even describe. It's like a tightness in my stomach, only more pleasant. I want to be the one biting her lip, our bodies pressed together as she lets me do things to she's never even imagined.

Our drinks arrive and I take a sip slowly. I want to lure her in, and I don't want to play nice about it. If I handle her wrong this date could blow up in my face, she could get scared and run like an animal caught in a trap, but given the way she's watching my throat as I swallow my drink, I think I'm safe.

After a few moments I tilt my head at her. With my voice low and silky I say, "I'm not here to be your little experiment."

"I never said that…" she whispers, looking away.

"But you're acting like it. What did you think would happen when you hit me up on a dating website?"

"I don't know…"

I take another sip of my drink and meet her gaze straight on. There's something about this pixie girl with the big grey eyes that has me fixated. I want to push her; to crack that calm facade she's wearing until the only thing she can think about is me. Until she's consumed by what I can do to her, how I can make her feel. Calm down Ava. The girl doesn't even know why she's here… but I do. I

## Let's Try Love

can read her body, the way her legs are almost touching mine and her lips gently part when she looks at me. I know lust when I see it. She doesn't seem to have a clue.

She shrugs, the alcohol kicking in as she loosens up. "I guess I was having no luck otherwise, and I'm not averse to trying something new."

I raise my eyebrow at her. "Something new?"

She laughs and it almost sounds like a tinkling noise, "Okay, so maybe you are an experiment of sorts."

I grin, "I don't know how I'm supposed to feel about that."

She thinks about it for a moment, twirling her glass between her fingers before answering. "Flattered? I mean, I still chose you out of all the messages I received."

It's my turn to chuckle. I bet she had lots of messages; she looked like a goddamn fairy who was begging to be loved. "Okay, I'll take that. What is it exactly you want?"

She stops playing with her glass and looks at me, "What do you mean?"

I lean forward, giving her a brilliant view of my tits in my low cut playsuit. "Well, I know who I am and I know what I want. I know why I'm here. You're still a lost little girl."

She frowns at that, and I think I've struck a nerve. She straightens up a little as if I provoked her, or lit a fire inside that beautiful body of hers.

"What do you want?" Her voice is sultry as she openly looks at me, eyes lingering on my lips. She's caught in my web and she never even had a clue I was drawing her in.

"I want to kiss you." I say it simply because it's the truth and sometimes the truth can be hotter than any romantic flowery shit I could spout. 'I want to fuck you' will always get me more riled up than 'making love' ever could.

Her little elf-like ears have the cutest pink tinge to them. Bingo! There's that blush I was after. My words hit the spot, and I have to restrain myself from touching her. She's mine.

"I want to slide that little black dress up over your knees and push your legs apart until there's that burn. That gentle, delicious burn as I run my hands over your smooth ivory skin." I say, my voice hushed as the bar gets busier and the noise around us rises. She leans even closer in, her eyes locked with mine, dying to catch every word that drips from my lips.

"Oh." She breathes. The blush has crept down her neck and across her collarbone now.

"And what if I let you?" She asks, never breaking eye contact. This girl has guts, but someone like me would eat her alive.

I ask with a coy glance, "Would you?"

"Yes." She's firm with her answer and I grin. She's hooked already. So am I.

# Lila

Fuck. I'm in deep water and drowning in everything that Ava is. She's gorgeous. Smart. And that mouth of is making me wet. When she approached me at the bar I almost choked on my drink. Her dark hair is silky and cut with precision, there's not a strand out of place as it frames her high cheekbones and bright eyes. Her body is toned and she looks amazing in her striped, low cut white, pink and black playsuit. It's classy, stopping at her ankles rather than exposing her ass like some of the other girls in here tonight. She's well put together, and for some reason that makes my heart hammer in my chest.

When she started talking about what she'd like to do to me, with me, that's when I felt it. That zing. The spark. The thrill I'd been missing on all the other dates. I didn't want to curl up inside myself and hide away from Ava. I wanted to open myself to her, I wanted her to touch me. Heck, when she started talking about making my thighs burn I almost begged her to touch me. Was this everything I'd been dreaming of?

"Prove it," she dares me.

I pause for a moment, how do I prove what I mean in a public place? She grins and sits back with her arms crossed, pushing her boobs up. She wants to see how much I'm comfortable with, how far I'll go, but more fool her. I'm tipsy and horny. I want anything she'll give me.

I copy her, shifting back and in the darkness of the club it looks like I'm adjusting my dress as I wriggle in my seat. After a moment or two my lacy thong slides down my legs and I reach down and scoop them off the floor. Shuffling around the booth so I'm next to Ava, I place my underwear in her hand with a sweet smile.

"Your move." I whisper into her ear, my lips brushing gently against her lobe.

A thrill shoots through me, I've never been so bold. Never been so brazen. God, my parents would kill me if they could see me now or, at the very least, send me to some reformation workshop at their church. Another thrill runs through me, Heather was right about some aspect of this fulfilling my need to rebel.

Ava doesn't bat an eyelid as she takes me by the hand and pulls me into the growing crowd. It's busy tonight, and the dance floor is full of sweaty bodies grinding against each other as a beat thrums through them. She manoeuvres us into yet another dark corner and presses her body against mine as she dances.

"Truth or dare?" She asks, her arms coming around my waist.

This was almost like some sort of test, was she trying to push me to see how far I'd go. My body wanted me to say dare but my mind was still holding me back.

"Truth…" I say with a grin.

She spins me around and presses herself against my back, her lips against my ear. "Are you glad you came tonight?"

"Yes." I don't need to think about my answer or over analyse how I feel. In this moment, I'm glad to be here. With her hands on my hips as we move together, I feel like my body is in sync with hers, I feel alive.

I turn again to face her, wrapping my arms around her neck. "What about you? Truth or dare?"

She gives me a sultry smile which creates a dimple on her left cheek. "Dare, always."

Feeling brave I whisper, "I dare you to kiss me."

## Let's Try Love

There's that smile again and it melts me a little. It makes my heart flutter faster and every other damn cliché I can think of as she grinds her hips against me.

Ava presses her lips gently against mine, and it's like a spark has ignited under my skin. My hands move up to cup her face and I deepen the kiss, she tastes spicy and intoxicating with just a hint of sour from the vodka. I want more. I want it all. She kisses me like I'm the air she needs to breathe, each touch frenzied and desperate. Her teeth nip against my bottom lip before she pulls away, her hands roaming down my body until she's cupping my ass. I'm more than just interested in this woman, I'm obsessed. Every touch is like a drug, addictive and I never want it to end.

"Lila, dare or truth?" she breathes against my neck.

She's backed us against a wall, her knee coming between my thighs. I can't help myself as I move against her. Fuck, who knew my inner lesbian was such a hussy?

Feeling braver, I respond with "Dare."

She slips a hand under my dress, which has now ridden up. I'm still covered, but barely. Her fingers dance across my pussy, teasing me and I groan. I can feel how wet I am without having to see her grin.

"Come home with me. I'll even let you stay for breakfast." She peppers my collarbone with kisses as she eases a finger inside me.

"Do your dates not normally get offered that?" I tease, as her thumb finds my clit. There are no words for how full, how complete I feel with her inside me and taunting my clit at the same time. My knees threaten to buckle as she continues her assault on me, her mouth covering every inch of exposed skin as her fingers work their magic.

She doesn't stop what she's doing, not that I want her to, but Ava moves away to look me in the eye. "No, never. But you're different."

Her lips move along my jawline as the pressure climbs and it's like I want to burst out of my own skin. Her touch is tender and unyielding, she doesn't let up despite my groans and little whimpers. I shift my body, writhing against her hand as I lose control of my thoughts. I am consumed by her. She is all I see.

I have no words as my orgasm builds so I do the only thing I feel like doing, and I kiss her. We're intertwined underneath the pulsing lights, surrounded by sweaty bodies and shrouded in shadows as I come.

"Let's go," I beg as my body trembles, wanting more of what we've just done. Wanting more of her. I'm lost to the stranger with a cute dimple and magic fingers, but then again, I knew that the moment she walked into the bar.

# Ava

I wake up late and there's an arm around my waist. I pause for a moment, my whole body tensing before I spot a flash of pink and remember my pixie girl, Lila, from last night. I relax into her, enjoying her warmth and the smell of cherry blossoms that seems to linger on her skin. I'm reluctant to move, I don't want to leave the safe haven of the bed this morning, but if I don't move soon, I never will.

I gently push her arm away and slide out from under the covers. Grabbing my dressing gown, I head into the kitchen and get the coffee brewing before calling my brother on Facetime. Nia answers for him, her big grin making me wince a little. How can a person be so cheery every morning? She hands the phone to him and he gives me a softer smile, knowing how grumpy I can be before lunchtime.

"How was your weekend?" He asks and I resist the urge to tell him about Lila. He'd only read too much into the fact that she was still asleep in my room. I get a warm feeling when I think about her wrapped up in my sheets. I'd already made up my mind about her.

"It was good, yours?"

He chuckles, "The same old same old. We're like an old married couple who never do anything exciting these days."

It sounds like a moan, but I know he loves it. Where I've always been driven, my brother has preferred a quieter kind of life. He loves being self-employed with his landscaping company and spending his weekends working on his own garden with his green fingered wife. Thinking about it, spending my weekends with someone special doesn't sound that bad.

## Let's Try Love

"I've got this week's matches from the website if you're ready for me to send them over. You can spend your Sunday afternoon perusing beautiful ladies, all handpicked by the Ava experts." He wiggles his eyebrows at me and I crack a smile.

I woke up this morning feeling different, invigorated almost and while I snuck out from my bed, I realised I was tired of all the endless women. Nothing was ever a good fit or the right one... until this unexpected match.

"No," I say slowly, "I think I'm going to take a break from the dating website for a while."

"Are you sure? You might miss out on the one?"

"Yeah. No more hook-ups." As I say that a pair of arms snake around my waist and Lila buries her face into my neck.

My brother's mouth drops open with surprise. I pause, I hadn't wanted to tell Jack about her just yet, I didn't want to be premature, but Lila was a force of her own and I doubt I could keep her hidden, even if I wanted to.

"Sorry, am I interrupting?" Lila murmurs her voice still heavy with sleep. Damn, she's so cute. And hot. How the hell did I get her to come home with me?

"No, Jack this is Lila. Lila, Jack."

Lila gives him a small wave and wanders off to the other side of the kitchen.

"Ava," my brother whispers as Lila makes us the coffee I brewed earlier. "She stayed over."

"Yeah," I say, trying to keep the surprise out of my own voice.

"She's still there," he presses.

I shrug and avoid his gaze. "Yep, looks like she is."

"You haven't scared her off…" he whispers again.

"I guess not…" I stage whisper back with a small laugh.

"How?"

"Jack!" Nia interrupts from somewhere behind him.

"She is there willingly, right?" He carries on.

"Jack, I'm warning you…" I say, making my voice as stern as I can manage.

I hang up on my brother and make an apologetic face at her. I hear Lila chuckle as she hands me a steaming hot mug as if we'd been here before even though we were strangers. But I was going to change that.

**The End.**
**Or the beginning.**

## About the Author

Alice La Roux is a dirty minded, mouthy Welsh author who is still trying to find her genre while dabbling in erotica, fantasy and horror. She owes her husband, best friend and sister everything—without them she wouldn't be writing. She's a bookworm who reads anything and everything and is addicted to social media.

If you want to stay in touch and get the latest updates (or just see pictures of her dog) then don't forget to stalk her!

Facebook: www.facebook.com/asmadasAlice/
Twitter: www.twitter.com/AliLaRoux
Instagram: www.instagram.com/alicelaroux/

**Don't forget to check out her other books:**

Firebird
Two's Company
TAG (written as AJ Everheart)

# Brokenhearted Click

## by Fey Simmons

Shane Thorn hates blind dates; the last one he had was a disaster. His friends decide to help him out by creating a profile in "Let's Try Love," a dating site with a high success rate. Deciding to give love one last try, he discovers his blind date is exactly the person that he has been trying so desperately to stay away from.

Sparrow Callahan's luck with love is nonexistent; her family convinces her to join the popular dating site, much like Shane. The last thing she expected is to be matched with the one guy who was always mean to her.

Despite the couple's lack of enthusiasm with their blind date situation, there are other forces working to keep them apart and will use any means necessary to keep it that way. Will the connection they found be strong enough to survive the reality that surrounds them?

# Brokenhearted Click by Fey Simmons

## One

Shane took several deep breaths before entering the small café. This would be his seventh date since his two idiotic "best friends" uploaded his profile to the dating site "Let's Try Love". He took the time to read all about it and came across lots of success stories, but still he couldn't shake the feeling that he was doing something…wrong. This was absurd. He was a twenty two years old single male about to graduate. Ready to start a whole new chapter in his life. And yet…here he was. His steps so damn slow that he was sure his own turtle walks faster than him.

"I´m not going to be executed…I´m going on a damn date with a gorgeous woman," he whispered to himself, a reminder of what was about to happen. With that in mind, he willed himself to, at least, present a calm façade.

## Let's Try Love

He had merely walked a few steps into the cozy little place when he spotted her. It wasn´t difficult to find her. With her long blond hair falling free and the tight ivory dress she told him she was going to wear, she looked so out of place it surprised him. Surrounded by the simpler décor, she reminded him of the expensive Diamond Opera Necklace from Tiffany & Co., whose campaign he has been working on. For a second, he was tempted to simply turn around and leave, but he knew he couldn't stand her up.

"Shane?" She waved at him as she rose from her seat.

"Karen, right?" He immediately offered his hand to shake, not wanting to get any closer than what was necessary. Which was so unlike him that if it wasn't for already knowing about the damn family "blessing" he would have gotten an interview with a shrink in a heartbeat. Instead, there he was, trying to find some sense into whatever cosmic alignment mojo had happened during the bonfire two weeks ago. He still held firm to the belief that since he wasn't a Gray like his cousins…he didn't catch the damn curse. Or did he?

Frustrated, he forced himself to smile and be the perfect gentleman with the woman sitting across from him. She wasn't to blame for what was happening. Besides, it could perfectly well be something else….Mars aligning with Venus…the moon about to become a super moon. If he thought hard enough, he was sure he could find a perfectly logical explanation to what the hell was wrong with him. Because, to be pining after Sparrow Callahan, when it was obvious that she was his cousin Phoenix's girlfriend, was wrong. And yet, of the cousins who had found out about his little "secret", they didn't even seemed to be worried about it. As long as they didn't end up trying to kill each other.

"What a drag"

"Excuse me?"

"Can you imagine something more boring than coming here to sit by yourself...to write? That's pathetic." Karen's nasal voice, which he hadn't noticed before, began to irk him as he followed her gaze, only to get lost in a pair of vibrant blue eyes that he had come to know really well. But he soon realized that they weren't really looking at him and were more focused on whatever she was thinking about. Because, they were soon focused on what seemed like a journal as she scribbled with impressive speed on its pages.

"Sparrow..." he whispered before he could stop himself.

"You know her? Right....you have a whole bunch of younger cousins. Is she one of them?"

"No. She's my cousin Phoenix's...girl." He had barely managed to say those words out loud without choking on them. Because every single time he thought about it, he wanted to beat the ever loving shit out of him.

"Oh! Maybe she's waiting for him. We could totally do a double date with them!"

"No!" He didn't mean to sound harsh. But there was no fucking way he could survive seeing Phoenix all over Sparrow without throttling him if he so much as held her hand or sat too close.

"All right...I...mmm...I'm going to the restroom." Karen sounded uncomfortable as she said those words. Shane barely nodded, his gaze still focused on the girl that was writing as if her life depended on it. He wondered what she could be writing about and then he remember that she was in high school, a senior about to graduate, but a highschool student nevertheless.

As if her relationship with Phoenix didn't already put her out of his reach.

"Take a picture. It will last longer." It was merely a whisper, but he had heard it loud and clear; and soon her amazing eyes were once again on him, this time accompanied by a glare. "I'm sure your date won't like seeing you distracted like that."

"It's not a date. We are having some coffee," he shrugged as he answered. He didn't want her to get the wrong impression.

"Right. Because this is so not the place where you would come for a first date with a person you barely know." Her voice dripped sarcasm and he couldn't help but smile at it because she was totally right.

"And what is your reason for being here?"

"Wanting to be on my own…away from all of them"

And that was when something clicked. He was sure that right there in the café, it was the first time he had ever seen her without her sisters by her side. Those four seemed to be joined at the hip and even though Dove and Grey were totally crazy about each other, the bond between the girls was truly strong which ended with several of the Gray cousins spending a lot of time with the group of girls. And yet…there she was, all by herself.

"Are you sure?" Hhe had only seen her being nice with everyone. This new side of her was completely unexpected and for a few seconds he wondered if Phoenix knew about it or if he was the first one to discover it.

"My family owns a café. I could have stayed there, but I didn't," she finally added. "And you should go back to your date before she notices that you are entertaining another person."

"You are definitely not 'another person', Little Bird," he answered, not wanting their conversation to end.

"Please, Shane, I just want to be alone…" This time her eyes were heavy with sadness.

Shane knew he should shut up, make up some stupid excuse and focused all his energy on getting to know Karen, but the look in

Sparrow's eyes felt like a blow to his stomach. He didn't know her, or what could have made her feel like that; but still, he wanted to see her smile at him...if only for a few moments. No, he needed to see her smile.

"Shane? Is everything all right?" Karen's voice felt like a nail against a chalkboard, but he still turned slightly around to look at her as she stood by the table.

"Yes. I was just about to offer Sparrow a ride to her house. She's not feeling well," he smoothly told her and cutting their "date" short was the most logical and expected curse of action.

That seemed to cause a reaction on both of them because while Karen's face turned as red as a tomato, Sparrow's got pale as she scrambled to her feet.

"I'm more than fine now. Please, enjoy your date. Phoenix will pick me up in a little bit," she rushed out the words as she put all her things away. Before either of the two could answer her, she rushed out of the place as if the hounds of hell were after her.

"Sparrow! Wait!" But though he tried to follow her, the moment he stepped out of the café, she seemed to have vanished into thin air.

Cursing under his breath, he went back inside and saw Karen holding a small leather journal in her hand. Though it wasn't the same one Sparrow was working on, the tribal bird engraved on the cover was unmistakable. It was definitely hers.

# Two

Sparrow was thankful that she knew the town as the back of her hand. In situations like the one that just happened, it was really helpful, especially since the café was really near the dense forest that rounded the entire area. Exactly the place she needed to be before heading back to the house.

It was her eighteenth birthday and the only thing she had wanted in the last few days was to be left alone. She still hadn't told anyone about what was going on. Except for Phoenix, and he had been the best at keeping her secret. But she had been avoiding everyone. Even him.

And that's how she ended up in "Midnight Café"… and running into the last person she wanted to see. Shane Thorn. One of Phoenix's older cousins. She could still remember how she felt the moment their eyes connected. It had been as if she finally found the one thing she had been missing and wasn't even aware that she had lost it in the first place. And that had scared her…badly.

He was the one man that could cause the butterflies in her stomach to take flight. And those little traitors had been crushed when they saw him on a date with that stunning blond model like woman. Older and sophisticated, she looked like everything she wasn't.

The last thing she needed in her life was more confusion and stress. She already had enough of it as it was. And wasn't even sure what to do about it. Her plans had always been so clear. She had wanted to go to the university and become a writer, but all that changed the moment she went to that party.

Thunder boomed over her head, announcing the coming of the storm; and though she knew she needed to hurry, for a moment she was tempted to simply find a somewhat safe shelter and stay out in the forest.

By the time she arrived at the house, twenty minutes later, she was soaked and chilled. Her eyes were puffy after all the crying she did while walking back.

"Happy Birth…What happened to you?!" Raven and Dove, her cousins, stared in shock at her as she went into the house through the back door that led directly to the kitchen, where they both seemed to have been waiting to surprise her.

Sparrow was aware of the fact that she looked like a drowned rat, but she couldn't care less. She just wanted to change her clothes, make herself a hot cup of tea and sit on the couch with her latest eBook, "Sweet Land of Liberty" by Samantha Rae, and forget everything about the outside world.

"Sis… are you all right?"

"I´m fine, Rav. Don´t worry. It's just a little bit of water," she whispered while dragging herself up the stairs. She hated how tired she had been feeling lately. Especially because it was getting harder and harder to hide the truth from her family and friends. She knew that eventually someone would find out about it and tell everyone, but she kept hoping to have a little bit more time and prayed that she was the one to finally tell everyone what was going on.

"That's not a little bit of water and you know it," Raven answered and was about to follow her when Dove stopped her.

"Let's make her something warm to drink before she freezes. Go and take a shower, cousin." Dove, after making sure that Sparrow was almost on the first floor, dragged her other cousin behind her. "Were you able to do it?"

Let's Try Love

"Yes. I just set it up. Good thing they don't care about the exact time of your birth." Raven muttered while checking the webpage where, between the two of them, they created a profile for Sparrow.

They knew she wasn't going to be thrilled at first. But, though she was supposed to be in some kind of relationship with Phoenix, they had noticed that they behaved more like best friends than two persons in love.

"Let's Try Love" seemed like a good and safe option. Though their town wasn't exactly huge, they found several profiles...one in particular, that they thought were perfect for Sparrow. Now, they only had to convince her to agree and, at least, contact the man.

They were so focused on the screen, they didn't hear her enter the kitchen.

"I'm not doing it," she told them as soon as she peeked from behind them.

"You have to!"

"Come on, Sparrow!"

"Are you both nuts?! What if he's a serial killer or something like that?!"

"We swear they aren't! It's a very serious place. They even run background checks on everyone who wants to join"

"Come on, sis. For example...look at this profile" Raven pushed the laptop toward Sparrow and clicked on the profile they both had been checking out. Though it didn't have a proper image, the rest of it seemed like an odd match for their cousin, but at the same time...he was perfect.

"And...we didn't use a picture either. Only this." Dove smiled proudly as they showed her the image of a Sparrow. Luckily, the place allowed the user to maintain their privacy as long as they provided them with their required legal information.

"I´m going to kill you both. I don't need a matchmaking service. I already have Phoenix."

"You do…?"

"What do you mean by that?"

"Sparrow, we have no idea what is going on between you two, but we are sure about one thing…you are not in love," Dove whispered, not wanting to call her cousin out.

"Come on. You´ve got nothing to lose. And, even if it doesn´t work…free tea!" Raven exclaimed.

She stared at both of them for several long minutes until she finally nodded.

"But…only for a month. If after that I´m still not happy, we are erasing the profile."

"Woohoo!" Both girls threw themselves on her. "You are not going to regret it!"

# Three

*Almost a month later…*

Sparrow checked her cell as she rushed into the café. A few days after accepting to "cyber date" or whatever her cousins called it, she ended up really getting along with the owner of the profile they had shown her.

Though she only knew him as "Shadow" that had become the least of her worries. Talking with him had felt easy. They´ve had been doing it every single day and all throughout the day. Though always without seeing each other. Just text messages. This had been absolutely perfect for her. This allowed her to maintain certain distance, though it did nothing to quiet down her imagination…which she was having a hard time reigning in.

Since he finally asked her out a week ago, her mind had been coming up with all kinds of scenarios. She was only one step away from transforming him into a Russian spy that was trying to uncover a government secret related to the six weird towns that were located all along the mountain road. And she was one of the few persons that could certainly attest to how creepy some of them were, especially after what happened to them two months ago when Dove began to date Phoenix´s cousin, Gray.

Taking a deep breath, she glanced around until she found the one table that had a beautiful jasmine flower on it. She couldn't help but smile at it. Though she was sure they didn't exist in that size, but it wasn't until she touched it that Sparrow realized it was made of paper.

"Your boyfriend went to get something from his truck. May I bring you something while you wait?" the waitress, which she didn't recognize as one of the regular ones, asked her.

"I...yes, please, a cup of tea," Sparrow finally answered. She couldn't pinpoint what it was, but something in the way the woman was staring at her was making her uncomfortable. And it wasn't until she left that she managed to relax.

Once again her attention focused on the delicate flower, she knew Shadow made it for her and thought it was an extremely sweet gesture. She just hoped they clicked as well in person as they seemed to do though their constant messages. Besides, she really needed to think of the baby.

The sound of a message entering her cell distracted her from her thoughts, and at the best time possible, before she panicked and ended up cancelling the date before they even saw each other face to face.

She hurried to take it out of her small backpack but, as it only happened to her, she ended up dropping half the contents of her purse on the floor. Sparrow cursed softly as she started to pick everything up. She had already managed to lose a journal, she didn't want to lose anything else.

"Sparrow?"

"Shadow?" She had barely managed to gather everything when she found herself staring at the person she least expected "Shane..."

"Did you like the flower?" The smile on his face was radiant, as if she had invented instant coffee or something like that.

"It's so beautiful, but how do you...?" Realization suddenly dawned on her. "You are Shadow."

"And you are...you." He still smiled as he sat down in front of her. "I know I'm not your favorite person so...let me get this out in

## Let's Try Love

the open. I'm really sorry for the way I behaved at the bonfire. I was a prick."

"You totally were." She wasn't about to cut him any slack. The day they met at the café had been the first time he had been civilized with her, so Sparrow wasn't feeling particularly inclined to be lenient.

"And also all the other times…It's not that I don't like you"

"Then…what is the issue? I didn't know you before that day and yet, you kept behaving like a moron"

"That's exactly the problem. Ok. Not a problem…or maybe it is"

"What are you talking about?" Sparrow was confused as she went over his words inside her head. They made no sense at all.

"You're Phoenix's girlfriend…and I like you. A lot," he finally blurted, just as the waitress was leaving the tea on the table.

Sparrow stared dumbfounded at him. She had no idea what to say. Especially because she never considered that Shadow was Shane, the one person she had liked the instant their eyes met. And yet, there they were…on a date.

"Did you lie?" For a second, she considered that it might all be some kind of sick joke.

"No…never. That was completely me. Every lame joke, every nerdy comment…it was all 100% me," he told her as a slight pink hue seemed to covered his cheeks. Which she found awfully adorable. If he could admit that, then she could at least be somewhat honest with him too.

"Phoenix's not my boyfriend," she finally whispered.

"He…isn't? But…" The shock soon turned into a panty melting smile and Sparrow discovered she was having a hard time resisting it.

"He's just being a good friend and trying to protect me," she admitted as she played with the napkin that was next to her cup of tea.

"From what?"

"Can we...not today, please," Sparrow practically begged, and she could see the curiosity in Shane's gaze, but he finally nodded and grabbed her hand while he started to tell her about the reason for his presence at the bonfire in the first place.

Half an hour later, she was having a hard time trying to catch her breath among all the laughter. She was truly having a fantastic time and decided that, once she got back home, she was making her cousins lots and lots of giant chocolate cupcakes as a way to thank them for their idea.

# Four

Shane felt ecstatic. Not only was the girl he had been falling for the same girl he was crazy about, which shouldn't surprise him since he had heard how no matter what they did the "blessing" would assure that they would keep on running into each other until they were finally together.

"So, about our date, would you like to...?"

"Shane? Shane! I knew it was you!" The unexpected and unwelcome intrusion immediately irritated him. Frowning, he glared at the woman that now stood next to their table. She was vaguely familiar, but he couldn't recall from where. Though he was sure that he should; with the violet hair, he was sure few people forgot her.

"I´m sorry. I don´t…"

"Come on! It's me! Cara!" her answer seemed a little overeager and made him feel uncomfortable. Not to mention, Sparrow was looking at the two of them with a certain amount of distrust. "I'm sorry. I'm interrupting. Hi, hon, I'm Cara Mitchels. Shane and I met at a nightclub right before he came here. It was such an amazing night. You wouldn't believe how good he was…"

Sparrow rose from her seat as if someone had set on fire and while mumbling several things, she gathered her things in a rush and was on her way to the door in record speed.

"Oh, I´m so sorry, I didn't me to…"

"I'm sure you didn't." Now, Shane was simply pissed off and, after throwing some dollars on the table, he went after Sparrow. He needed to stop her. He needed to explain himself.

## Let's Try Love

"Shane, wait!" He barely managed a few steps before the woman clung to his arm, stopping all his movements...unless he wanted to drag her after him.

"No. Stay the fuck away from us"

"Us? You mean...you and that little girl?"

"She's more woman than you"

"That wasn't what you said while you were fucking me...and Cira"

Suddenly, it all came rushing back to him. He had been completely drunk that night. They were supposedly celebrating with his teammates after having earned a new campaign and he drank too much. This led him to a wild night, only to wake up naked with a girl on each side of him, and in an unknown apartment. In less than ten minutes, he had gotten himself dressed and out of the place as if the hounds of hell were chasing him. Since neither of them tried to contact him, he thought that would be it, but...it seemed like he was wrong.

"That was a mistake. And one I immediately regretted the moment I woke up," he growled "It meant nothing and you better get that in your head."

"No, honey. You should be the one getting into your head one thing. And only one...I would be really careful about who you get close to. You never know when an accident can happen"

"Are you threatening me?"

"Me? I would never do something like that." But the triumphant smile on her face made him look toward the entrance where he saw Sparrow talking with another woman that had rainbow hair...Cira.

***

Sparrow stopped on the sidewalk as she held the jacket in front of her tummy while she caught her breath. Though it wasn't obvious, she knew that if someone looked closely they would probably guess her secret. After all, she was three months pregnant.

When she accepted the date, it had been her intention to come clean at some point if everything went as awesome as it had been while they texted each other. The last thing she expected was to discover that Shadow was Shane…or that he was a playboy. That had hurt, especially after what he had admitted to her. But it seemed that in the end, it had all been a well-played game to get in her pants, which wasn't going to happen.

"I'm really sorry you had to find out about it this way…," the female voice startled her and as she turned around she came face to face with another woman with colorful hair, this time. It reminded her of rainbow sherbet. "I´m Cira, Cara´s sister."

Stunned, Sparrow merely nodded. Unsure of what was going on, she managed to put her jacket on while holding her backpack between her legs.

"Shane has always been like that. I´m not sure about numbers, but he had slept at least with half of the girls in the campus." the woman gave her a sympathetic look "At least, you´ll be able to save yourself from the heartbreak."

"I…we…he's not my boyfriend. Just a friend," she whispered.

"Then, it's true. You are Phoenix's girl. Shane shouldn't even be asking you out. Especially with the baby and everything."

Sparrow suddenly felt like she couldn't breathe. Besides her, and her OBGYN, there was only one other person that knew about her secret and he had promised her to keep it quiet. It seemed like he didn't. The sense of betrayal cut her deep and she knew that if he had been standing in front of her, she would have punched him square on the nose.

"Don't worry. I won't tell anyone. Though you shouldn't trust anyone from Shane's family. Not even Dove's boyfriend." The woman kept talking like she knew a lot about all of them and that was starting to freak her out big time. "There are a lot of rumors going around about them, if you just dig a little bit."

"Rumors are nothing if there isn't some real evidence to support them." She had had her fair share of them as the daughter of one of the members of the infamous quartet of "Season girls". And when it came to her, she couldn´t be more different from her own mother. So…rumors were bullshit.

"But, there is evidence Sparrow..." She immediately found herself staring at an image of Shane, on a bed, the two girls lying on his naked chest. If he had been sleeping, she would have given him the benefit of the doubt; but instead, he was gazing straight at the camera, a huge smile on his face.

Shane's voice calling her told her that he had finally escaped from the other woman and was approaching them. But she didn't want to hear any of his excuses. Also, she finally had enough and refused to give the woman another minute of her time, so she grabbed her backpack and hurried the same route as last time,through the forest. The quickest and easiest way to lose someone. Especially if they weren't familiar with it.

## Five

Shane was beyond furious by now. He had seen the other woman talking with Sparrow outside and he had to appeal to all his manners not shove Cara away from him. But before he could go after Sparrow, she had disappeared once again.

"You prefer her instead of us?" Cara practically screamed as she left the café right behind him

"Always!" He wasn't in the mood for games. And once he discovered who had convinced those two to ruin his chances with Sparrow, blood was going to be spilt.

"That's rich considering she's spoiled goods and forever will be...," Cira muttered "Maybe you should ask her who the father of her baby is..."

"Oh my God! Sis! He has no idea! She didn't tell you about her little bun of joy. Did she now?" Cara hugged her sister as they both stare at Shane, who had visibly paled as he took in the unexpected news.

"You...are lying," he finally managed to choke out.

"Are you sure? I think Phoenix has a thing or two to say about the baby." Cira smiled as he answered.

Those were the last words Shane could recall hearing because twenty minutes later half his cousins had to intervene when he threw himself on Phoenix and tried to punch the daylights out of him.

"What the fuck is wrong with you, Shane?!" Gray shoved him again once more

"That fucker got Sparrow pregnant!" he shouted and finally managed to land an uppercut that left Phoenix sprawled on the floor.

## Let's Try Love

The silence in the room was so loud that it was almost deafening and everyone stared at the two of them.

"And why do you care about that?" Phoenix answered as he stood up. He had made a promise and, even though the cat was out of the bag, he was going to keep it.

"Because she's mine!"

"Mine like..." Phoenix stared at him in shock. He had no idea how Shane felt about Sparrow, but that explained his shitty attitude toward her. Especially if he truly believed that she was with him. "You need to speak with her right now, Shane. I´m not kidding."

"Did you give anything to her?" When Gray spoke again, he was dead serious as he stared at them.

"A flower...a paper jasmine," he finally muttered, still glaring at Phoenix. "It's her favorite..."

"Gray...call Dove and get her to bring Sparrow here. And you...contact her. Somehow. You two really need to speak." Phoenix was so insistent that Shane began to panic and, after several minutes of his messages being rebound, he decided to try and contact her though the dating site. But was crushed to discover something else. He didn't hesitate to show his cousins the message: "That profile no longer exists".

Sparrow had blocked him completely out of her life...his only chance was that it wasn't forever.

"I made a promise, but you need to know something. The baby is not mine either." Phoenix told him as soon as they were out of hearing reach from the others. "What are you going to do about it?"

"All right. Let´s go. Sparrow just arrived at the house and she's taking a hot bath," Grey shouted while he ushered both of them towards the door.

"I'll be there for Sparrow and the baby…if she lets me," was his immediate answer as they climb on the truck.


**If you want to know more about Sparrow and Shane…and how their story ends.**
**Winter Sparrow**
**Winter 2019**

# About the Author

Fey Simmons is new to the English market.

She began to read when she was 4 years old and never stopped.

It always felt natural to get lost in a book. English has always been a part of her life having grandparents that interacted with her in that language.

Despite what people believe characters do speak to the writer. In her case, despite being Argentinian and having Spanish as her first language, half of her characters speak in English and that's how they want their story to be told.

Writing in English at first was scary but with the help of two friends, she finally decided to jump headfirst into it because... if you do it, pour your entire heart into it.

# Never Too Old for Love

## by Judy Swinson

Julie married her high school sweetheart, Jerry. For forty plus years they had it all; a beautiful home, three lovely daughters, several dogs throughout the years, her husband's successful insurance business, and Julie's nursing career . They were completely devoted to eachother and were making plans to travel throughout Europe when they retired.

Then one sunny August afternoon in 2014 Julie's world came crashing down when she found her husband in the back yard laying face down by a running lawn mower. She called 911 but the para medics said it looked like he may have had a massive heart attack. He had no pulse and no heartbeat.

Jerry has been deceased for almost five years and Jessica, the youngest daughter is getting concerned her mother has no social life. She is spending every Friday and Saturday night at home watching movies on telvision with her yellow labrador retriever, Jake. Jessica decides to encourage her mother to go on an on-line dating site, Let's Try Love. After seeing the concern, Jessica has about her being alone. Julie agrees to give it a try for a thirty day trial membership.

There are several prospects but will Julie take a leap of faith and follow through or will an emergency with Jake put an end to her on-line dating activities? Will Let's Try Love bring her a second chance at love or will faith intervene and bring the right man at the right time. One thing is for sure. You are Never Too Old For Love.

# Never Too Old for Love by Judy Swinson

## One

I am sitting in the kitchen drinking my second cup of coffee when I hear the screen door to the back porch open and then slam. I know it has to be Jessica, my middle daughter. She is the only one who allows the door to slam, every time. I walk over and grab a clean cup from the dish drain and hand it to her as she walks into the kitchen.

"Hi Mom. I know I slammed the door again. You know I don't mean too." She grabs the cup from my hand and walks to the coffee pot as I turn and sit back down in my chair. Jake, our big yellow lab, trots into the kitchen to greet Jessica, he also knows when the back door slams, and Jessica has arrived.

"Jessica, do you slam doors in your house? I ask.

## Let's Try Love

"No, but I don't have a screen door." She leans over and kisses my cheek while placing her cup on the table and stoops down to hug Jake.

"Jessica, I didn't expect to see you this early, I thought it would be after lunch."

"Oh I have some errands to run and I ran out of coffee at home, so I thought I would stop by and visit and have coffee with you."

"Well, it's always a pleasure to have a cup of java with my daughter."

"Mom have you given any thought to our discussion last week?" She blows on the coffee in the cup to cool it before placing it to her lips while nervously looking up at me.

"What conversation might that be?" I know what she is talking about but I am going to play this scene out a little with her and chuckle inside because I know she is nervous.

"You know, Mom, what I am talking about. I think it's time you put yourself out there again. Dad has been gone for almost five years now, you are still a good looking woman and I want you to be happy. Being alone will just make you grow old sooner."

"Jess, I am not one foot in the grave, but I am not a young woman either. I am sixty-six."

"You and Dad got married right out of high school and you have given it more than a reasonable amount of grieving time.

"Jessica, I am not lonely or sit around the house and mope the way you and your sisters think I do. I still volunteer at the Hospital two days a week and I enjoy reading and going to my writing group once a month. What makes you think, I need a man in my life?"

"Mom, we girls know what a great marriage you and Dad had and how this house was filled with love with us girls growing up. It was a shock to all of us when he had a massive heart attack while cutting the

## Let's Try Love

grass in the back yard. But we want you to live, to enjoy life, to have some fun and be happy.

"Jessica, sounds like you and your sisters have had this discussion, what makes you think I am not happy?" I ask as I stand up and open the screen door so Jake can go out in the yard.

"Mom, we just think you live in this big house all by yourself. Stacey is married and I don't think she plans on having children. Cathy is traveling abroad and will probably end up living somewhere in Europe. I am busy at work, I try to spend time with you, but you need someone your age to enjoy life."

"Okay, tell me what you girls have in mind? Do one of you already have my next husband picked out?" I laugh.

"No, we have talked about it, well not picking out a husband, but it's because we don't know of anyone we think would be a good fit for you. But we do have an idea."

"Well go ahead, Jessica, you might as well at least tell me what you girls are thinking."

"On-Line Dating."

"Is that where you go and do on-line dancing? No, Mom that is called Line Dancing." She looks at me and we both start to laugh.

"Mom. You are just teasing me now. I am sure you have heard about On-Line Dating. It has become very popular and kind of the in thing now for single people to meet other single people who have similar interests. There are a number of dating sites on the internet, I could help you pick one out."

"Jessica, oh my. On-Line Dating, are you kidding me? I have seen some pretty crazy cases watching Phil Donahue in the afternoon and some are not safe. I am not sure I would even want to do this or even know where to start."

## Let's Try Love

"Mom, I have to get going this morning. I have errands to run. Why don't you check out some of the information on the internet today. I will pick you up for Church tomorrow at the regular time. I assume we will get lunch afterwards?"

"Yes, at the country club for the buffet."

"I will help you with a profile tomorrow afternoon and we can just do a trial period and see if you are comfortable with it. Is that okay?"

"This is something you girls really want me to look into?"

"Yes, Mom, we do." Jessica stands up, puts her cup in the sink and hugs me goodbye.

"Okay Jessica, I won't promise I will go through with this, but I will read up on the sites and gather more information this afternoon."

"Just have an open mind and let's just see. I'll see you in the morning."

"Bye Jessica, thanks for stopping by and don't slam the ... ... SLAM. Too late."

* * *

I just put a load of whites in the washing machine when I hear the phone ringing. I quickly pour the laundry detergent in the machine and close the lid for it to begin its cycle and go to answer the phone, it's not one of those Robo calls.

"Hello?"

"Julie, it's Mrs. Woods with the Hospital Auxiliary can you talk for a couple of minutes? I would like to go over the schedule with you for next couple of months, with the holidays coming up there are some changes."

"Of course, I was just doing some laundry. Let me grab a pen and paper to take notes."

"Julie, Janice is taking the entire month of December and January off and going on vacation with a new boyfriend."

## Let's Try Love

"Good for her! I didn't know she was seeing someone, although several of us ladies in the gift shop have noticed she has been happier in the last few months. Do you think he's the reason? Did she meet him at the hospital?"

"I don't think so, in fact rumor has it. You know Julie, I don't like rumors, but I have heard she met him on one of those On-Line Dating sites."

"Well Mrs. Woods, I am happy for her. My daughters have said they are popular now, I am just not sure they are safe."

"Julie, I am sure it's like anything else in this day and age, we all have to be careful."

"Mrs. Woods, I am sure you are right. What can I help you with?"

"I know you volunteer in the gift shop two times a week, but do you think you could possibly pick up a morning every other Saturday to fill in for Janice's shift? It would be 9:00 am until 1:00 pm. I would really appreciate it. There are several volunteers going to be out of town and the gift shop does well financially during the holidays. I would hate to close it down and have unhappy customers."

"Mrs. Woods, I would be happy to help out in a pinch like this, but I wouldn't want to do it more than the two months Janice will be gone."

"Julie, you are a sweetheart. I want you to know how much I appreciate your helping out with this and I give you my word it will only be for December and January."

"I will mark it on my calendar, happy to help, Mrs. Woods."

"Goodbye dear."

I hang up the portable phone and place it back on the table near the sofa and walk into the kitchen for a cold drink from the

## Let's Try Love

refrigerator. After pouring some tea, I stand at the sink and look out into the back yard noticing several varieties of birds enjoying the fresh seed put out this morning.

Thinking about the conversation I just had with Mrs. Woods and about Janice finding a fella on an On-Line Dating site has me curious. Before I know it, I am walking down the hall to my small office off the bedroom, pulling out the chair, and sitting down. I look at my computer for a few minutes before turning it on and typing in the search engine On-Line Dating sites.

To my amazement, there were numerous web sites popping up filling the page with their names and this is just the first page. Looking down at the bottom, I see there are more than seven additional pages of on line dating sites listed.

My Jessica was right when she said this is a popular way to meet singles now. Laughing out loud at some of the headers; Try Us for the Love of Your Life, Second Chance Romance, You are Never too Old to Love Again, Active Love at Any Age, Guaranteed Love, Love on the Go, Pick Your Lover, Let's Try Love, Want a Date this Weekend; Click here. Thirty Days to Find Love, Do you want to Date a Millionaire?

I scrolled through several pages until I found a site advertised that caught my eye, Let's Try Love. I start to hesitate, but then click. It takes several seconds before a web site appears. I spend the next couple of hours reading information on the site; its history, location, rules regulations, and membership fee. I am impressed but also cautious. I like the fact they have an entire section on how to be safe while talking or meeting someone on the dating site. If a person was to try this On-Line Dating, I think this is the site I would choose. Being a Christian, I wasn't interested in playing games or hooking up,

## Let's Try Love

but having a male companion to have dinner with, go for a walk, the movies or a concert would be nice.

I had missed those moments with my husband being gone, and a man was just different to converse with, their opinions, emotions, and behaviors were just different than a woman's.

I decide to talk to Jessica the following day and she can help me put together a profile on this site. I decide to try a three month membership. If nothing else, it may prove to be an interesting chapter of my life.

## Two

    Jessica picks me up for church in the morning and like every Sunday we go to Hills Creek for their Sunday buffet. Hills Creek is a very old and established country club from the fifties; a lovely well maintained country club with thirty-six holes of golf, three swimming pools, tennis courts and a large dining room where Sunday brunch is served each week. Both my family and my husband's family have been members here for years. In fact, my husband and I actually met here playing golf during a family day tournament. We were both juniors in high school, but went to different schools.

    We walk in and Jessica takes my coat to the coat closet. The morning has been chilly and she insisted I wear a heavier coat. Entering the dining room, the host greets us and takes us to a table for two near the large windows overlooking the golf course. A few couples are playing, even though it is quite chilly.

    "Julie, is that you?" a voice calls out as I look up and see Janice walk toward me with a tall and handsome man, who looks familiar, walks beside her. As she approaches our table, I see her loop her arm through his, almost in a possessive manner.

    "Hi Janice, how are you?"

    "Julie, I am fine, she almost giggles, as she smiles and looks up at the man standing beside her. I would like you to meet my friend, John Howard."

    Mr. Howard steps closer and extends his hand. "It's nice to meet you Julie."

    "Nice to meet you, and this is my daughter, Jessica." I respond while trying to think why he looks so familiar.

"Julie, Mrs. Woods called me yesterday afternoon and told me you were going to cover my shifts every other Saturday while John and I are on a cruise. Thank you." Janice says and smiles lovingly at John.

"Janice, I am pleased to help out. When will you and John be leaving?"

"We leave in a couple of weeks, I am so excited. You know my late husband Phil, never wanted to go anywhere. It was all about work, and then when he retired, he just dropped over and died."

I glance over at John who appears embarrassed at the remarks Janice is making. I quickly change the subject.

"Janice, I hope you have a lovely trip. Be sure to take lots of pictures and share them with the volunteers in the gift shop when you return. I promise to keep the hospital gift shop running on Saturdays while you are gone."

"Thank you Julie. John, I think we should be going now", as she takes his arm and walks away. I look at him and he mouths "thank you." I just nod.

Noticing Jessica and I have placed our menus to the side, our regular waiter, Harry, appears with the crystal water pitcher to fill our glasses.

"Mrs. Grayson, you and your daughter having the buffet today?'

"Yes, Harry. I think we need a couple of Bloody Marys too."

'Yes Mam."\

"Mom, Janice hasn't changed a bit. She is still the talky gossipy woman she has always been. Who was the man she was with? He was extremely good looking with the white hair and those cobalt blue eyes. He looked so professional and seemed very nice. Wonder where she found him?'

"I have been told she met him on one of the dating sites you talk about."

"Really?" Jessica's eye brows shoot up, the same look she has since she was a teenager when something happens she can't quite believe.

"Yes, that is what I have been told, and if my memory serves me right. I think I know him."

"How?"

"He looks so familiar, but now I remember. He used to play golf with your Dad on occasion, but that was a long time ago. I met him briefly at a country club social after a golf tournament."

"Do you know anything else, Mom? Apparently, he's not married. Do you know what he does for a living?'

I look at Jessica and just smile. I see the wheels turning in my daughter's mind.

"Come on Mom, tell me what does he do?"

"He's a physician at the Hillsboro clinic in Brooksdale. Your Dad saw him a couple of times for the flu when Dr. Jacobs was out of town."

"It just goes to show you there is some potential, Mom, to this On-Line Dating. I wonder how he and Janice got together, if she keeps talking about her dead husband, John may not stick around. Do you know how long she has been seeing him?"

"A couple of months, I was told.

"I bet it was her idea to go on that cruise." Jessica laughs.

Let's Try Love

"Let's go check out the buffet, I am ready to eat."
"Okay Mom."

\* \* \*

In the afternoon, Jessica and I sit down at my computer and I pull up the on line dating site for Let's Try Love.

"Okay, Jessica. Here is the site I think I want to explore. What do I do next?"

"We need to find a photo in your picture file first, that may take some time for you to pick out the one you want to represent you best. I would go with a casual shot, maybe you in the garden with your flowers or one in your volunteer uniform."

"What about me and a picture of Jake, I have several?"

"We can look at some if you want, but I would stay away from animal pictures, at least at first."

We look through the picture files for about ten minutes and both agree on a picture of me standing with Jessica at the nursery with flowers behind us.

"I can crop me out of the picture, Mom. But this looks just like you and its casual and the flowers in the back ground are pretty."

"Okay, now what?"

"Let's go to the profile section. You need to answer these questions."

**What are you looking for?** Casual    Friendship    Dating    Long term    Marriage

"Jessica, I don't know."

"Okay, let's choose Dating."

**What age group do you prefer?**    18-30    30-45    45-60    60-75

"45 -60"

Let's Try Love

**What is your status?**     Single   Married   Separated   Divorced Widow

"Widow"

**What personality are you?**     Quiet   Outgoing   Sense of Humor

"Outgoing, but I enjoy some humor."

"Let's stick with Outgoing, you don't want a clown."

"How many questions are there?"

"A few more, but you can finish this part later. I will show you how to save it, but let's upload your picture and write an introduction and get you started.

"Jessica, are you sur about this?"

"Mom, it's a dating site you can check out, if you don't like any of the potential prospects, you can check out others."

"Jessica, I am going to go fix us a glass of tea and let Jake out in the back yard. You go ahead and write the introduction. Do not put it out there until I can read it." I hear Jessica start typing as I call Jake and walk down the hallway into the kitchen and to the back door. I fix the two glasses of tea and put some snickerdoodle cookies on a plate and smile as I wonder what introduction this girl of mine will come up with. Lord knows.

"I am almost finished Mom, just correcting a couple of typos and then I will read it to see if it meets your approval."

I hand her the glass of tea and offer her a cookie, as I take one myself and stand to look over her shoulder as she reads the profile she has written.

"Here it is Mom, let me read it."

*Hi, my name is Julie. I am a retired nurse, but still active volunteering with my local hospital. I was happily married for over forty years. My husband passed away almost five years ago. I have*

269

*three grown daughters and a dog named Jake. I am an outdoor kind of gal who enjoys walking, swimming, and bicycling on the miles of trails we have here in Florida. But I do enjoy dressing up at times for a nice dinner out. I attend church regularly and looking for someone to spend time with that may enjoy some of the same activities. Sorry, but I am not interested in a long distance relationship, but prefer to meet someone in Dolphin or Manatee counties of Florida.*

"Well, Jessica, this sounds nice. How many of these introductions have you written? Are you on a site?"

"I have a couple of friends that I helped write intros, they have met some nice guys. I thought about going on a site, but then I met Eddie at work and he's a cool guy so there was no need for me to join a site. None of my friends have met anyone special, but they haven't had any unpleasant experiences either, so that's all good."

"Okay then, go ahead and put the picture and the introduction on and choose the 30 day free trial for me. I will mark on my calendar to cancel at 30 days if I am not pleased."

Jessica does all the technical work on the computer and shows me how to get to the site to check for messages, she also informs me the dating site will send me a confirmation within 24 hours and each time someone looks at my profile, or sends me a message I will also get an email. I have a sea of emotions going through me as Jessica gets ready to close my computer down and go home. I am excited, nervous, and uncertain. All emotions I choose not to share with my daughter.

# Three

I wake the following morning to a wet nose on my face and hear a tail hitting against the side of the bed. Moving over in the bed and patting the space that is now vacant gives Jake the invitation to jump in the bed and lay down beside me. This is a ritual we have had since my husband died and no longer occupies the space beside me. Jake not only brings me comfort by filling the empty space I have in my bed, but also in my heart.

"Okay big boy, let's get up."

Wagging his tail, he jumps down and walks to the bedroom door, turns and waits for me. Another morning ritual. What comes next is my putting my robe on, walking into the kitchen, hitting the button on the Keurig to warm the water and letting him out in the back yard. I fix a cup of coffee, check on Jake who is laying patiently under the large oak tree waiting for the squirrels to scurry on the tree branches. The phones rings and before I even have the receiver up to my ear, I hear Jessica's voice.

"Mom, did you have any hits on the dating site last night?"

"Jessica, I don't know. I haven't checked it yet."

"Mom! Mom, Mom. You might be missing opportunities."

"Honey, if it's going to happen, it will happen. I promise to check the site later this morning, I will let you know. Stop worrying about me and go back to work. Love you."

"Love you too, but if there is anything exciting going on, call me at work. Promise?"

"Okay, I promise, now scoot." I laugh as I hang up the phone.

\* \* \*

## Let's Try Love

It's late morning and I am in the green house replanting some flowers with Jake laying by my feet when I remember I promised Jessica to check the dating site. I must not be too interested in this new adventure of on line dating if I have already forgotten to check it out.

But I promised Jessica and knowing her if I don't at least look at it when she calls she will be on her way over here after to work. She can be so bossy at times.

* * *

Sitting at the computer, I follow the brief instructions Jessica left to go to the web site, but decide to check emails first. I pull up the Gmail account and see a number of unread new emails, eleven to be exact. There is a confirmation from the dating site for a 30 day trail period and a reminder that it automatically renews if I don't cancel. I look over at my calendar and see the note in 30 days   Julie, are you canceling the site today? In red ink. Other emails have come from the dating site. I have 5 smiley faces, 3 waves, 2 kisses, and 2 messages. I laugh out loud.

I open the dating site and go to the notifications and click on it.

I have a smile from Eric, John, Tyrone, Billy and Jessie. There are waves from another, a Blake and Jim. Two messages follow from Henry and Lawrence.

I click on the message first from Henry and read
*Hi Julie*
*It was nice to see you on this site and even nicer to know you live in my county. I am not into long distance relationships either they just don't seem to work out or perhaps one or the other just isn't interested in making the effort. I haven't decided what the reason is.*

## Let's Try Love

*I will tell you a little about myself and see if you have any interest in meeting me.*

*I am sixty two years old, work in banking for the last twenty years and have been divorced for seven years. I have two sons who are married, happily I might add, and a daughter who hasn't married yet, but has a steady boyfriend. I enjoy the outdoors and have a small 18 foot pontoon boat that I keep at the marina at Lake Manatee. I am looking for a friend first and maybe more later.*

*I look forward to hearing from you. Regards, Henry*

Sitting back in my chair I decide to chick on additional photos, he sounds nice. Jake comes in and nudges me, his signal to let me know he needs to go out.

"Let's go big boy." After letting him out and see him settling under the large oak, I fix myself a second cup of coffee before returning to the computer. Glancing at the screen, I see photos are now open and a sense of excitement flows over me. The pictures of Sam are casual, one with his two boys, I assume are his sons and one with a very large Doberman pincher. If I were a dog, seeing that picture, my hackles would go up. I love most dogs, but I am leery of that particular breed. I have never had any bad experiences with them, but I did have a close friend in school who was seriously injured trying to break up a dog fight between two dogs at the dog park, one was a Doberman. Should I send a message back to Sam, thinking for a few minutes I decide I don't want to appear over

273

## Let's Try Love

anxious so I close his message out and move on to see what Lawrence has to say. This is at least entertaining.

*Dear Julie, Good morning. I trust you are having a nice beginning to your day. You must be new to this site, I haven't seen you on here before and I am aware of most of the single women who live in this county. But maybe you are on some other sites, I just haven't discovered yet. LOL.*

*I read you like the outdoors, I do too. I really like tent camping, it's a little more intimate for me, if you get my drift? So Julie, would you like to go camping with me this coming week end? I have a 2 person sleeping bag and that way we don't waste any time getting acquainted over several months, that is just a waste of time, don't you think? Well I will be checking my emails today waiting for a response. .Don't keep me waiting too long, there are other mermaids in the sea.     Larry*

Oh my. Now what do I do? I don't know if I am amused or frightened.

# Four

Jessica stops by the house on her way home from work the following afternoon. I know immediately she has arrived with the slamming of the back door. I actually smile to myself as the noise is actually comforting now that the house is so empty. Immediately Jake gets up from laying on the floor beside my office chair and trots down the hallway to meet her.

"Hey Mom, where are you? She yells out. I hear the footsteps stop. Hey Jake."

"Back in the office, Jessica."

"Hi Mom. What are you up too? Have you checked the dating site today?" She asks as she enters the room as she sees me on the computer.

"Yes, I have." While trying to maintain a demeanor of being nonchalant with my daughter.

"Well? Talk to me. What did you find out there? Any one send you messages?"

"Maybe."

Jessica walked around and looked over my shoulder, but I had closed the site when I heard the back door slam, knowing it was her.

"Come on Mom, play hard to get with the men, but not with me. Please open the site so I can see if there is anyone out there that looks promising."

"Oh, so Jessica, you think you are going to have to approve anyone I might want to meet?"

"It's been a long time since you have dated. Maybe it might be a good idea for us to check these guys out together, don't you think?"

## Let's Try Love

I open the site and let Jessica read over my shoulder wondering what her opinion and comments will be.

"This first guy doesn't sound bad. He likes the outdoors and not bad looking. What did you think?"

"I thought he sounded polite, not pushy and nice looking. I liked he worked in banking, a good honest and professional job. He has a boat, I have missed going out on the boat when we had our boat. And he wants a friend first. That is important to me."

"Okay, let me see the next one."

"Jessica, I think that will be a waste of your time to even read it."

"Now, I really want to read what he said."

Jessica reads the remarks from Larry, "Oh my, this guy is something else. I understand what you mean. I would respond to him."

"Why? What would I say? I don't want to encourage anything with him."

"Just be polite, thank him for his message, but you are busy and have other plans or something like that. Let's write Henry a message back."

"Jessica, don't you think I should maybe wait a couple of days? If I respond right away he may think I am too eager?"

"He seemed nice from his email and I think it would be nice to respond. Here, why don't you get up from the chair and let me sit down and put something together and see if you like it and we will send it."

I pause long enough for Jessica to take my elbow and hurry me out of the chair. She sits down and pulls up the message from Sam

## Let's Try Love

and reads it over again and then hits the reply button. She starts to type as I look over her shoulder. We work on the message several times before I approve her sending it.

*Henry,*

*Thank you for the nice message I received from you today. I appreciate your telling me a little about yourself. I am a widow for almost five years now and to be honest, my daughter suggested I give this On-Line Dating site a try. I have three daughters. One is married, but no grandchildren in the forecast, one is traveling in Europe this year and one who is in her last year of college. I also have a big yellow lab named Jake who provides me with company and entertainment while watching him chase squirrels in the back yard. I am a retired nurse and do volunteer a couple of days a week at the hospital.*

*I enjoy the water and my husband and I used to have a boat years ago when the children were still living at home. I am familiar with Lake Manatee, it's a lovely lake. I hope to hear from you again. Julie*

"Mom, wait a day or two and then send a note to Larry if you want too. You may never hear from him again. He sounds like he's full of himself. He may send that same note to several women and wait to see if any mermaids respond." We both laugh in reference to his comment *there were plenty of mermaids in the sea.* Jessica kisses me goodbye and leaves the house, slamming the door behind her.

I sit at the computer and read Henry's message one more time and my response wondering if I will hear back.

* * *

Several days pass and I find myself going to my computer and checking the dating site for an email from Henry. Each time walking

## Let's Try Love

away feeling disappointed and discouraged. This is ridiculous. Deciding I am not going to check anymore and think seriously about canceling this membership. I think it's crazy for a women my age to be on a dating site. Just crazy. It is not like me to get this emotional over one email from a stranger. I decide to take Jake to the dog park. On the way home, jake and I stop at the Burger Haven, a plain burger for him and a salad for me.

Pulling into the driveway, I see Jessica's car. Oh No! I don't want to deal with her right now. I know she's just being Jessica and wanting to find out if anything is going on with the dating site.

I open the back door of the SUV for Jake to jump out when Jessica comes out the back door of the house.

"Hi Mom, where have you been? I was just getting ready to leave. You are usually home at dinner time."

"I took Jake over to the dog park and we went by Burger Haven. I didn't feel like cooking tonight. I have a big salad if you want to join me."

"No, I just stopped by for a few, see if anything new is going on? I have a night class in an hour, so I need to get home and change."

"Sorry you missed me, you run along, nothing going on here." and I walked into the house.

*  *  *

Before going to bed, against my better judgement, I decide to check for any emails. Not the dating site, just my regular emails from friends and business acquaintances. There were several from the nursing retirement group I am a member and a couple of advertisements, I was getting ready to close the computer down when I noticed an email from the dating site that read,

## Let's Try Love

*There are three people interested in you, Julie. Check your email on our site.*

*Love may be waiting.*

Making a decision wasn't hard. It only took one click to open Let's Try Love site, telling myself I was doing it more out of coursity than any expectation of finding anyone. There were three emails in my mail box. I had an email from Rick, Henry and Sam. I clicked on Rick's first. It was nice but he lived in California and I lived in Florida.

I responded thanking him for his email explaining I was not interested in a long distance relationship. I moved on to Paul's email, it was interesting and it seemed we had some similar interests and he had a lab. Saving Sam's email till last I clicked on Sam's.

*Hello Julie,*

*I saw you on this site and you look like a nice woman. I have not done this before, I guess you can say I am more old school where you meet a lady through your friends or at an organized outdoor event; hiking, kayaking, or maybe a social event like wine tasting or a church pot luck. I am almost seventy years old, but healthy and active. I have a Silver Sneakers membership. My wife passed away several years ago and I have a black lab, Coal, who keeps me busy especially when I take him to the dog park on Saturday mornings. You mentioned you have a dog too. Do you ever go to the dog park off Turner Peak Road? Maybe we could meet there one Saturday and talk or take a walk around the park. I look forward to hearing from you. Sam*

*Dear Sam,*

# Let's Try Love

*I received your nice email today and wanted to respond. I agree with you, I think this is a very different means to meet someone. Who would have ever thought we would be dating at our age, much less through a dating site. Yes, I have a yellow lab and I don't live too far from the dog park. Jake and I go to the park several times a week, mostly in the morning when they open. It would be nice to meet you one morning and get acquainted. Julie*

Just as I decide to save Sam's email to read in the morning, the hall clock chimes and a memory flashes before my eyes of my husband giving me the clock for our anniversary the last year he was alive. I remember as I opened the box and recognized the clock I had admired in an antique shop months before, he stooped down in front of me and took my hand in his and said, *"Julie, Happy Anniversary. This clock represents our love is timeless."* If only I had known two weeks later he would have a massive heart attack and die.

## Five

In the morning Jake is whining and nudges me with his nose before the alarm goes off. I pat the side of the bed inviting him to jump up beside me like every morning, but he refuses. He starts to pace and continues to whine.

"Jake, what's wrong boy? Do you need to go out?"

I locate my slippers beside my end table and grab my robe off the hanger by my closet. Jake walks slowly behind me with his tail tucked between his legs to the kitchen. I open the door and he slowly walks down the few steps to the back yard and over to the corner where he usually does his business. His whines are getting louder and he seems to be struggling to go to the bathroom.

Walking over to get a closer look, I see he is constipated and there is some blood. He then starts to vomit a green bile substance. I panic. Leaving Jake in the yard, I run in the house and grab the phone and call the vet.

"Grey's Animal Hospital, this is Sarah. May I help you?"

"Sarah, Hi. I am so glad it's you who answered the phone. This is Julie Brownstone. Jake is sick, can you fit me in this morning?"

"Hi Julie, what seems to be his problem?"

"He woke me up whining this morning. He's pacing and panting. He's constipated and there was blood in his stool." Then he started vomiting a greenish colored bile."

"Julie, sounds like he's eaten something that upset his stomach, but because of the blood in his stool, you need to bring him in and let the doc check him. Can you come in about 10:15 this morning?"

"Yes, I will be there. Thanks Sarah."

"And Julie, bring us a stool sampled too."

## Let's Try Love

Checking on Jake in the back yard, I see he's lying under his favorite tree, but his head is down and he is not interested in the squirrels this morning. Looking down at my wrist watch, it's almost nine. I need to get dressed. I am just going to the vet's, so I grab the jeans from yesterday and my Virginia is for Lovers t-shirt and comb my hair. Today is definitely a no make-up day.

* * *

At the vet's office, Jake doesn't want to jump down out of the car, I try to coax him but he just lays in the back seat.

"Jake, come on big boy. I know you don't feel good, but we have to find out why."

Jake just continues to look at me but doesn't budge. I try to tug on the lease but it's like he is dead weight, he doesn't even lift his head. Just then a man comes out of the office walking a big black lab.

"Can I help you, Miss?"

"I have a sick dog but I can't get him to budge."

"Let me put my dog in the truck and I will see if I can pick him up and carry him in there for you."

"Oh, thank you. That is very kind of you."

"Come on Coal, let's get you in the truck so I can help the lady."

The man reaches down and picks Jake up in his arms and follows me into the vet's office. Sarah sees us coming through the door and tells me to have Jake carried back to the treatment room. I follow the man and Sarah leads the way.

Once Jake is placed on the treatment table, the man excuses himself and leaves. I wonder why there is something familiar about him, then Dr. Grey enters the room and smiles.

"Julie, what seems to be the problem with Jake this morning?"

"I don't have a clue Doc. He woke me up this morning whining, wouldn't jump up on the bed like his normal routine. Pacing, constipated, blood in his stool and then vomited bile. I couldn't get him out of the car until a nice man coming out of your office stopped and offered to carry him in here for me."

"Did you bring a stool sample?"

"Yes."

"I know he is up to date on all his vaccinations. We will test the stool, but I think I would like to run just a couple of routine blood tests, okay with you?"

"Yes, of course."

Dr. Grey checks Jake over and draws three tubes of blood and leaves the room. Twenty minutes pass and I continue to watch Jake as he begins to start whining again and becomes restless. I call for Sarah. As she enters the room, Jake tries to get up and falls back down on the table as though he has no energy or strength. He starts to pant and is drooling and then he starts to shake. Sarah calls Dr. Grey on the intercom and requests that he come to the treatment room and gives a code number, I later learn it's a code for an emergency situation.

"Dr. Grey, what is happening?" I ask in a frightened voice that doesn't even sound like my own as he walks into the room.

"Julie, Jake is having a seizure." He says as he touches my shoulder and then gives Sarah instructions for obtaining medications from the pharmacy. I learn it's a sedative to calm him during the seizure.

The seizure lasts only a couple of minutes, but it seems like hours to me. I pray. Please Lord, don't let Jake die.

\* \* \*

Over the next twenty four hours it is touch and go for Jake. His blood tests come back with an extremely elevated white blood count, meaning there is infection somewhere. He has a couple of more seizures, but not as severe as the first one. Dr. Grey has him on IV antibodies every twelve hours. The Animal Hospital is open twenty-four hours for emergencies and Dr. Grey recommends Jake stay there to be monitored. I agree and go home alone.

## Six

The drive home is filled with tears and sobs, I can barely see the road. I can't lose Jake, not now. He has been my constant companion since Jerry died. He fills the house with the noise of his nails on the hard wood floors, and his tail hitting against the side of the bed in the morning, and watching him chase squirrels. I pull into my drive way and walk out to Jake's tree. I can't imagine not seeing him lie under the tree and waiting for the activity of the squirrels. The gates holding back my tears erupt and I sit on the grass below the oak tree and hold my face in my hands as the tears come uncontrollably. I pray.

*Lord, please, I beg of you help Dr. Grey with Jake. I know some may feel he is just a dog, but to me he is my companion, I need him Lord. Please.*

\* \* \*

During the evening I walked to pick up the phone a dozen different times to call the Animal Hospital and check on Jake, but Dr. Grey promised if there was any change someone would call me otherwise I should rest and call in the morning.

Jessica called and I told her what had happened. She stopped by after work and brought dinner from the family diner down the street. I wasn't hungry, but realized I hadn't eaten all day.

"Jessica, thank you. This is good."

"Mom, you always called the diner food, comfort food because it wasn't fast food when we were growing up." She reaches over and touches my arm.

"I remember. It seems so long ago."

The phone rings and startles me as I drop my fork and it hits the floor.

"I'll get it Mom." Jessica pushes her chair back from the table and grabs the phone off its cradle.

"Hello."

"Yes, my Mom is right here, Jessica hands the phone to me. I think it's the Animal Hospital."

"Hello, this is Julie. That's good news, I am so glad you called. I understand it may only be temporary, but for now Jake is resting and the seizures have stopped. I will call you in the morning. Thank you" I am shaking when I get off the phone and Jessica gets up and wraps her arms around me.

"I could only hear your side of the conversation, Mom, but it sounds like Jake is going to be okay." Jessica hugs me tight.

"Yes, I have been praying and the tech said he's doing much better. They will continue to monitor him and do some other tests in the morning, but I might be able to bring him home in a day or too."

"Mom, do you want to watch some television or go out and sit on the deck for a little while. I don't have to go home right away."

"No, honey. It's been a long day, a very exhausting and stressful day. I am tired. I think I will just take a hot bath and get ready for bed."

"Okay, then I am going to leave, but call me if you need me."

I walk Jessica to the door and wait and watch as she pulls out of the drive way and waves. I shut the door and feel the loneliness of Jake not being home cover me like a heavy blanket. A hot bath will feel good tonight.

\* \* \*

The next morning I call the Animal Hospital and am told, Jake had a good night and ate a little of his breakfast. Dr. Grey hadn't seen him yet, but he would call me with a report within the hour. I tried to keep myself busy and my mind occupied. I watered the flowers and filled the bird feeders and drank three cups of coffee. I was anxious, my routine had been altered and I was restless. I decided to go check the dating site while I waited for Dr. Grey's call.

I forgot I had not read Henry's email now was several days old. I signed on to the site and clicked on his email.

*Dear Julie,*

*Hi. I am sorry I haven't been in contact with you. I was away at a conference last week and had several issues to deal with when I got back to work this week. I hope this week has been good for you. I plan to take my boat out on the lake this week end, if you would be interested in joining me, please let me know. If you would prefer just to meet for coffee one morning to get acquainted, that would be nice as well. I look forward to hearing from you. Henry*

*Dear Henry,*

*Thank you for your email. This week, or at least the last couple of days, have been difficult. My lab, Jake, became quite ill yesterday and is at the Animal Hospital. He has some type of an infection and actually had several seizures yesterday. He was doing better last night and Dr. Grey will call me this morning. I am sorry, until I hear what the diagnosis is with Jake, I don't want to make any plans. I hope you understand. Julie*

I read over the email Henry sent and my answer and hit send just as the phone rings.

\* \* \*

"Jessica, I just got a call from Dr. Grey. He's pleased with Jake's prognosis. He wants to keep Jake for another twenty-four hours and give him another round of IV antibiotics. If Jake stays seizure free

Let's Try Love

during that time, I can pick him up and bring him home tomorrow afternoon."

"Mom that is wonderful news. I am so happy he's improving. I guess it's a good thing you got him in to Dr. Grey as soon as you did."

"Yes, a blessing for sure. Honey, I will let you get back to work. I just wanted to let you know the good news."

"Okay. Thanks. I have a class tonight but I will stop by on my way home tomorrow night and welcome Jake home."

* * *

The following day I receive a call letting me know Jake is cleared to be discharged and I can pick him up after 2:00 o'clock. I make Jake his favorite meal, chicken and rice in a little broth. It's easy on his stomach and I want him to know I am glad he is home. I wash the cover on his dog bed that sits in a corner of my room. The only time he gets in bed with me is in the morning when he wakes me up and I invite him to jump up beside me. I can't believe I am this excited. The house has not seemed the same with him being gone. No one to feed or let out and then back in and then back out. I laugh at the silly things he does and realize what an empty part of my life he has filled.

I am in the lobby waiting to be called back to Dr. Grey's office for discharge information when Sarah, the receptionist steps from behind the counter and comes over to speak to me.

"Julie, I almost forgot to tell you. Sam called yesterday to check on you and Jake."

"Who is Sam?" I asked confused.

"Sam Brothers. Your friend that carried Jake in the other day for you."

"Sarah, I don't know anyone named Sam Brothers. The man who carried Jake in was a stranger. He had a black lab and saw I couldn't

## Let's Try Love

get Jake out of the car and I was getting upset. He offered to help me."

"Oh, I thought he was a friend of yours when I saw him carry Jake in to the office. Anyway, I just wanted to let you know he was concerned and called to check on you and Jake."

My conversation with Sarah ended when my name came across the intercom at the desk with instructions to go to Dr. Greys' office.

"Julie, please sit down. Dr. Grey said and motioned me to a chair across from his desk.

"How is Jake? I can take him home today, right?' I said with more than a little excitement in my voice.

"Yes, Julie. He smiled and his whole face lit up. You can take Jake home. It was good that you got him in here as quickly as you did. Seizures are scary to watch and I was immediately available to give him a sedative to calm him. Some dogs don't survive and some dogs have to be on medication for the rest of their lives.

"Will Jake need to be on medication?"

"Not at this time. The seizures were not severe and he only had a couple. If he has another one within the next thirty days, then I might reconsider, but for now I think this was an isolated case. He has started to eat. I wanted to see him start to have an appetite before I let him go home.

"Are there other instructions or information I need?"

"Keep him quiet for the next day or two. Today is Thursday. No chasing squirrels in the back yard. I want him to build his strength up, seizures can drain a dog of their energy. You are a member of the dog park out on Turner Peak aren't you?"

"Yes, why?"

"Maybe by Saturday or Sunday you can take Jake out there for a nice walk around the grounds. But no running. Keep him on a leash if he will not walk quietly by your side. Now let's go get your big boy."

"Thank you so much for taking such good care of him, I really appreciate it. I don't know what I would do without him. Since my husband died, he has become my best friend and companion."

"Julie, our dogs are our family. You don't hesitate to call the office if you need anything. I want to see Jake in ten days just for a checkup." Dr. Grey calls Sarah to get Jake and bring him to the lobby for me.

The kennel area door opens into the lobby and Jake walks through and sees me. He seems to be a little sluggish, but his tail is wagging as fast as it can. He walks up to me and nudges me with his nose. I look down into his soft brown eyes and tears form in mine as I take his leash from Sarah. Jake and I are going home.

## Seven

The next several days are uneventful. I spend a lot of time paying attention to Jake. I think he likes being spoiled. I know he enjoys his chicken and rice because he licks the bowl clean and looks up at me like more please. I think his energy level is improving. He hasn't tried to jump up on the bed in the mornings, but I haven't pushed it. He did drag his bed from the corner over closer to my side of the bed. I guess he wants to be close to me. I found an old ramp in the garage and put it up next to the SUV to see if he would walk up it. He did so I decide on Saturday we will go for a nice walk at the dog park.

I haven't looked at my emails since I brought Jake home or checked on the dating site, my concentration and attention has been devoted to Jake. I know I will have to look at the site soon because Jessica will be asking me. But for this week, this week is about Jake.

\* \* \*

Saturday morning comes and the weather is beautiful. The sunlight is making shadows from the trees on to my deck as I look out the window and see Jake under the oak tree. After breakfast, I decide to take Jake to the dog park for o get more exercise for him. We will stop by and get Chicken Nuggets on our way home as a treat for Jake.

I finish the dishes and find Jake's leash and head out the door. I ask Jake to sit and wait while I get the ramp from the garage and attach it to the back of the SUV. He walks up it without hesitation and we head for the park. I am hoping it's not too busy. I want Jake to relax but get more exercise than what he can get from our small back yard.

Pulling into the parking lot, I see more cars on the little dog side and I sign relief. I open the back door, put the ramp down and have

Jake walk down it. He acts like we do this all the time. Pleased with his ability to trust and engage with the .ramp, I take a hold of his leash and walk to the gate to enter.

"Julie" I hear someone call my name and turn to see Susan the park owner, walking toward me.

"Hi Susan. How are you?"

"The better question is how you and Jake are?"

"Oh, you heard about my week?"

"Yes, I ran into Jessica at the store the other night. So he looks like he is recovering nicely, I am so glad for you. Seizures can be scary."

"Dr. Grey suggested we just take it slow and take a nice walk around the grounds to give Jake a little exercise. I can't let him out in the yard, because Dr. Grey doesn't want him running yet and I know my Jake he would be chasing the squirrels. Here I can walk and keep him on the leash."

"Well, enjoy your walk. Good to see you Julie and glad Jake is doing better."

"Thanks, I was sure worried for several days but Dr. Grey is an exceptional vet so I am sure we are on the road to a full recovery."

The distance around the outer edge of the large dog side is almost like a walking trail. My GPS shows it to be about 1.25 miles, a good walk for Jake's first time out. Some of my friends and their dogs have gathered at the pond where some of the dogs are swimming and chasing balls. I wave and several see me and wave back. I wonder how many know Jake was sick this past week.

The sun has been behind clouds most of the morning, but now it is starting to clear up, the sun is shining bright and it is getting hot. I notice Jake is panting a little and so as not to have him overheat, I get off the walking path and go over to a bench under a shade tree for

## Let's Try Love

both of us to rest. After a few minutes we start back on our walk. We are more than a mile into the walk, when I see a black lab and the black lab sees us. He wags his tail and bounces happily up to Jake. I see a man come around the corner up ahead and I assume the dog is his. The man gets closer and the dog runs back to him. The man continues to walk toward me and stops.

"Hello, he says. You look familiar. I mean I think your dog looks familiar. Is your dog's name Jake?"

"Why yes. How would you know that? I don't think we have met."

"Not officially. Last week at the Animal Hospital, I helped you by carrying Jake into the facility. He was quite sick."

"Oh. Then you must be Sam Brothers."

"Yes, I am. Sam replied and held out his hand to shake mine. I know Jake's name and yours?"

"My name is Julie Brownstone. Thank you so much for your help last week, I am not sure I even thanked you. I was so frightened Jake was so sick." I look down and see the dogs are laying side by side looking up at us with tails wagging.

"Julie, Do you mind if Coal and I walk with you? It seems our dogs have become friends."

"Of course, I would like the company, Sam."

We walked for the next thirty minutes just taking our time. Coal was off lease but stayed beside Jake the entire time. We talked about the weather and our families. Sam had two married sons who lived out of state and a couple of grandchildren. He was a widow, his wife had died from a brain aneurysm in July of 2014. My husband had died of a heart attack in August of 2014. Sam was retired as a supervisor with Duke Whitehall Energy Corporation and he had traveled quite a bit prior to his retirement last year.

## Let's Try Love

"Sam, I have to say somehow you look familiar, but I know I haven't met you before."

"I thought the same thing when I first shook your hand, like there is something so familiar about this woman. I just can't put my finger on it. I even thought maybe I had met you at one of my wife's business functions."

We continue to walk a short distance further before we see the entrance and exit gates out of the park.

"Julie, Let's Try Love!"

"Excuse me?" I am stunned at his remark and it appears he is amused.

"No! No! Don't get the wrong idea as he starts to laugh. We are both on the same On-Line Dating site, Let's Try Love. I saw your profile a couple of weeks ago and sent you an email. You sent me one back, but then I never heard any more."

"I think that's it. Sam with a black lab named Coal who likes to be outdoors and kayaking, beach, etc. You are one and the same? You have to be kidding."

"Yes, Julie the same. Disappointed?"

"No, not at all." I laugh.

"Are we considering this our first date, Sam?"

"Oh, no. Let's consider it our meet and greet, but we could take it a step further today and go to the little family diner not far from here and get an ice cream cone. They have outside seating and the dogs are allowed."

"Sounds like fun."

*Three Months Later*

## Let's Try Love

The week after I met Sam at the Dog Park, I got an email from Henry asking about Jake and telling me he had met a nice lady on the dating sight and she raised Dobermans. They had a lot in common and he wanted me to know he wanted to see her and he wasn't one to date more than one woman at a time. I responded with appreciation for his concern for Jake and his kindness wishing him also the best with his new relationship.

Sam and I have become a couple. Any misgivings I had about dating again vanished a little more each time we were together. We enjoy most of the same activities; swimming, the beach, kayaking, craft fairs and Christian concerts. He is an avid reader like me and we even like some of the same authors; James Patterson, Michael Connelly and Tim Green. He is encouraging me to continue with my writing and says he wants to see my name on the cover of a book as an author. My daughters have met him and approve. In a few months we are meeting his sons and their wives for a get together in the Cayman Islands. I have talked with his family on the phone and they all seem as nice as Sam. I think they are as excited to meet me as I am to meet them.

Sam is bringing Coal over to the house to stay with Jake while we are gone and Jessica will house and dog sit.

Sam and I talk frequently about how we met. Was it the result of both of us being on *Let's Try Love* or was it faith that brought him into my life when Jake and I needed him? Maybe a little of both. We both agree You are *Never Too Old for Love*.

**The End**

# About the Author

Judy Swinson is a Virginia native with a diverse background from Airline Stewardess in the 60's to healthcare worker from the 70's until retirement in 2015. More recently, she has been working with shelter animals, rescues and foster groups. Loves to travel especially to Florence, Italy.

Member of RWA (Romance Writers of America) and Sunshine State Romance Authors. Dreamed of being a children's author, but life took her in a different direction and her first publication was a key article published in The International Journal of Volunteer Administration. In 2018 Judy became a multi-genre author publishing stories in four anthologies from paranormal to flash fiction to sweet romance. Judy's preferred writing is sweet contemporary romance as shown in her debut novella, Autumn Love in Italy released in October 2018. Judy makes her home in central Florida with her two dogs, a lab named Jake and a minature Australian labradoodle named Libby.

Judy loves to hear from her readers and can be reached at JudySwinson.com or her face book page JudyLoomanSwinsonAuthor.

# Unexpected Love

## by C.L. Williams

Being too busy with their careers, Victor and Diana meet on Let's Try Love. Upon their first date, they not only realize they have similar jobs, they actually work in the same building and realize why it took an online dating service for the two of them to meet.

# Unexpected Love by C.L. Williams

After months of failed dates and the nagging of his friends, Victor agrees to set up a profile on an online dating site. After searching through every site, app, and pages on social media, Victor settles on trying the dating site/app called *Let's Try Love*. It has the highest review scores of any site he checked and it's both a website and an app, that way, he can check the app when he is on his lunch break and look at the website when he is at home. He also plans to look at it on his computer at work, whenever his boss isn't around. He sets up everything and within minutes, Victor already has five messages in his inbox. Victor isn't a pessimistic person, but he knows he's not the best-looking guy on the planet. For five women to message him immediately after setting up his account, he's a little surprised.

The first message read *Hey baby! Wanna have some fun?* Victor is unimpressed and deletes the message. The second message is more of what Victor would expect, *You look cute and we have similar interests. Wanna talk?* But Victor looked at the profile picture and it is a man citing himself as a woman. Victor's little brother is gay, and Victor does his best to support LGBT rights, but Victor is straight and is looking for a woman to date. The third message was from a woman named Diana, it was a simple hand-waving emoji. Victor decides to check out her profile after he reads the remaining two messages.

The fourth message is from a girl named Yuri. He looks at her picture and he thinks Yuri is cute. Her message reads *We should talk sometime.* Victor decides to respond to Yuri before moving on to the fifth and final message. He responds with *You're very cute in your picture, I'm down to talk.* He then moves on to the fifth and final message, a girl named Victoria. Victor thought it was funny his name being Victor and hers being Victoria. Her message simply read, *Hey sexy* ☐. He replies with *Hello sexy yourself :D!* After answering the last two messages, he's about to respond to Diana, the girl that simply sent a hand-waving emoji. Before he can respond, he gets a response from Yuri. Her response to him calling her cute; *LOL Thanks sweetie! It's my senior pic! Took them last month* ☐. Victor sees her saying it's her senior picture and decides he is not responding to her. He goes back to Diana's message and says, *Hello Beautiful! We should talk sometime.* Victor isn't expecting much of a response. He knows he lacks flirting skills and his previous messages were a possible underage girl, a guy pretending to be a girl, and someone he's sure is only interested in a hookup. Much to Victor's surprise, Diana responds him.

She responds; *WOW! You're the first guy to respond to me that is not asking for sex!* Victor laughs to himself knowing he was thinking Diana was about to ask for sex as well. He responds to Diana, *I'm looking for a real relationship, not some random hookup with some girl I don't know.* He then sends the message and before Victor can

## Let's Try Love

continue looking at other profiles, he gets another message from Diana, *Where do you live? Last guy I tried talking to lives 50 miles away from me.* Victor reads the message and responds *Trekton and I work in Enterprise.* Seeing that Diana is responding quickly to him, Victor quits looking at other profiles and waits for Diana to respond. He is not let down, *OMG! I live and work in Enterprise!* Victor is finally to a point where he feels bold enough to ask *Since I work in Enterprise and you live in Enterprise, would you like to do dinner this week? I like eating at this place called Outpost.* Victor sends the message and sees that he has a message from Victoria, the only other girl to send him a message that he didn't find weird or creepy, but he also wanted to see if Diana will respond.

Even though it was only a few minutes, Victor felt like he had been waiting hours when he got a response from Diana, *I LOVE OUTPOST* followed by multiple smiling heart emojis. She then sends another message *Is Friday good for you?* Victor smiles as he knows he is about to have his first date in almost two years, he responds with *Friday sounds good. Is seven good for you?* He sends it and sits there again anxiously waiting for a response from Diana. Again, even though Victor is only waiting a few minutes, his anxiety makes it feel that he is waiting for hours. She then responds with *7 sounds good! See you there. I'll be wearing a red dress, that way you know who to look for.* Victor did not realize it until she said what she plans to wear but Diana is not using her own picture for her profile picture. She's using an animated character for her profile picture. Victor then makes a run to his closet, looks inside, and runs back to his laptop to give his response. *I bet you look good in that red dress, I'll be wearing a black polo. See you Friday!* He sent the message and smiles to himself. He can say he finally has a date and with someone who lives nearby. Even though Victor has his concerns about Diana not using her own

## Let's Try Love

picture for her profile, he is not going to complain given he has had very little luck leading up to Diana responding to him.

****

Friday is here and Victor is putting on his black polo and is getting ready to make the travel from Trekton to Enterprise for his date with Diana at Outpost. Victor goes to the hostess and requests his table, he informs her his date will be here momentarily. As the hostess is leading Victor to his table for his date with Diana, he notices something. He is one of many guys in the restaurant wearing a black polo. Victor feels he needs to inform Diana about the issue, but he is currently without her number. He's been using the *Let's Try Love* website, not the app. Victor quickly opens up the app store on his phone and rapidly goes through each app until he finds *Let's Try Love*. He finds it and begins downloading the app. While waiting for the app to download, he looks around to see if Diana has arrived yet. He does not see anyone wearing a red dress and resumes staring at his phone in hopes of the app downloading faster. The app is done downloading and Victor types in his log in information. He notices he has one unread message from Diana, *Sorry sweetie, I'm running late.* Victor responds, *It's all good. BTW, I'm one of many dudes here wearing a black polo. I'll be looking for you. I'll stand up when I see you. I'm about 6'2, kinda skinny, and I wear glasses. I've already got us a table.* Victor hits send and impatiently awaits a response from Diana.

Victor places his phone on the table as a waitress comes over to ask for his order. He tells her he would like a glass of water until his date arrives. After the waitress leaves to get Victor his water, his phone's notification tone begins buzzing. He picks it up and it's Diana. She responds with, *I'll message you when I'm at the door. That way you'll know when to stand up. OMW!* Victor responds with

## Let's Try Love

a thumbs up emoji and the waitress returns with his glass of water. When she hands him the glass of water, Victor asks if she can bring two menus to the table before his date gets here. She smiles and walks away to grab the menus.

Victor is waiting for the waitress to return with the menus when his phone goes off. He checks and it's Diana *I'm here! You can stand up now. LOL.* Victor stands up and even though Diana didn't put a picture of herself on her profile, Victor can already tell Diana is easily the most beautiful woman he's ever been on a date with. He stands up and notices his nerves are getting the better of him and he feels he is starting to sweat. Diana sees Victor in his black polo, noticeably tall stature, and glasses. She smiles at him as she walks over to him. She automatically goes in for a hug and begins talking.

"Hello, I'm Diana." She says, starting off the conversation, followed by a smile that can make any man melt.

"Hi. Victor," Victor says in a speedy tone as they end the hug and sit down. "I've got to be honest, I'm feeling a bit nervous."

"Why?" She asks.

"I was not expecting the most beautiful woman in the room to be my date for the evening. You look amazing." Victor says as he gives a crooked smile to Diana.

"Thanks." She responds as she blushes from the compliment courtesy of Victor.

Victor is about to say something, but the waitress comes over and hands menus to Victor and Diana. Seeing the woman Victor is with, the waitress whispers in his ear, "She's pretty"

The two look at their menus for a moment before Victor breaks the ice with an unusual conversation starter. "If you don't mind me asking, why is someone as beautiful as you using a dating site? I could see men throwing themselves at you."

## Let's Try Love

"Well, I have a job that requires a lot of my time and so many men talk a big game but when the time comes to step up, they just can't. Why did you resort to online dating, and what made you pick *Let's Try Love*?" Diana asks.

"I've been single for a while and my friends are giving me a hard time about it. Like you, I work a lot. I don't consider myself good-looking, so I thought I'd go for the anonymity of online dating. I chose *Let's Try Love* because it had the best review scores of the other sites, and it had the highest scores of any site/app hybrid." Victor responds.

"I think you're cute, and you've been more of a gentleman than any other date I've had recently. Where do you work if you don't mind me asking?" Diana asks.

"Data analytics at Troi office park."

Before Victor can say anything else, Diana interrupts him. "Did you just say you work in the Troi office park?"

"Yeah, why?"

"I work in Office Q over there! How have I never seen you before?" Diana asks in excitement.

"I go in, do my job, and leave. None of my friends work there and other than my boss, I can't say I'm close with anyone there."

"Well, come Monday, you and I will be having lunch. What time do you usually take lunch? That way I can coordinate my schedule."

"I usually go around one, that way I can go somewhere *after* the craziness of a lunch rush."

"Tell me about it," Diana says, "I went to lunch around noon ONCE, a mistake I'll NEVER make again." She then concludes her venting with some laughter.

Diana and Victor share a laugh before the waitress comes back over to take their orders. Diana orders some pasta and a sparkling water while Victor orders a burger and a soda. After the waitress leaves, Diana asks Victor something about what she noticed.

"Usually I see guys order a beer with their food." Diana says to Victor.

"I live in Trekton and I didn't know if you drove or not. I don't want to take any chances. Can I ask you the same thing?" Victor asks.

"This may surprise you, but…." Diana pauses, "I don't drink."

"Not too surprising, I know plenty of people that don't drink."

The waitress comes back with their orders and their drinks. Diana and Victor spend the rest of the evening engaged in small talk and enjoying the food they are eating. At the end of the date, Diana gives Victor her number. That way the two of them can talk without needing to go onto *Let's Try Love*. She tells Victor to text her when he arrives home. Victor pays for the meal and he walks Diana to her car. They talk for a brief moment before Diana kisses Victor and gets in her car to go home. Victor then heads to his car and makes his way back home. As promised, he texts Diana when he gets home, letting her know he has arrived home safe. The two text one another for the majority of the night.

*Monday*

Monday is now here, and Victor is at work; Data Analytics at Troi Office Park. While he is finishing up some work on his computer before going to lunch, his boss stops by his cubicle.

"Hey Victor, there's someone here for you. She said you promised her lunch." Victor's boss says in a confused tone.

"Thanks Bruce," Victor says to his boss, "I'm almost done, then I'm going to lunch."

## Let's Try Love

"Victor," Bruce says in a serious tone, "Ever since I became president of Data Analytics, I've never known anyone to come here to see you, especially someone that gorgeous. Just save what you're doing, take some extra time for lunch. Don't worry about pay." Bruce then steps aside and makes a phone call. Within a few minutes, he returns and pulls out his wallet. He gives Bruce fifty dollars in cash, "Victor, there's this nice steak diner on Riker Street. I already have your reservation set up. Here's some cash. Now take your time on the date and make that woman happy."

"You don't have to do this Bruce." Victor says, feeling uncomfortable about taking the money and the reservation from his boss. "I'm just taking her somewhere for lunch. We can do something when we're not on a time clock."

Bruce, insistent that Victor take the deal, replies, "I told you, don't worry about pay and I think this will help. Trust me!" Bruce says as he holds out the money once more.

Victor accepts the offer from Bruce. He saves everything he needs on his necessary reports. He then goes outside of the Data Analytics office and Diana is standing outside the office door, waiting on him.

"Sorry it took so long, my boss took one look of you and said I needed better lunch plans. Gave us a reservation for some steak diner on Riker Street." Victor tells Diana.

"You mean your boss wants you to take me to House of Glory Steakhouse?!" Diana says in shock.

"I guess so, I'm not in that part of the city too much. I know how to get there, but I've never been much of a steakhouse person."

"Don't worry about that, they have other amazing food. You do know we'll be more than an hour in there?"

"My boss told me I *need* to leave a good impression with you and to take as much time as I need. He even told me that I'll still get paid." Victor tells Diana.

"All I need to hear, let's go!" Diana responds as they walk over to the parking garage and get in Victor's car.

They go to the House of Glory Steakhouse and end up spending three hours at the steakhouse. When they get back, Bruce, Victor's boss is at the main entrance of Troi Office Park waiting to see how things went for his employee.

"So......," Bruce says with a cheesy grin upon his face.

Diana responds before Victor can say anything, "It was great, and my boyfriend told me I have you to thank!" Diana says as she extends her hand to Bruce.

Bruce is complimenting Diana while Victor stands in shock that not only is his boss happy for him about his date, Diana just referred to him as her boyfriend. While in a state of shock, Bruce then snaps Victor out of his trance.

"VICTOR!" Bruce yells.

"Sorry boss, what's up?" Victor asks.

"Take the rest of the day off. Take Diana to your place and enjoy the evening. If you need tomorrow off," Bruce then gives Victor a wink, "That's fine by me!"

"Thanks boss!" Victor and Diana make their way back to the parking garage, before Victor can give Diana directions to his house, Diana gives him directions to hers. He then follows her to her place and the two of them sit in the living room and watch movies while engaging in some small talk.

"Diana, things have been going very well for us. Is something bad about to happen?" Victor asks.

## Let's Try Love

"No! I think we both found what we're looking for. You need someone who understands you have a busy lifestyle with work, and I need someone who is interested in me and not just getting me into bed, by the way, you won't have to wait too much longer on that," Diana says as she smiles at Victor and follows it up with a kiss.

"Sooooo," Victor says as he tries to tell Diana what is on his mind, "I guess me asking what I need to ask is not going to be a problem then."

"What would that be?" She asks.

"With everything going well and you calling me your boyfriend to my boss, I think I should go ahead and delete my profile on *Let's Try Love.*"

"Good idea!" Diana then gets up and races to her bedroom. She then comes back into the living room with her laptop, opens it up, and makes her way to the website. She then logs into the site, goes to account settings, and requests delete profile. When she was prompted to explain why, she replies with *OTHER*, in the comments section, Diana responds, *"Met the man of my life in Victor. He's charming, sweet, and everything I could ever ask for. I'm deleting my profile because Let's Try Love truly worked!"* She then hits send and her account is now deactivated. Diana then hands her laptop to Victor who also chooses to delete his profile. When asked why, Victor responds, *"I tried the website because my friends kept harassing me to. What I never expected was that I would meet Diana, she's beautiful on the outside and her inner beauty surpasses that. Let's Try Love is a true success and I will be happy to recommend it to all of my single friends."* Victor then hits send and his profile is now deactivated. He then gives Diana the laptop and she puts it away and the two of them resume watching their movie.

Let's Try Love

Shortly after both of them deleted their accounts, Victor's phone starts buzzing. He checks his phone to see he has an unread email. He reads it to himself before reading it to Diana. The email reads:

*Hello Victor,*

*This is Adam, co-founder of Let's Try Love. I just read your reason for deleting your profile and while it's upsetting to lose someone, my wife and I could not help but notice how quickly you and Diana met one another using our website. With her permission, I'd like to ask if you and her can submit a picture of the two of you for us to put on our website as a way to show those in doubt that Let's Try Love can work?*

*Thank you,*

*Adam*

Victor then asks Diana, "Wanna take a pic of us for them to put on the site?"

"YES!" Diana says before pulling out her phone for a quick picture of her and Victor. She snaps two quick pictures; one of them smiling and one of them kissing. She then texts the pictures to Victor, who in return replies to Adam of *Let's Try Love.* Victor puts his phone down and resumes his cuddling and movie watching with Diana before his phone starts buzzing once more. It's another email from Adam of *Let's Try Love.*

*Victor, it's Adam again. My wife loves the picture you sent me. I'll be doing a site update later this week. When the picture of you and Diana is added to the homepage, I'll contact you again, that way the two of you can see it and give your approval.*

*Thanks again,*

*Adam*

"This is exciting," Diana says, "I've never been featured on a website before," She then moves in to kiss Victor, "And I get to be

311

featured on this website with you." Diana then looks Victor deep into his eyes and says, "Victor, I love you."

"I love you too, Diana," He then moves in to kiss Diana once more. The two continue watching the movie on television before both of them eventually fall asleep on the couch with Diana wrapped in Victor's arms.

## Epilogue

Victor and Diana eventually see their picture on the *Let's Try Love* homepage. It remains part of the homepage for nearly a year. Around the time their picture goes down to show off the new couples that have found love. Victor decides the time is right and proposes to Diana. While the two of them never thought online dating was the best option, they found love with one another and have *Let's Try Love* to thank for the reason that they found love.

## About the Author

C.L. Williams is a multi-genre author from central Virginia. His most recent release is a romance novella titled The Next Step: First Valentine's. In addition to writing his own books, C.L. Williams has also been featured in various anthologies and magazines. When not writing, C.L. Williams is reading and sharing the works of other independent authors.

### LINKS

www.facebook.com/writer434

www.twitter.com/writer_434

www.instagram.com/writer434

writer434.wordpress.com

### SELECT RELEASES AND FEATURES

Aspects of Love 1.5 (Love Poem Collection)

META- (Complete) (Poetry)

The Paradox Complex (Poetry)

Shades of BWWM (Anthology includes "The Next Step", "Moving In", and "Unexpected")

Starting Over (Anthology includes "Saved by a Siren"

The Next Step (Romance novella)

The Next Step: First Valentine's (Romance novella)

# It Started With a Click

## by Terri A. Wilson

As a high school principal, Owen Chatman was prepared for anything except for tonight's date. Thanks to the app Let's Try Love, he found a wonderful woman, but his nerves were about to get the better of him. Now after years of being a widower, he' ready to try again. Will this first date make the positive impression he wants or will he crash and burn?

# It Started With a Click by Terri A. Wilson

As a high school principal, Owen faced grumpy teenagers, angry parents, and overworked teachers, all the time. None of that prepared him for what he had to do tonight. One woman, at a restaurant, with other adults, and no kids. A date. His last one was with a fellow pollster during the Bush-Clinton race. He married her and loved her every day until she passed.

"I still can't believe you created a profile behind my back," Owen Chatman said to his oldest daughter.

"You would have never done it by yourself. I gave you a little push." Zoe pointed to a tie on the bed. "Try that one again."

He picked up the blue swirled one and held it under his chin. "You're sixteen. What do you know about pushing?"

Zoe rolled her eyes. "I don't like that one. Try the red tie. Isn't red a power color?"

He switched ties. "This is harder than prepping for a job interview."

Two mini-versions of Zoe walked in and sat on the bed.

"Did you finish your homework?" Owen said to his youngest daughter.

She scooted to the top of the bed, leaning against the headboard. "I did it at school."

Own gave her a side glance. "At school? Are you sure?"

She hugged a pillow against her. "Yes. I'm sure. Shesh."

He waked closer to her. "Mia, forgive me for questioning your ability to complete homework. I sat in a parent-teacher conference two months ago."

"The teacher made a big deal out of nothing. She picks on me because I'm your daughter."

Owen rubbed his chin. "Is that so? Your teacher picks on you because I'm a handsome guy."

She batted her dad with the pillow. "No. Gross. Everyone treats us differently since you won Principal of the Year."

He studied his three daughters. "Are all of you receiving special treatment?"

The youngest daughter sat up on her knees. "My teacher let me go to the library first. Then she asked me how we were celebrating. Mrs. Timpleton asked if you were doing something special with someone. I don't get why she asked that. You celebrated with us."

Rosie didn't understand how women saw her father, and that was fine with him. Since Alicia died, almost every woman in the district tried to wiggle her way into his private life. "And we had a great time."

"Why can't we go out with you tonight?" Rosie asked.

Zoe threw a pillow at her little sister. "It's a date, Dork."

Rosie reached across Mia hitting Zoe with the pillow.

## Let's Try Love

Mia hit Zoe, got off the bed, and stomped out of the room. "You're such a disease."

"Mia," Owen called, but she ignored him and slammed her bedroom door.

"What's going on here?" Owen asked the other two.

"I don't know what you're talking about. They always fight." Zoe scrolled on through screens on her phone.

"How do you help?" Owen tried another tie.

"What am I supposed to do?" Zoe popped her gum.

"You are the oldest. I expect you to help when I'm not around. Setting a good example is important."

Zoe swung her legs off the floor. "I didn't ask to be born first. Why should all the responsibility fall to me?" She huffed out of the room.

He pinched the bridge of his nose. A dull headache settled in the back his head, waiting for an opportunity to pounce.

Rosie wrapped her arms around his waist. "I set a good example."

He held her. "I know you do, Nugget." He stepped back. "What do you think? Do I look good?"

Rosie nodded. "Whatever you do, don't wear a hat and you'll be fine."

Owen took off a black fedora from the ornate mirror frame. "You don't think she'll like my hat?"

"No one likes your hat, Dad."

He shrugged. "I like it. Maybe I'll just take it then. Go tell your sisters we're having a family meeting in five minutes."

Rosie ran the hall calling her sisters. They responded with grumbles, but he heard them head downstairs. He put on the hat and checked out his reflection. A framed picture of Alicia smiled back at him.

"I wish you were here, Ali. You'd know exactly what I should wear and tell me what to say or avoid. What if she doesn't like me? What if I make a fool out of myself?" His hand rested on the frame. "Are you okay with this? Is a year long enough? Did I do all right?" He slumped on the bed.

"Dad? Dad, we're here waiting. Are we going to do this or what?" Zoe's voice was dripping with annoyance.

None of Owen's work at the high school ever compared to dealing with his own daughters. "Hold your horses."

He put the hat back on the finial atop the mirror frame. Without the hat, it was obvious a few gray streaks ran throughout his hair. He put it back on, saw his reflection, took it off, and walked out of the room. Before he left the hall, he hurried back to the room for the hat. Just in case.

The three girls waited around their kitchen table. Zoe's attention focused on her phone, Mia ate crackers, and Rosie tempted the dog with a cookie. Owen checked his watch. It wasn't too late to cancel.

The dating app, Let's Try Love, had a stick policy about last-minute cancellations. The teacher's strike canceled his last date an hour before it started. His date told him she understood but reported him anyway. Another negative rating would not help.

"Zoe, you need to make sure everyone gets to bed on time," Owen said.

She didn't look up from her phone.

"Zoe." Nothing. He slammed his hands on the table. "Zoe."

She jumped and dropped her phone. "I heard you. You don't have to overact. Dinner. Bedtime. Everyone on time. Don't burn the house down, keep the door locked, and no one has any sugar after we've brushed our teeth. We've been alone at home before. I've got this."

## Let's Try Love

Zoe pursed her lips and glared at him. For a heartbeat, Owen thought Alicia was sitting at the table. "I know you've been alone before but never because I went on a date."

"Dad, it's just one date," Mia said.

He sat down with them. I won't go if you guys aren't fine with this."

Zoe put her hand on his arm. "It's cool dad. Have fun and be home by curfew." She went back to her phone as she headed out of the kitchen.

"Zoe," Owen called.

She flipped her ponytail around and spun around. "What?"

"I love you. Thank you for watching your sisters." He opened his arm.

She ducked her head and melted into his hug. "I love you, too." Zoe walked away.

"I don't see why I need a babysitter." Mia said. "I'm fourteen."

"You're right, but you're here and Zoe is the oldest, so she's in charge. Don't think of her as a babysitter, but rather like a manager."

She wrinkled her nose. "Whatever. That's the same thing."

Owen hugged her and kissed the top of her head. "We still need to talk about those missed homework assignments."

"Tomorrow. I promise to turn in everything I'm missing."

"Mm-hm."

Mia left for her room.

"Dad, are you bringing us a new mom?" Rosie picked up the dog and held him close.

"What makes you ask that?"

"My friend LaLa's mom started dating, and she got a new daddy."

"Are you okay with me dating?"

"I guess." She looked down to the floor.

# Let's Try Love

"Rosie, what's wrong?"

She didn't respond.

Owen moved to the chair next to her, pushed her chair back, and settled in knee to knee with her. "Rosie, what's wrong?"

"If you bring home a new mom, does that mean we have forget our old mom?"

Owen brought her and the dog into his lap. She lowered his head onto his shoulder. "I don't know what will happen on this date. It might lead to more and it might be the last one. But no one will ever replace your mom."

"You always tell me I can leave if someone is mean to me. If she's mean, come home. We'll watch a movie."

"You bet. If she's mean, I'll come straight home."

They kissed, and she left to her room.

No more excuse. Get out of here.

He picked up his keys, walked out the garage, then walked back in for his hat. Just in case.

****

Owen walked into the restaurant. His clammy hands were buried deep in his pockets. The ambience of this place was like nothing he was used to. Had he not been running five minutes late, he would have turned around and gone home. Damn the rules of the dating app.

Dating shouldn't be this hard. When he was twenty-one and weighed all of a hundred pounds, soaking wet, women only focused on his stupid jokes. He didn't exist as a man. But that awkward kid was dead. He had a lot to offer any woman who went out with him; sincerity, politeness, and a great sense of humor.

"May I help you, Sir? Do you have a reservation or are you meeting someone?" The hostess asked him.

## Let's Try Love

"Yes, and yes. The reservation is under Chatman, but I don't believe my date is here yet."

"Uh, excuse me. Owen Chatman?"

Owen turned to see the woman he was meeting. Her online profile picture did not do her justice. Straight, long, brown hair hung down her back. Her eyes invited him into her world, and her smile sealed the deal.

"Madeline? Madeline York?" He reached out his hand to meet her extended arm. Not knowing what to do next he leaned in to kiss her on the cheek, he lost his balance when she moved in the opposite direction and groped her breasts on accident. "Oh my god. I am so sorry that was an accident." He stepped back, his face reddening and burning hot.

"Well, that makes for an impressive beginning to our date. Most men wait at least until dessert before making a move."

This would not end well.

Owen racked his brain to think of an excuse to leave. "That was perhaps one of the most embarrassing things I've ever done. I can't tell you how sorry I am."

Madeline laughed. Owen noticed her eyes twinkle. "I promise, it's okay. I know you meant nothing by it. It was just an accident."

"Yes, let's chalk it up to be an accident. Uh, it's been a long time since I've been on a date but I'm sure that's not how I should conduct myself. Let's try this again."

They shook hands, and she said, "Owen Chatman, I'm Madeline York. We met online through the dating app, Let's Try Love. It's nice to meet in person."

"It's a pleasure to meet you in person, Madeline. I look forward to getting to know you better. Hope you're hungry because I've heard great reviews about this place."

Owen turned back to the hostess. She gave him a plastered-on smile, "Mr. Chatman, if you and your party will follow me, I will seat you."

Owen waved his arm, indicating Madeline should go first. It gave him a chance to see her from behind. He liked what he saw and reminded himself this was a getting-to-know-you date and nothing else.

"Your server will be with you in just a moment. Enjoy your meal." Owen was positive the server smirked at him as she returned to the front of the restaurant.

He buried his face behind the menu giving him a chance to calm his racing heart and wait for his face to cool. It had been a long time since he went to a restaurant that didn't serve macaroni and cheese or chicken strips. He didn't recognize some of the dishes on the menu.

"Welcome to the Belle House. I will be your server and my name is Jo Anne. May I start you off with a cocktail or a glass of water? Perhaps you're ready to order an appetizer. Might I suggest the charcuterie platter?" Owen lowered his menu and realized Madeline was staring at him. He gave her a closed-lip smile. "Madeline would you like to start with a cocktail?"

"Perhaps a glass of water, for right now."

Owen placed his menu on the table. "That sounds good. We'll start with two glasses of water."

"Very well. Do you have questions about the menu?" the server said.

Owen raised an eyebrow in a quizzical look.

"I have no questions," Madeline said. "I would like a few minutes to decide, though."

"Absolutely. Please, don't feel rushed. Again, my name is Jo Anne but if I'm unavailable, any of the servers can help you with your needs." She left them alone and another server holding a water pitcher appeared.

Owen thought of asking her to return to explain every item on the menu. The more talking she did the less talking he'd have to do.

"Congratulations on your win." Madeline moved her water glass to the edge of the table making it easier for the server. "That's a big honor."

"Yeah, I guess. Are you referring to the Administrator of the Year Award?"

"Yes. It seemed like a big deal. The newspaper said you were advancing to the state level. What does that mean?"

Owen took a long drink and cleared his throat. "It sounds more prestigious than it really is. My portfolio will be forwarded on to another set of judges who will read it along with all the other winners and then make a choice."

Madeline loosened the scarf tied around her neck. "From what I've heard, it was a well-deserved honor. My children are in college now, but if they were in high school, I would want them to go to your school."

"That's right. You told me your son played basketball at State. And your daughter was studying in London."

"Actually, my daughter plays basketball for State, and my son is studying abroad."

I'm going downhill fast. "Sorry about the mix-up."

"Have you decided on a drink? An appetizer?" The server stood next to the table, waiting.

Owen nodded to Madeline.

"What do you have on tap tonight?" she asked.

"I'm sorry we have bottled Heineken, and Stella Artois. We do not have any taps."

What kind of weird place was this? Owen wanted a beer way more than anything else.

Madeline frowned. "Oh, okay. I'll take a glass of the house Chardonnay, then."

The server turned to Owen.

"That sounds good. Make it two."

"And have you decided on an appetizer?" Jo Anne asked.

Owen opened the menu and scanned the appetizers again. He studied Madeline for any reactions she might have to the menu. Better to let her give the cues. "Do you see anything you would like?"

"I think I'll take the muscles," Madeline said.

"Oh, er." Owen gulped.

"Do you know something about the muscles I should know?"

Owen cleared his throat and took another drink. "I'm allergic to shellfish."

Madeline closed her menu. She loosened the scarf a little more. "I forgot. How about we go for the platter she mentioned in the beginning?"

Owen watch a subtle glow of red flush her cheeks. Was it possible she was a nervous as he was? "That sounds good." Owen turned to the server and said, "We'll take one of those platters you mentioned."

"A charcuterie platter? That's an excellent choice," the server said. "I'll bring your wine right over and give you more time to think about your meal."

Madeline finished her water. "You must think I'm an idiot for not remembering your allergies."

"It's no big deal."

"It could have been a big deal if I had made you dinner at my place and served shellfish."

"Trust me, it's okay."

Let's Try Love

A pianist played a Barry Manilow song.

"This is my mom's favorite song," Madeline said. She smiled and thanked Jo Anne for bringing the wine.

"You haven't shared much about your parents." Owen held out is glass. "Let's toast."

"Okay. To what?"

Owen scrunched his brow. "How about to smooth first dates?"

They clinked glasses, and she smiled. "I almost didn't come tonight. It's one thing to chat online with someone. It's different chatting in person."

"I was nervous about coming tonight too. I've already had one last minute cancellation, though."

"Oh, yeah? What happened?"

An older couple got up and swayed to the piano music.

Oh, great a dance floor. "Teacher strike. I had an hour to figure out how to corral twelve hundred students with no certified teachers."

"Get out. What did you do?" She rested her elbow on the table and put her chin on top of her hand.

"I made every non-teacher staff member a substitute teacher and did what we had to do. A lot of kids stayed home so that made it easier."

"You didn't strike with them?"

A different server brought the appetizer. Madeline and Owen sat back making room on the table.

"May I help you with anything else?"

Owen smiled at the server. "No, thank you."

The server handed Madeline a small plate.

"Thank you," She served herself and started eating.

## Let's Try Love

He helped himself to the bread, meats, and cheese. His fork made the perfect spear for an olive; however, Madeline must have eyed the same olive. Their forks linked as they went for the tasty morsel.

She lifted her eyes to his and the same red flush returned. "I guess you like olives, too."

"I do, but I'll take this one." He lifted his fork and took a different one. "You asked me if I went on strike with my teachers."

"Yeah, how does that work?"

"Our contracts are negotiated differently. I sympathize with them, but admins aren't union. We can't strike. I would have lost my job."

She finished her wine. "That doesn't seem fair."

He shrugged. "It is what it is. I agree our teachers need more money and better working conditions. I supported them in other ways."

"What did you do?"

"A portion of my budget is discretionary. I used money from that category to make sure everyone had donuts and coffee in the morning then snacks later in the day."

"That was nice of you."

Jo Anne returned. "How is the charcuterie platter?"

"It's fantastic." Madeline held her hand over her mouth because Jo Anne caught them mid- bite.

"Make sure you try to the honeycomb with the meat. It makes a great salty-sweet combination."

They smiled at her and finished their bites.

"Would you like to hear about our specials tonight? It might make it easier to decide on your entrée?" Jo Anne pulled out a small pocket folder and read off the various meals on special for that night.

"Oh, the sea bass sounds good." Madeline's eyes brightened.

# Let's Try Love

"Excellent choice. Would you like that with the vegetable medley or creamed spinach?"

"The spinach, please."

"Perfect." Jo Ann faced Owen. "And you, Sir?"

"I'll have the steak with the mushroom risotto."

"And how would you like your steak?"

He handed his menu to the server and held out his hand for Madeline's. "Medium rare. Thank you."

"Excellent. Would you like another glass of wine?" Jo Anne asked.

Owen smiled at Madeline. "I'm game if you are."

"Two more, please," Madeline smiled and said to their server.

Jo Anne nodded then walked away.

"How is work going for you? When we chatted the other night, you were getting ready for a launch."

"I'm excited about this one. It's the first book I've worked on with another author. It comes out in three days."

"Was it hard working with another author?" He reached for a cracker and spread cream cheese on top.

"Not really but I've known this author for years. We released our first book about the same time. You could say, we've grown up together."

"And you do all of it yourself? No publisher involved?"

Jo Anne returned with two more glasses of wine.

"I am a publisher. At first, it was just my books. Now, I have ten authors who regularly publish."

"I find all of that fascinating."

The piano player moved on to Frank Sinatra songs and two different couples danced close to the piano.

Owen to a deep breath. "Do you like to dance?"

## Let's Try Love

For a second, Madeline's face lost all expression. "I can't remember the last time I danced on a date."

"I'm not much of a dancer, but we could get in one or two before our dinners get here." He wiped his mouth and put the napkin on the table.

She tilted her head. "I can't think of any reason not to, so sure." She pushed back her chair.

Owen jumped up and helped her with the chair. He presented a bent elbow and she linked her arm with his.

By the time they made it to the dance floor, the pianist switched to a love song from the Seventies.

"My parents played this all the time," Owen said.

"No one does it like Clapton," she added.

He wrapped one arm around her waist and held her hand in the other. "I keep telling my girls, the music from today cannot compare to the music I listened to."

She snickered. "And how does that go over?"

"About as well as you think."

They swayed to the music.

"Did you tell your girls the truth about tonight?" she asked.

"Yeah. Zoe, my oldest, was the one who created my profile."

She leaned back. "Really? How did you feel about that?"

"I grounded her for two weeks. Then, I corrected her grammar and spelling and looked at other profiles."

The song ended, and Owen saw Jo Anne headed to the table.

"Our food's here."

Jo Anne waited until they were seated, then put their dinner dishes in front of them. "Let me know if there is anything else I can bring you."

# Let's Try Love

Owen went for the cherry tomato on the side first. He missed, and it fell on the floor. Madeline reached for the salt and knocked the mini flower vase over spilling a little water on his leg. She took the napkin from her lap to blot the spill. The corner of the napkin settled on top of the candle and caught on fire. Owen used his hand to smother the burning fabric and burned his finger.

His steak had no hint of pink on the inside. They cooked his steak well-done, so he sent it back. Madeline refused to eat while he waited so her food cooled.

This time, they cooked his next steak to perfection, and he breathed a sigh of relief, thinking all the chaos had ended.

He looked up from his meal to pay better attention to Madeline. A big piece of spinach stuck to a front tooth. He couldn't focus on anything other than her spinach-tainted smile.

Do I tell her? That will go over well. "Madeline, there's some food on your teeth." That's what every woman wants to hear on a date.

He made exaggerated movements hoping to send her a message. First, he ran his tongue over his teeth. Then he wiped his mouth with the napkin. When those didn't work, he rubbed his upper lip with the side of his finger.

"Owen, are you here? I think you zoned out a bit. Is everything okay?"

He shook his head. "I'm sorry. I don't know how to tell you this, but you have spinach stuck to your tooth."

She opened her eyes wide and covered her mouth with the napkin. The red flush started at the base of her neck and rose to her eyes. She took off the scarf and placed it next to her on the table. "I'm so sorry. I can't believe that happened."

## Let's Try Love

Owen reached for her hand. "Don't worry about it." He glanced at his hand. She glanced at his hand. They gawked at each other and yanked their hands away.

"Um how is your meal?" Owen ducked his head.

"It's great. How's yours?"

"Great. Real great."

They ate the rest of their meal in quiet until a couple walked by the table on their way to the door. A faint smell of perfume tickled his nose. He sneezed. The floral scent increased when the stranger turned around a blessed him. A sneeze. Another sneeze. He gasped for air, reached for the napkin and continued sneezing. With the last sneeze he rested against the back of his chair but stared in horror as a living Rube Goldberg machine made of servers and patrons ran its course.

The last sneeze startled a child sitting at the next table causing her to toss her lovey, which landed on a well-balanced set of entrees as a server walked next to the table. The added weight tipped over one plate. A pile of mashed potatoes landed on the floor and the hostess slipped falling to the floor. The menus she carried flew in the air and landed in a fish tank splashing water on the surrounding tables. One man jumped from his seat knocking back his chair into the next table. The commotion startled the lady sitting at the table and her wine spilled from her glass and onto the one woman Owen wanted to impress. Madeline.

He stared at her and the mess in the dining room. A simple apology didn't seem strong enough. He searched for Jo Anne and found her stifling a laugh. "Check, please."

Madeline cleaned herself as much as possible while Owen settled the bill.

He followed her out the door. They stood in the parking lot.

## Let's Try Love

Owen knew there would be no second date. "Um, I guess tonight didn't, uh, er, go as planned."

She sighed. "No not really."

"Well, thank you for going out with me." He held out his hand.

"Tsk. This isn't a business transaction. I had a terrific time."

Owen gave her a half smile. "What was the best part? The part where I spoiled your dinner plans because I'm allergic to shellfish? The part where I embarrassed you? Or maybe you enjoyed the wine spilling on you?"

She stepped closed and took his hand. "It was an unforgettable date, that's for sure. But you have to be one of the nicest men I've met. You know on all the dates I've been on since I started dating again, not one of them held out my seat or showed as much concern and interest in me."

"Oh."

"I'll tell you what. Would you like to go someplace else? I know a great bar that has plenty of taps for good beer."

He met her gaze. "That sounds great. You aren't scared?"

She ran her fingers through her hair. "I've got a hat in my car. The worse has happened. What else can go wrong?"

"You wear hats?" His voice cracked. Get it together. You're not twelve.

"I love hats. I think they are a great accessory to complete any outfit. Besides, hats hide my gray."

"I didn't see any gray hair."

"The lighting in there was low. I've got 'em, trust me." She pointed to the corner of the lot. "I'm parked over there. I'll meet you at the entrance and you can follow me. Are you familiar with the bar on Sixth called The Cauldron?"

"I've been meaning to go there, but it's hard to get to a bar when you live with three minors who have to be in bed by nine."

She leaned in and kissed him on the cheek. "Follow me. You'll love it there. Way better than this stuffy place."

"Hey," he protested. "The Belle House was voted most romantic spot in town."

She stood with her hands on her hips. "Be honest. Is this the kind of place you frequent?"

He chuckled. "I've never been here, and I probably won't come back."

They headed to their cars and met at the parking lot entrance. He followed her to the bar but had to park a block away. He checked his watch. *Why are there so many people out this late on a school night?*

*Did he just worry about being out late on a Wednesday? You're old, man.*

For all the cars parked on the street, the bar was only had full. Madeline waved to him from a high-top table in the middle of the bar. A gray fedora sat on her head.

"Fedora, huh?" He sat across from her.

"It's a classic. I'm not going to wear an Easter bonnet in a place like this." She waved over the server. "What's your favorite kind of beer?"

"I like IPAs, but since I have to work tomorrow, I'll just keep it easy."

"Oh, I forgot you can't sleep in tomorrow. What time do you have to go to work?"

"I try to get there before everyone else does. It gives me a chance to ease into the day. It's around six."

## Let's Try Love

"Are you kidding me? I sometimes don't go to bed until six. If I get a good train of words coming, I don't stop until I can't keep my eyes open."

The server stopped at their table.

"I'll take a Blue Moon unless you still have Sam Adams Oktoberfest," Madeline told her.

"We've got both. So, Sam Adams?"

Madeline nodded.

"And what about you?" The server turned to Owen.

"Do you have any pale ales on tap?"

"We added Evil Twin Hipster Ale, last week."

"That sounds good," he said.

"Okay, I'll be right back. Do you want any wings or pretzels? Our nachos are popular, too."

Owen held out his hands toward Madeline. "I'm good, unless you want to split something."

"Nah. We'll just stick to the beer for right now."

A loud cheer echoed around the bar. Owen saw a hockey game on the TVs hanging on the wall. "I can't believe they are ahead by that much. They weren't supposed to win tonight."

"Are you a Penguins fan?"

"I learned to skate before I learned to walk. My whole family lives and breathes Penguins hockey. What about you?"

"I have season tickets. I never miss a game if I can help it. Maybe we can go the next home game. I think it's late next week."

Owen cocked his head. "Next week? You want to go out with me again?"

"If you'd like to go out with me?"

"For tickets to the game, you bet."

"Hey, you'd only go out with me because I have tickets?"

## Let's Try Love

"Well, the tickets, and," he paused, "the company too." Owen winked.

"Oh, thanks." She patted him his arm.

"Okay, I have a Sam Adams and an Evil Twin. Did you change your mind about something to eat?" The server set the beer glasses on the table.

"No, we're fine," Owen said. He held up his glass to toast Madeline. "I think we'll be just fine."

They clinked their glasses and settled in to watch the rest of the game.

For someone who hadn't dated in a long time, Owen felt confident in how the night went. Maybe his daughter was right to set up an account for him on the app. He had a good feeling there would be more than one more date in his future.

## About the Author

Terri is a former English teacher and librarian. She taught middle and high school and college. Now she works from home homeschooling her two daughters and living out her dreams via her stories. She began escaping into books a little later than most but was hooked after the first book. It has been her dream to give back to the book world since second grade.

When she's not writing or reading, she enjoys binging on Netflix and painting. Due to her crunchy lifestyle and free spirit, she considers herself a recycled hippie. Her most important goal is to help others jump and learn to fly.

To find out more about her characters and the lives they live, check out her website, http://www.terriawilson.com. Follow her on Amazon and Goodreads, or connect through Facebook, Twitter, and Instagram.

Newsletter- http://eepurl.com/dCKgkj
Website- http://www.terriawilson.com
Goodreads- https://www.goodreads.com/TerriAWilson
Twitter- http://twitter.com/terriawilson
Facebook- http://www.facebook.com/wilsonterria/
Instagram- http://www.instagram.com/terria.wilson/
BookBub- https://www.bookbub.com/profile/terri-a-wilson

Made in the USA
Columbia, SC
15 May 2019